D0679683

WEAPONS OF MASS DESTRUCTION

MARGARET VANDENBURG

THE PERMANENT PRESS
Sag Harbor, NY 11963

For information, address:
    The Permanent Press
    4170 Noyac Road
    Sag Harbor, NY 11963
    www.thepermanentpress.com

Library of Congress Cataloging-in-Publication Data

Vandenburg, Margaret—
    Weapons of mass destruction / Margaret Vandenburg.
        pages ; cm
    ISBN 978-1-57962-401-9 (hardcover)
        1. Marines—Fiction. 2. Suicide--Psychology—Fiction. I. Title.

PS3572.A647W43 2015
813'.54—dc23   2015020500

Printed in the United States of America

for Grandpa and Cousin Rick

—*ᴧᴧᴧ*—

Corporal Jess W. Hammer
US Marine Corps
World War I

Staff Sergeant Richard W. Rohweder Jr.
US Army
Iraq and Afghanistan

In Memoriam

PETER SWAN

November 16, 1983, to September 10, 2001

When they were boys they performed rituals in the aspen grove. They used the same knife to slice their thumbs. It was an old knife dating back to the nineteenth century when Pete's great-great-grandfather still herded wild horses in the high country. There were notches in the handle. They told stories around the campfire explaining how they got there. A record of buffalo killed. Or stallions broken. The darker the night, the more gruesome the stories. One notch for every cavalry officer massacred. Or scalped.

Pete let a few drops of blood spill on the ground. He did it with such conviction, Sinclair did the same. Dry leaves drank the offering. They pressed the wounds together, working their thumbs to make sure the blood mingled enough to last a lifetime. No one needed to tell them what to do. The only way for men to bond was to shed blood together, either their own or the blood of another. They did it to relieve the agony of separation they felt because they were so close.

To question their motives would have been unpatriotic. American troops were sent to the armpit of the world to defend freedom. It was a scary business. They learned on day one in Iraq that fear and survival were inseparable. If you weren't afraid you were dead, plain and simple. Sinclair understood this instinctively. He chalked it up to the fact that he was raised in a military family. His grandpa claimed the Sinclairs were reluctant warriors, but there were medals locked in his desk drawer. He had survived Hürtgen Forest. Grandpa's humility didn't fool Sinclair a bit. Reluctant soldiers ended up dead, not decorated.

Nothing made Sinclair feel more alive than death. His first love was hunting. He and his buddy Pete had killed spike elk by their tenth birthdays. Pete was an even better marksman than he was. Sinclair always pictured him on sniper duty, how he would have sighted the target without squinting and squeezed the trigger without flinching. There were plenty of ace shots in the US Marines, even more than they'd known as boys in the backwoods of Montana. None with as keen an eye and steady a hand as Pete. Old timers on the ranch used to say he could shoot ticks off a buck's balls, no sweat. Turns out there's such a thing as too good a shot.

Everything was most certainly not fair game. There were strict rules, and Sinclair loved to obey them. Hunting animals out of season wasn't just illegal. It was immoral. When Sinclair bagged his quota, he tracked mammals he had no intention of shooting, just to see that look in their eyes. He felt it himself with his finger on the trigger, a kindred terror and defiance. The boundary between hunter and prey is permeable. Real hunters raise their rifles not to kill but to consecrate the instinct to survive.

"Don't shoot!"

He remembered the time they hunted sage grouse with Grandpa. Pete wandered between a bear and her cub and raised his rifle when the sow threatened to attack. Grandpa rushed right past her, almost within swiping distance, and tackled Pete. They rolled down the hill out of reach. Grandpa had risked being mauled to avoid shooting that bear. Fair was fair, and hunting was ignoble when you robbed an animal of its right to protect its progeny. They had trespassed.

Of course they had no choice but to bust into Iraqi homes. Orders were orders. They had to meet the enemy on his own turf. But mistakes were easier to make in Fallujah than in Baghdad. Americans in uniform seldom confronted actual troops anymore. The enemy had a thousand faces, all of them masked. Terrorists posed as civilians. Ba'athists hired mercenaries. Iraqi citizens were alternately insurgents and innocent bystanders, depending on the day of the week. To win battles, you need to know who you're fighting.

The war hadn't started out that way. Operation Iraqi Freedom was a glorious campaign with clear-cut rules of engagement. More often than not, even Saddam's Republican Guardsmen conducted themselves honorably. But in Fallujah it seemed like everybody was hunting out of season. Sinclair's instincts were confused by the wavering distinction between civilians and soldiers, the one boundary that should never be crossed in war. Just last week on an evening raid, he had stormed a bowl of soup on a kitchen table, a spoon poised on its porcelain lip. His platoon had been told the house was filled with insurgents. They burst through the door, already shooting. He wanted to believe a die-hard Ba'athist had been eating shorbat adas just seconds before. Then they found the kid in the next room, draped bleeding over the windowsill.

"Shake it off!" Lieutenant Radetzky shouted.

"Delay and you get blown away."

Radetzky was a prudent officer. But an invisible chain of command was calling the shots, expecting his platoon to pull the trigger. Military intelligence kept trying to distinguish between civilians and insurgents. The enemy was equally intent on blurring this distinction. Their objective was to make United States Marines look like terrorists. And finally, in the wake of the lynching on Brooklyn Bridge, they almost succeeded. Four Blackwater security contractors hung from the girders, smoke still leaking from their charred limbs. Teenagers pumped their fists for the benefit of an ecstatic crowd. The most brutal act of war to date had been committed by what looked like a mob of men on their way home from work. Husbands and fathers. Retaliating without terrorizing their wives and children seemed next to impossible.

The entire world was watching. But nobody actually witnessed the atrocities firsthand. Sinclair's platoon had been patrolling a neighborhood on the other side of town. Back at the base, they tuned in along with everyone else, watching the same images over and over on television and online. Exaltation on the bridge. Bodies burned beyond recognition. Al Jazeera was the only press with access, so the coverage was impassioned. Newscasters kept harping on what they called the infidel occupation. The footage reminded Sinclair of videos showing al-Qaeda celebrating the bombing of the Twin Towers.

His buddies couldn't stop talking about the bodies, even over meals. McCarthy had a morbid streak that alternately amused and disgusted Sinclair. It's true you had to make light of all the blood and gore or you'd go stark raving mad. But there were limits.

"Did you see the shapes of those things?" McCarthy kept saying.

"Or lack thereof," Wolf said.

Nobody played devil's advocate better than Staff Sergeant Wolf. Quintessentially cool himself, he liked to rile up everyone else. The more steam his men blew off at the base, the less pressure they felt on the battlefield. He was the only noncommissioned officer in the battalion who deigned to eat with grunts in the mess. He never pulled rank because he didn't have to.

"Do you think they hacked off the arms first, or did they melt?" A native Ohioan, McCarthy could pass for a corn-fed choirboy until he opened his mouth. "Talk about a hot mess."

"Barbecue," Wolf said. "Good old-fashioned barbecue, Fallujah-style."

Sinclair's bunkmate, Logan, picked up his tray and moved to another table. He had given up trying to insist on decency. In turn, the platoon stopped making born-again jokes. They were willing to live and let live as long as he shut the hell up about God. Not that they wouldn't lay down their lives to defend Christian values against jihadist fanatics. But they didn't need to harp on the big guy upstairs to know he was on their side.

Sinclair almost followed Logan, but he didn't want guys to think he had a weak stomach. Wolf made them bunk together because they were both poker faces. Sinclair didn't mind. Logan liked fly-fishing magazines and the same heavy-metal bands.

"They'll fry for it," McCarthy said. "Washington's pissed."

"Fuck Washington," Trapp said. "Since when do they run the show?"

Trapp was the oldest member of the platoon, a lifer who had despaired ever getting the chance to prove himself. He had served in the Gulf War. But that was child's play, more like a computer game than combat. There was pretty much no one left to fight after all the laser-guided missiles hit home. Iraq was like a dream come true. This war was being fought on the ground. He could see the whites of the enemy's eyes. Judging from their murderous expressions, Fallujans weren't convinced that major combat operations in Iraq had ended.

"Don't get your hopes up," Wolf said. "Baghdad's the main attraction. We're just a sideshow."

"More like coming attractions," Trapp said. "Wait till folks back home in Mississippi hear about those Blackwater dudes."

"Crispy critters," McCarthy said.

"Hanging from what was left of their necks, no less."

"Could have been their thighs. Hard to tell."

"One good lynching deserves another, don't you think?"

"Not in Harlem," Wolf said. "Anyway, why waste good rope when you can blow them to smithereens?"

"Now you're talking," McCarthy said. "If they'd strung up marines instead of contractors, I wouldn't even wait for orders. We'd wipe this goddamn town off the face of the map. No more pussyfooting around."

Central Command took a more measured approach. Kilo Company was ordered to cordon off a half-mile radius around the bridge. Once the area was secured, Sinclair's platoon moved in to patrol its southern perimeter. As usual he was posted on sniper duty. He was the best shot in the platoon, maybe the whole company. All that hunting had paid off, provided you liked sniper duty. He was ambivalent about it. It offered a bird's-eye view, but sometimes he felt left out. That particular day, he was relieved to be off the streets where the excitement they witnessed on TV bubbled beneath a superficial calm. Their platoon commander kept warning them to exercise extreme caution.

"Fallujah's a powder keg," Lieutenant Radetzky said. "A few itchy trigger fingers and the whole province will explode."

"Bring it on," McCarthy said, out of earshot.

"Don't let Radetzky hear you say that," Sinclair said.

"Yeah, right. Like he's got time to listen, with Centcom barking his ear off."

Sinclair thought he heard cheering in the distance, an ominous sound in the wake of the Blackwater ambush. But it was probably just boys playing soccer, which they continued to do even in the midst of sporadic urban combat. He was stationed on a rooftop in Queens. Fallujah was laid out on a strict grid, like Manhattan, so the US Army had renamed neighborhoods after the Big Apple. They even posted makeshift signs next to Arab street names. Sinclair had taken these substitutions for granted until they heard the news that four desecrated bodies were hanging from Brooklyn Bridge. Somehow it brought barbarism too close to home.

His battalion had been redeployed to Anbar Province just two weeks before the attack. They had spent a furlough back in the States after having distinguished themselves in the Battle of Baghdad. Most of them were raring to get back to Iraq. They were enlisted men, not National Guardsmen, lifers and patriots who answered the call of duty after 9/11. They hadn't joined the US Marines to get an education. If the War on Terror wasn't a holy war, it came pretty damned close.

The first two weeks in Fallujah had seemed hopeful. They only realized in retrospect they had been kidding themselves. The departing Eighty-Second Airborne Division was disillusioned, but that was typical of the army. Marines were far more versatile. They were better equipped to carry out the next phase of operations, building a new free Iraq from the ground up. Sinclair's battalion had already helped restore municipal services in several Shiite towns on the Tigris River. They prided themselves on a history of humanitarian campaigns, including the peacekeeping mission in Somalia. Winning the hearts and minds of the people of Fallujah seemed entirely possible after the liberation of Baghdad.

Scores of military engineers and private contractors flooded into Fallujah. With the exception of occasional raids to round up suspected insurgents, marines shouldered their guns and worked with locals to rebuild the city's infrastructure. They handed out candy and yo-yos to bashful kids with reticent mothers. Sinclair was usually stationed atop buildings, to make sure nothing happened to his buddies mingling with the crowd below. The idea was to neutralize the enemy by cultivating local support. Psychological operations units called it meet-and-greet detail. Hard-core gunners like McCarthy called it shooting the shit, a poor substitute for shooting bad guys.

"Looks good on paper," McCarthy said. "Not so good when you're meeting and greeting suicide bombers."

A PSYOP officer pulled out an official report. They were always quoting statistics, like anyone gave a damn.

"It worked in Habbaniyah," he said. "Meet and greet outperformed search-and-destroy missions two to one."

"Habbaniyah isn't Fallujah," McCarthy said.

"It's a Sunni town."

"It's Disneyland compared to this snake pit."

Sinclair was less skeptical. But then he was a sniper, not a gunner, more apt to bide his time than rush headlong into battle. The mood on the streets seemed to support the long view. Fallujans appeared optimistic, almost buoyant. Looking back, Sinclair wondered if it had all been an act. Either the people were complicit, or anticoalition forces hadn't yet successfully infiltrated Fallujah.

The Brooklyn Bridge debacle derailed everything. Sinclair's outrage was more nuanced than that of the average consumer of the evening news. Those four security contractors had no business traipsing through Fallujah without military authorization. No doubt they were in a hurry, trying to squeeze in one last supply delivery before payday. Anything to make an extra buck. It wasn't the first time Blackwater guards had taken matters into their own hands, threatening the success of the peacekeeping mission in Anbar Province. So much for meeting and greeting the Iraqi people.

Central intelligence had identified the ringleaders responsible for the mutilations on the bridge. Within a day or two, US Special Forces would be ready to start hunting them down one by one. With such highly specialized assassins on hand, there was no earthly reason to launch an attack on the city. A full-force assault would only fan the fire of resentment smoldering in Fallujah, giving Ba'athists and jihadists the momentum they needed to recruit a steady stream of insurgents. Fallujah had not yet reached the tipping point. There were still more allies than enemies among civilians.

The general of the Marine Expeditionary Force was already on the phone with Washington, explaining the volatile situation on the ground. He had never spoken directly with the White House, not even during Operation Iraqi Freedom. The voice on the other end of the line was peremptory. Impatient. The spectacle of hanging bodies dominated the conversation.

"Cut to the chase, General. Somebody needs to pay for this."

"Special Forces will track down the Brooklyn Bridge insurgents. That way marines can keep cultivating local support."

"Sounds like a mixed message to me."

"Sir?"

"We need to broadcast, loud and clear, that nobody terrorizes Americans with impunity."

"Make no mistake. Sparing the innocent won't compromise our vigilant resolve to punish the guilty."

"What about all those people cheering on the sidelines? You call them innocent?"

"I'm not following you."

"Does the word *insubordination* mean anything to you?"

"Yes, sir."

"I'm handing you a big stick, General. Use it."

Military men are trained to make strategic rather than emotional decisions, calculating the best way to achieve their objective with the least number of casualties. They never play to an audience. The image of those brutalized contractors, invading American homes on television, horrified the general no less than anyone else. But four bodies were never cause enough to put an entire battalion of soldiers at risk, let alone a city of civilians. The order to launch Operation Vigilant Resolve came from the top. The only traces of the general's recommendations were the words *vigilant* and *resolve*.

In Washington, the tactical shift from meet and greet to search and destroy was initiated before the bodies were even lowered from the bridge. Engineers and contractors were airlifted from the city. Tanks and bulldozers rolled in from Ramadi. Usually they spent weeks planning and rehearsing major offensives. This time the attack was scheduled to begin in forty-eight hours. Three of the four mutilated bodies had already been surrendered to the authorities. The fourth was purportedly en route. Everything was under control in Fallujah long before the commander in chief intervened.

Back at the base after an uneventful night patrol, Sinclair and Logan prepared their gear for inspection. They had heard through the lance corporal grapevine that Special Forces were hot on the trail of the monsters responsible for the lynching. Presumably their platoon would back them up when they moved in for the kill. Sinclair and Logan never talked much. They both relished silence after the belligerent bravado of their buddies. Not that they didn't love them. Military men seldom spoke of the bonds of blood that bound them. For all their talk of freedom and Christian values, or vengeance and retribution, the real reason they rushed headlong into battle was for each other.

Sinclair cleaned his machine gun rather than his rifle. Special Forces would bring their own snipers. Sinclair noticed Logan's barrel rag was shredded, so he handed over his own. When he finished reassembling his automatic, he sat with the gun on his lap, half listening to Logan's whispered prayers and the crackle of AK-47 fire in the distance. A soft breeze blew through an open window. Dusk was his favorite time of day. The last trace of desert sunset faded into darkness before he stretched out on his cot. Logan was already snoring overhead. He always slept on the top bunk.

"Closer to God," Logan liked to say.

"More exposed to air strikes," Sinclair pointed out.

"I'm not worried," Logan would say. "He's got me covered."

The call came at 2100 hours. The platoon was instructed to report to the staging ground. Their battalion commander, Colonel Denning, was very old school. He always insisted that his troops hear official orders in drill formation. Captain Phipps was also on hand, along with several other company commanders. Colonel Denning approached the podium and adjusted the microphone. He towered over Captain Phipps, who stood by his side, stone-faced. McCarthy called them Mutt and Jeff.

"Central Command has issued the order to invade the city of Fallujah," Colonel Denning said. "Code name Operation Vigilant Resolve."

He waited until an almost imperceptible wave of excitement subsided in the ranks.

"Three battalions will coordinate offensives. 2/1, 1/5, and the Thundering Third."

Colonel Denning turned to Captain Phipps. They exchanged salutes and Colonel Denning left the field. Captain Phipps stepped forward and grabbed the mike, yanking it down to his level with excessive force. Sinclair expected him to brief them on the rationale of the offensive. He was an approachable officer who believed in sharing strategic information with his men. But his presentation was short and sweet and inexplicable.

"Kilo Company will be responsible for clearing and holding the area east of Highway 10," Captain Phipps said. "Platoon commanders will issue specific directives."

Captain Phipps seemed to look each of his men in the eye. He paused, on the verge of continuing, and then apparently decided against it.

"Dismissed."

"Rock and roll," Trapp said, slapping Wolf on the back.

Sinclair and Logan exchanged furtive glances. This game plan flew in the face of everything they'd learned about warfare in Iraq. Attacking the city to apprehend the Brooklyn Bridge insurgents would be like dynamiting a stream to catch a school of trout.

"Somebody's in one hell of a hurry to make an example of Fallujah," Logan said.

Sinclair refused to believe it. Military men were above scapegoating an entire city for the actions of a handful of embedded insurgents. Their objectives were more strategic, less symbolic. The logic of Operation Vigilant Resolve escaped him, but he blamed his own shortsightedness. No one trusted the wisdom of his superiors more than Lance Corporal Sinclair.

The platoon was ordered to prepare for a week's foray into East Manhattan. Their base was several miles outside of Fallujah. They packed thousands of pounds of ammunition, leaving precious little room for anything else. Stuffed to capacity, their rucksacks held 3,200 cubic inches of whatever they needed to stay alive. Grenades and clean socks were about the same size. Foot rot was smelly and painful but not lethal. You do the math.

At 0800 hours they reported to the northern perimeter of Queens to help evacuate citizens to camps outside of harm's way. Tanks with loudspeakers were broadcasting warnings of the impending attack. Fallujah's elders and sheikhs had been asked to spread the word in neighborhoods, and local media outlets had been notified. They were too pressed for time to distribute leaflets promising clemency to allies and death to everyone else. Most of the population had already seen them anyway, the last time Americans blew through town.

Sinclair's platoon proceeded on foot to Highway 10, which cut straight through the heart of the city. All four lanes were clogged with traffic moving slowly enough to allow inspection of passengers jammed beyond capacity into vehicles ranging from Mercedes-Benzes to patchwork taxis made of cast-off parts. Vast numbers threaded their way through the creeping cars, fleeing on foot. Teams of marines were responsible for patrolling an eighth of a mile of highway. Sinclair paired up with McCarthy. Interpreters were available in case Iraqis had questions or needed to be questioned. The evacuation was primarily humanitarian, but it was also considered an intelligence-gathering opportunity.

"Unbelievable," McCarthy said.

"All these people?" Sinclair asked.

"All the time we're wasting. Last I knew, we were marines. Not glorified traffic cops."

"Damn right."

Once the offensive was officially announced, even Sinclair was anxious to mobilize. McCarthy kept griping until a car bomb exploded fifty feet from their post. When the smoke cleared, they rushed over to the burning shell.

"Stand back!" Sinclair shouted.

A circle of spectators looked blandly at the approaching Americans. The studied blankness of their expressions conveyed the prevailing myth that no one was responsible for the flames leaping from the car. Feigned indifference on the faces of Fallujans was far more ominous than blatant hatred. You never knew where you stood with them.

"Fucking cowards," McCarthy said.

Miraculously no one was hurt. The bomb was more a calling card than anything else, a greeting from insurgents camouflaged in the crowd. McCarthy stopped complaining about being a traffic cop. Sinclair adjusted his body armor to calm himself. They started rotating duty, taking turns directing the flow of so-called civilians and covering each other in case someone decided to take potshots at infidel invaders.

People rolled up their windows as they passed. Never mind the fact that the temperature had already topped eight-five degrees. Roasting in a closed car was presumably preferable to breathing the same air as Americans. This was their first evacuation, but Fallujans had heard plenty of horror stories about Baghdad. When asked to leave home for your own safety, odds were against having a home to return to when the threat subsided. Trunks were bulging with valuables, secured with twine to maximize the load. Refugees on foot labored under the weight of backpacks and suitcases. Anyone empty-handed was probably up to no good.

Usually only men and emboldened teens gave Americans dirty looks. Now mothers with crying children glared at them as they rushed by. Their burqas covered everything but their malice. Extended families followed wizened patriarchs, more abled generations supporting the enfeebled and carrying the very young. Men in the prime of life were conspicuously absent from the throng. Teenagers roamed in packs, pretending to evacuate. Two young boys pushed an old woman in a wheelbarrow, a rangy dog yapping at their heels. She alone seemed oblivious to the sweltering stream of hostility.

A few hours into evacuation patrol, Sinclair started noticing a pattern. Car doors opened, and no one climbed in or out. Shortly thereafter, gangs of teenagers carried things away from the site, disappearing down side streets. Insurgents were evidently taking advantage of the exodus to disguise ammunition drop-offs. Sinclair signaled McCarthy.

"Are you thinking what I'm thinking?"

"Time to teach those punks a lesson."

Sinclair radioed Lieutenant Radetzky for permission to pursue.

"Request denied," Radetzky said. "The offensive isn't scheduled to begin until 0500 hours."

"By then they'll be armed to the teeth," McCarthy said. "Let's take them out now. Before they dig in."

"Sit tight, gentlemen," Radetzky said. "You'll see plenty of action tomorrow. And then some."

Identifying insurgents was particularly tricky in Fallujah. If they were out there, they were adept at blending in. Or not. To the extent that they expressed the collective ill will of the evacuees, they would be indistinguishable from them. Sinclair had learned to be wary of people with cell phones, especially if they kept glancing in his direction. Looking back, he wished boot camp had taught him to read body language. Military training still lagged behind innovations in the War on Terror. Marines were accustomed to fighting armies, not jihadists playing the part of civilians. He wondered if monitoring body language figured into their training in the mountains of Afghanistan and Pakistan. He imagined hooded men indoctrinating bearded acolytes.

"Avoid direct eye contact with American soldiers."

"If they accost you, act like you're glad to see them."

"Pretend you're escorting a group of women and children."

"Trim your beards. Dress inconspicuously."

Many of the older men wore dishdashas, but T-shirts and trousers were more common overall. Those engaged in suspicious activities were just as likely to be wearing tennis shoes as sandals. Someone in a police officer's uniform lugged away what looked like a carton of AK-47 cartridges. It was impossible to tell whether he was confiscating or stockpiling them. Uniforms were a fickle sign of affiliation in Iraq. They had a tendency to stray into the wrong hands. In Ramadi, marines had even encountered insurgents fighting in army fatigues. Such blatant violations of the most basic rules of engagement were what separated terrorists from soldiers.

Police and National Guard uniforms were hot items on the black market. Most of them came from Anbar Province where desertions were rampant. Even when they didn't decamp, Iraqi security forces were notoriously unreliable. The American military was well aware that their involvement in strategic offensives was cosmetic, at best. The Pentagon was committed to the political imperative of joint efforts, which gave the impression that Iraqis were beginning to take charge of their destiny. In places like Fallujah, where Ba'athist militias sided with Saddam Hussein, entirely new security forces had to be trained. The United States poured money into recruitment and training.

"They might as well pour it down the drain," Wolf said.

Staff Sergeant Wolf was second in command in the platoon. But he was always first to pipe up when official policy threatened the safety of his men.

"Marines can barely afford body armor," Wolf said. "Meanwhile Iraqi soldiers have brand new equipment. Compliments of Uncle Sam. What's wrong with this picture?"

Lieutenant Radetzky seldom openly criticized military policy. He was a commissioned officer, not an NCO like Wolf, more circumspect by necessity as well as training. But when Wolf started ragging on coalition security forces, Radetzky couldn't resist chiming in. The Second Battalion of the Iraqi National Guard was slated to participate in Operation Vigilant Resolve. He was afraid their involvement might be counterproductive, putting his platoon at risk.

"Don't hold your breath, men," Radetzky said. "Even if they show up, watch your backs. When the going gets tough, they're usually long gone."

Iraqi National Guard retention rates were miniscule. Often as not, their officers had clandestine connections with deposed Ba'athist party leaders intent on recovering control of Anbar Province. The more ardent their expression of allegiance to the coalition cause, the less likely they were sincere. In Sunni strongholds like Fallujah, suspicion was prudent. Loyalty often masked an insidious intent to use American resources to subvert American interests. Sinclair's platoon had learned this the hard way.

When the First Marine Expeditionary Force arrived in the city, they were committed to changing the dynamic between civilians and military personnel, the first step toward reconstruction. Locals complained that the army had imposed martial law. To reverse this impression, Radetzky's men paired up with Sunni police officers for joint patrols. Like so many initiatives in Fallujah, the plan looked good on paper and fell flat in the field. Their Iraqi counterparts showed up once or twice before succumbing to pressure to quit. Nobody outside of Washington was operating under the illusion that they had enlisted out of love for the coalition interim government. The paycheck was hard to resist in an economy devastated by war. But there was no use putting food on your family's table when no one was around to eat it. Journalists weren't the only ones being abducted, or worse. Under Saddam, Iraqis had become accustomed to being caught between a rock and a hard place. Nothing much changed when the Americans showed up.

The army may have had the right idea after all. There were telltale signs that martial law was the only real option even before the mob scene on Brooklyn Bridge. Security force defections were the tip of the iceberg, if such an intrinsically American expression made sense in the broiling sands of the Syro-Arabian Desert. So many things were lost in translation. As a result, even civilians turned on them. If you extended a helping hand, chances were someone would bite it.

The worst was the soccer fiasco. Sinclair's platoon spent a week constructing a playing field out of a wasteland just north of the industrial quarter. Neighborhood kids were thrilled. Their parents seemed pleased, if a little subdued. Trapp orchestrated a ribbon-cutting ceremony. He and Wolf officiated the first game, an epic contest between the Jolan Giants and the Askari Argonauts. They even supplied official uniforms, red and black T-shirts with Nike logos on the sleeves. The Argonauts prevailed in overtime.

The next morning Wolf's squad swung by en route to patrol duty in Queens. The goal nets had been torn down and garbage was strewn over the recently graded surface. No one claimed responsibility, but the motive was unmistakable.

"Talk about kicking a gift horse in the mouth," Wolf said.

"More like kicking kids in the teeth," Trapp said.

Trapp was visibly upset. His buddies looked the other way while he recovered his composure. Nobody loved kids more than he did. He had four of his own and had a hard time accepting how war robbed children of their childhoods. Every warrior has a chink in his armor. Trapp could twist a knife blade in a fedayee's gut without flinching. But the thought of disappointing the Jolan Giants was too much for him.

"Let's rebuild it," Sinclair said. "We can probably salvage these nets."

"Good idea," Wolf said. "What do you say, Trapp?"

"Sounds like a plan," Trapp said. "Operation Kill 'Em with Kindness."

"There's more than one way to fight a war."

"In your dreams," McCarthy said under his breath. He didn't want to add to Trapp's disappointment. But as far as he was concerned, winning hearts and minds was a slogan, not an op plan. This wasn't the first or last time Iraqis would sabotage the peace process.

Sinclair was also shaken by the incident, though he would never admit it. He understood war and retribution, but not gratuitous violence. Vandalism was one thing. At least it followed a kind of sick logic. If you couldn't keep up with the Joneses, the next best thing was to trash their property. But wrecking your own stuff was like turning the knife against yourself. Or the gun, as the case may be. The worst were suicide bombers. People always said it was an Arab thing. But Sinclair witnessed the same will-ful self-destruction back home in Montana. His best friend, Pete, had ruined his high school graduation present from Grandpa, a brand new calf-leather saddle. He hacked it to pieces with a hatchet and threw it in a pile of manure behind the stables. A week later they found him dead in the mountains. He blew his head off with his favorite shotgun.

Sinclair had traveled halfway around the world, think-ing he could make a fresh start. But everything reminded him of Pete, especially the bond he shared with his bud-dies. They were brothers in ways that far exceeded the mere accident of birth. They shed blood together. With Pete, it had been the blood of animals. When Sinclair killed his first deer, Grandpa plunged his hands into the carcass and smeared the steaming blood on his face. They inherited the ritual from Pete's great-great-grandfather, a Sioux scout who corralled the first wild horses bearing the Sinclair brand. Grandpa repeated the ritual when Pete killed his first buck, washing his face with blood as though he were his own son. That's why it was so awful when things went south. They were like family.

It seemed to happen overnight. One day they were boys roaming the hills with their rifles. The next Pete was busting things up. He played hooky and started hanging around with dropouts on the reservation. He disappeared for days at a time. Even Sinclair couldn't find him.

"He'll end up in the slammer if he doesn't watch out," Sinclair's father said.

Almost every night over dinner, they tried to figure out what went wrong. Sinclair's sister, Candace, was uncharacteristically quiet during these conversations.

"Must be a guy thing," Candace said, excusing herself from the table.

In hindsight Sinclair wondered whether his sister withheld information that might have saved Pete's life. Nothing at the time made sense. Grandpa tried to explain that Pete struggled with things Sinclair took for granted. The Swan family had seen better days. They lived in one of the migrant-worker trailers down by the river. But Pete spent most of his time with Sinclair, eating meals in the big ranch house when his dad was on a bender. Grandpa had all but adopted him, even offering to pay his way through college. Sinclair assumed they'd ultimately run the ranch together.

"Pete's proud," Grandpa said. "Too proud to accept handouts."

"Takes after his dad," Sinclair's father said.

"What's that supposed to mean?" Sinclair asked.

"He'd sooner shoot himself in the foot than take a step forward."

"That's not fair."

"Doesn't mean it's not true," Grandpa said.

"Why else would they live in that ramshackle trailer?" his father asked. "The foreman's cabin is there for the asking. Always has been."

"You can lead a horse to water," Grandpa said. He thought better of finishing the adage. Pete's father could never be accused of refusing to drink, that's for sure.

"There must be something we can do," Sinclair said.

"Fact is we may have done too much."

"You can't save people from themselves."

But something didn't add up. Sinclair knew Pete would never shoot himself in the foot just to make a point. He wouldn't have shot himself in the head, either, if he hadn't been completely demoralized. They said it was an accident, but Sinclair knew better. No one handled a gun like Pete. If he were in Iraq, he'd head up the sniper squad, not Sinclair.

It defied explanation. You tried to help people, and they lashed out. Apparently gifts were easier to give than to receive. They carried an unseen burden, a kind of back-handed slap in the face. If even soccer fields gave offense, imagine the perceived aggression of liberating a country from sectarian tyranny. In Iraq, if not in Montana, freedom translated more readily into vandalism than Saturday afternoon team sports.

They should have seen it coming. Allegiances changed overnight in Fallujah, like shifting sands in the desert. Marines adapted to the climate, manicuring soccer fields one week, evacuating the city the next. They were in it for the long haul. There was something satisfying about pitting yourself against the region's timeless resistance to stability. If it took fifty years to usher the Middle East into the twenty-first century, so be it.

The evacuation was taking longer than anticipated. Sinclair started doubting whether the exodus would be over in time for the offensive. Highway 10 was still packed with people, mostly on foot by late afternoon. Car bombings and munitions smuggling had finally convinced the tactical operations center to restrict vehicular traffic. Civilians were forced to flee with nothing but the clothes on their backs. Most of the more affluent citizens were long gone anyway. According to official reports, the poor lagged behind, inexplicably reticent to leave their homes. From the vantage point of boots on the ground, they looked more resigned than reticent, too accustomed to being trapped to imagine an alternative. They lacked the resources, either emotional or financial, to escape the red tide of war. In order to flee, you have to have somewhere to go.

A man in a bulky jacket approached Sinclair. The temperature had climbed another ten degrees, and he was conspicuously overdressed. Sinclair confronted him, his weapon at the ready.

"Back off! Hands over your head."

In the heat of the moment, Sinclair forgot the few Arab phrases they'd learned in boot camp. If he had an Achilles heel, it was his phobia of suicide bombers. Improvised explosive devices were a far more pervasive threat, but he took them in stride. At least IEDs made sense, instinctively as well as strategically. Killing the enemy meant safeguarding yourself, your platoon, your country. War itself was an extension of this collective will to survive, not an excuse to indulge self-destructive impulses. Blowing yourself up sullied the ethics of war with senseless violence.

The man looked more perplexed than intimidated. He kept gesturing toward the moving throng of refugees, repeating the same words over and over.

"*Ummi. Kalb. Kalb.*"

Sinclair trained the barrel of his automatic on the man's head. Explosives strapped to his body could be detonated by a point-blank shot.

"*Ummi. Kalb.*"

McCarthy rushed over and frisked the man. It turns out there was nothing under his jacket but a sweaty T-shirt. An alarming number of people stopped to glower at them. Sinclair tried to reassure them that they were on their side. He used a stock Arabic phrase he'd been required to memorize, something about how searches and checkpoints were designed to protect ordinary Iraqi citizens. The exact translation eluded him. He knew damned good and well his accent was atrocious. Butchering the language had no effect whatsoever on the man's confidence in Sinclair's ability to communicate. He started talking the Arabic equivalent of a mile a minute, gesticulating adamantly and often.

"*La afham,*" Sinclair said. "*La afham,* goddamnit."

Sinclair kept repeating that he didn't understand, a phrase he spoke much more fluently than any other. Finally he radioed Radetzky to request an interpreter. The man talked nonstop until the terp showed up. Sinclair asked why he was dressed for a blizzard in the middle of a fucking heat wave. The interpreter was trained to edit out expletives and wildly inappropriate figures of speech. His delivery was still less than cordial. He was Syrian and had a hard time disguising his distaste for Iraqis, not that Sinclair or anyone else in the platoon noticed. Terps were increasingly hard to come by. Most of the Iraqis they used in Baghdad quit when they found out the battalion was headed for Fallujah.

"You must be dying of the heat in that get-up. The corporal wants to know why you're all bundled up like that."

"I'd rather be hot now than freezing to death tonight," the man said. "The camps are already full. We'll be sleeping out in the open."

"Did you approach the corporal for a reason?"

"I wanted to ask if he'd seen a woman in a wheelbarrow. I've lost my mother."

"The one with the greyhound?"

"Actually, a saluki."

Sinclair couldn't believe it. There they were, in the middle of a war zone, sorting out dog breeds. Two soldiers and an interpreter had been tied up for ten minutes because a man couldn't keep track of his own mother. The US Marine Corps was being transformed into a global babysitting service. Next thing you knew they'd be changing diapers. Good thing McCarthy had already resumed his post on the other side of the highway. No doubt he would have launched into one of his tirades about squandering military resources. McCarthy never needed an interpreter. He was a gifted communicator, fluent in the universal language of outrage and obscenity. Without necessarily understanding a word he said, Iraqis knew exactly what he meant. After editing out invective, there was nothing left to translate anyway.

The evacuation dragged on well into the night. The steady flow of foot traffic finally ebbed, but there were still stragglers when the platoon was ordered to report back to the base. Only five hours remained before Operation Vigilant Resolve was scheduled to begin. Sinclair and Logan lay on their cots, resting but too excited to sleep. Sinclair tried to relax by concentrating on the relative comfort of his mattress. Even if they bunked in abandoned houses during the offensive, there wouldn't be enough beds to go around. Just as well. Beds were a security risk. Insurgents could hide under them.

Their watches beeped almost simultaneously. Sinclair jumped up and started strapping himself into the hundred pounds of gear that would sustain and protect him. Logan knelt down to perform what had become a combat ritual. He extracted the crucifix lodged between his body armor and his chest, and they both kissed it. Sinclair didn't share Logan's faith in icons, but soldiers were even more superstitious than ball players. Rituals helped them believe they would survive.

"Lord Jesus, mighty warrior and prince of peace—"

Logan grabbed his automatic. There wasn't time to finish the prayer on his knees, but God would understand.

"—grant us the strength to fight the good fight."

"Amen."

Platoon after platoon boarded Strykers bound for East Manhattan, where they would dismount and split into squads. It was the first time they'd been in armored vehicles since their arrival in Fallujah. The effort to normalize their presence in the city included traveling in Humvees rather than Strykers and tanks, leaving them vulnerable to roadside bombs. There had been talk of forgoing body armor, but Radetzky had drawn the line there.

Rucksacks were lashed onto racks to make room for more men. Sinclair was wedged between McCarthy and Trapp. Their lower lips bulged with enormous plugs of Skoal. On campaigns they rationed cigarettes, alternating between fags and chew. Sinclair passed their spit cup back and forth as they waited for the signal to mobilize. By the time the Strykers finally lurched into motion, the cup was half full.

"Now this is what I call riding in style," Trapp said.

"Break out the party snacks," McCarthy said.

They bumped along Highway 10, which was now closed to all but military traffic. Scattered palm groves dotted the desert on either side of the road, silhouetted against the rising sun. Once they were under way, a boom box blared AC/DC so loud nobody could think or talk. They played the same CD before every major offensive, to help them get into the zone. The first disc had been incinerated by a grenade. Trapp's sister sent them another one. If "War Machine" wasn't your favorite song when you enlisted, it would be by the time you shot your way out of a few fire-fights, shoulder-to-shoulder with sixty-one other grunts who swore by AC/DC. They sounded like a karaoke band on steroids, clutching guns instead of microphones. Real heavy metal. Sinclair was tone deaf, not that it mattered. Wolf was the only one with anything approximating a singing voice, and he was usually half hoarse from shouting out orders. What they lacked in pitch they made up for in volume. Fists pumped in unison every time they reached the chorus.

The platoon was already in the zone, well before they reached the city limits. From base camp, Fallujah looked like a shimmering mirage in an endless expanse of desert sands. Straight out of a Hollywood film. Up close and per-sonal, it was a gritty, angry city ready to boil over. Its rigid grid of streets lacked the grace of the mosques towering overhead. Too much concrete with too little architectural imagination. Even the most affluent houses looked more like fortresses than mansions. Courtyard walls jealously hoarded the lush shade of hidden gardens. Poorer neighborhoods gave the impression that the city had lost its self-esteem in the wake of one too many military occupations. But from a distance, cooled by Euphrates breezes fragrant with the scent of flowering date palms, Fallujah looked like a miracle. Its mosaic domes glistened in the bluest of skies, transforming the punishing sun into a kaleidoscope of fractured incandescence. Minarets pierced the heavens, promising spiritual transcendence one minute, vengeance the next. The City of a Hundred Mosques, most of them preaching hatred of Western infidels.

Fallujah's radical Sunni clerics mounted powerful speakers on minarets. Once the evacuation was announced, they commanded Fallujans to hold their ground. Baghdad had already fallen to the Americans, who were buddying up with Shiites. This wasn't the first time barbarians had conspired against Sunnis. Broadcast after broadcast referred to the commander in chief in Washington as Hulagu II, a new millennial incarnation of the notorious Mongol invader who had challenged Sunni ascendancy in ancient Iraq. Five times a day, before and after prayers, imams called on the faithful to defend Islam against the infidel occupation.

"They're in bed with the Ba'athists," Logan said every chance he got.

"Must be awfully crowded in that bed," Trapp said.

"No joke," McCarthy said. "Ba'athists, Sunnis, fedayeen."

"Mujahideen, jihadists."

"Don't forget al-Qaeda."

"Sounds like a sectarian orgy," McCarthy said.

"What about Shiites?"

"They're in bed with us."

"No way," Logan said. "We're on our own, thank God."

"Spoken like a true celibate."

"Here we go again. Another sermon on abstinence."

"Don't knock it till you've tried it," Logan said.

"I tried it last night. It sucks."

"Or doesn't suck, as the case may be."

"There are other things in life."

"Like what?"

"Like annihilating our enemies," Logan said. "All we have to do is wait till they screw each other over."

"Then move in for the kill."

Logan must have thought being a born-again Christian made him an expert on sectarian squabbles. He was convinced that imams were in cahoots with local Ba'athists, fellow Sunnis excluded from the political process after the fall of Baghdad. Washington may have miscalculated, disenfranchising them so completely. A few minor mistakes were apparently fueling the insurgency. But Ba'athist fears that Americans would hand Iraq over to the Shiites were ridiculous. Americans had no intention of handing Iraq over to anyone, at least not in the foreseeable future.

Highway 10 was deserted except for the convoy of Strykers. The emptiness accentuated the ominous beauty of the desert. Everything was double-edged in Iraq. Oases concealed deadly snipers. Pristine mosques rose from rubbish heaps. Teenagers wearing American T-shirts shouted obscenities at American infidels. One minute shepherds waved their staffs, the next they opened fire with AK-47s. Sinclair's platoon had been ordered to assume that Fallujah's benign side had decamped. The fact that civilians were instructed to evacuate meant that everyone left behind was noncompliant, one of McCarthy's favorite euphemisms.

"You know you're in trouble when the military bothers to be politically correct. It's a sure sign they're gearing up to kick somebody's ass."

Enemies were noncompliant forces. Offensives were operations. Tank search-and-destroy maneuvers were officially called movement-to-contact missions, though unofficially they caused the same amount of death and destruction, otherwise known as collateral damage. Before the Brooklyn Bridge debacle, marines were actually required to knock before entering family homes or insurgent compounds, as the case may be.

"Military etiquette," McCarthy said. "Guess who's coming to dinner."

Hospitality left something to be desired in Fallujah. Civilians seldom answered the door before squads of marines stormed into their living rooms. Rules of engagement only authorized opening fire in self-defense, a slippery distinction at best. Jumpy marines had been known to gun down hapless household pets, if not their owners, with impunity. According to McCarthy, the self-defense clause was the military equivalent of no-fault insurance. Sometimes Sinclair wished he wouldn't kid around so much. It cheapened their mission.

Tanks had flattened guardrails on either side of the highway, allowing the convoy to fan out across the desert. One too many roadside bombs had claimed the lives of military personnel over the past few weeks. Humvees with mounted machine guns and grenade launchers flanked the Strykers. The farther they penetrated into the interior of the old city, the more labyrinthine the urban landscape. Humvees were more versatile and could thread the needle into alleys and courtyards too narrow for tanks and Strykers. Revised rules of engagement guaranteed that there would always be extra firepower to back them up when the going got tough.

While Sinclair's battalion moved in from the south, two others converged on the city from the east and west. With so many units moving in from so many different quadrants, the danger of friendly fire ruled out aerial strikes until everyone dug in. Thankfully everything was relative. Insurgents didn't have tanks and Humvees with mounted artillery. Their rockets and RPG launchers were like slingshots in comparison. It was David and Goliath all over again. Only this time the giant would win.

As they entered the city proper, concrete compounds replaced stone houses. Each residence rose two or three stories over cement walls tall enough to conceal whole squads of men. East Manhattan was a relatively upscale district. Its homes resembled tastefully decorated citadels. Every three or four blocks, a mosque dominated the neighborhood. Sinclair noticed that Hazelit earthen barriers had been piled around several of the mosques. This didn't bode well. Barricades were usually reserved for coalition and Iraqi Interim Government buildings. While marines were busy evacuating civilians, insurgents had been constructing defensive positions and stockpiling ammunition. Too much babysitting had jeopardized their strategic advantage.

"What did I tell you?" McCarthy said.

"Delay and you get blown away."

The other two battalions were authorized to use maximum firepower to flush the enemy out of the industrial sector and Queens. The Thundering Third would act as a kind of human net to catch insurgents as they fled into East Manhattan. Sinclair knew guys back home who used a similar technique, flushing deer into hunting blinds. Pete's dad, Eugene, claimed his ancestors used to stampede buffalo herds over the palisades of the Tobacco Root Mountains. But Grandpa taught them never to resort to traps. Real hunting meant engaging the animal one-on-one, matching instinct and endurance.

Sometimes Sinclair wished that war was more like hunting. It's true they had a lot in common. They were both blood rituals pitting cunning and courage against fear and death. But one was in service of civilization, the other a return to the primitive. You might think a battalion was like one mighty hunter with a thousand appendages. But hunters don't shed blood for the sake of others the way soldiers do. They don't kill to protect the innocent and safeguard freedom. A great deal more was at stake in war, and Sinclair knew better than to split hairs over strategies that worked. Orders were orders. At least he was in the battalion that would most directly engage the enemy. They were authorized to summon tank and rocket support when they encountered terrorist cells, often hidden in basements of well fortified homes. But most of their mission would consist of point-blank combat with insurgents in close quarters.

Commanders were equipped with aerial photographs of the city, digital images so precise every single building and back alley was clearly mapped out. Each platoon would be responsible for clearing a block at a time before advancing. To decrease the danger of friendly fire, they had to move at roughly the same pace. Straying into each other's quadrants was strictly prohibited, even in pursuit.

"This will require discipline," Radetzky said. "When one of your buddies is maimed or killed, you'll want to track down the enemy. To make them pay."

"Damn right."

"Damn wrong."

"Yessir."

"Coordinated efforts are essential," Radetzky said. "Radio alerts to adjacent squads. We'll nail the bastards that way."

When they reached the northern perimeter of East Manhattan, the Strykers parked at two-block intervals. The trek into the city had only taken twenty minutes, and already the temperature had jumped ten degrees. With one hundred pounds of gear and one hundred degrees of heat it would have felt like two hundred degrees in the shade, if there'd been any shade. Body armor was the worst. It chafed and caused heat rashes that itched like mad.

"Better scratchier than a dog with fleas than dead," McCarthy said.

Better anything than dead.

Lieutenant Radetzky ordered one last weapons check. Their flak jackets were loaded down with grenades and magazines. They carried sidearms and machine guns. Sinclair packed both a rifle and an automatic so he could alternate between sniper and raid duty. He had also strapped a Ka-Bar knife to his leg and sheathed a more compact blade on his boot. He was equally adept at long-distance marksmanship and hand-to-hand combat, which he had picked up from Pete's dad. Nobody ever knew whether Eugene learned to wield the blade in barroom brawls or from tutelage in the dying art of Sioux warriors. One way or the other, he could carve up a far sight more than Thanksgiving turkey. Several members of the platoon had Sinclair's knives to thank for the fact that they were still standing. He was quick as a cat, especially with a Ka-Bar in his paw.

The weapons check was more ritualistic than pragmatic. It was too late to run back to base camp, too late to retrieve forgotten gear, too late to call off the mission if conditions changed on the ground. Grunts complained that the big shots planning offensives didn't have their fingers on the pulse of the action. But the trade-off was worth it to Sinclair. What generals lost in proximity they regained in expertise. Nobody could deny that the big brass had seen more action than a flophouse madam.

The beauty of the military was its unshakable chain of command. When orders were issued, they were almost always respected and virtually always carried out. This was the armed forces' most powerful weapon, this steadfast devotion to duty. It's why Sinclair joined up in the first place, along with 9/11. He had been too young to articulate what bothered him about kids at school. The Marine Corps gave him the language to diagnose the problem. Entitlement. His boot camp sergeant claimed it all started in the sixties. Ask not what you can do for your country but what your country can do for you.

"Hippie chicken shits," Sergeant Troy shouted.

He paced back and forth, stopping periodically to dress down individual soldiers. They were all blundering blueheads, but at least they weren't hightailing it to Canada.

"Draft-dodging sons of bitches."

All day eight days a week he yelled, as though the lives of his men depended on a steady stream of abuse. Verbal, physical, psychological, you name it. Maybe he was right. By the time they deployed to Iraq, all vestiges of entitlement had been beaten out of them. They knew how to fight. Even more importantly, they knew what they were fighting for. Freedom. Justice. When he really wanted to get the platoon revved up, Sergeant Troy ranted and raved about the World Trade Center. It was his rally call.

"If 9/11 had a silver lining, which it didn't, at least it nipped that entitlement shit in the bud."

The Twin Towers should have been everyone's rally call. But after the first shock wave, Sinclair's friends back home picked up where they left off, worrying their pretty little heads over midterms. Sinclair was appalled. America had been attacked on her own soil, and all they could think about were their grade point averages. When news broke that the Japanese bombed Pearl Harbor, Grandpa had left an unfinished physics exam on a desk at the University of Montana. Before the end of the semester, he was in uniform and on his way to Algiers. The closest Sinclair's classmates came to giving a damn about their country was writing college essays about how 9/11 changed them forever. Which it didn't. They were no different than they'd been on September 10, judging from their indifference to the call of duty. Sinclair couldn't hide his disdain. He lost a lot of friends that year, not just Pete.

His parents flat-out refused to let him enlist right away. They forced him to stay in college, as though playing pattycake with a bunch of frat brats would somehow change his mind about the military. If he'd been a year older, he'd have enlisted anyway, without their blessing. There was no doubt in his mind the American government wouldn't let al-Qaeda get away with mass murder. It was just a matter of time before they declared war on the guilty parties. The summer before the invasion of Iraq, he joined the US Marines. Somebody had to do it. Heroism wasn't confined to the Greatest Generation, regardless of how many new millennials took freedom for granted. Sergeant Troy was absolutely right. The War on Terror had given America its balls back.

Weapons checks were a kind of meditation. Focusing the platoon's attention on the minutiae of arms and ammunitions was Radetzky's way of keeping them calm in the face of combat. Then some clown showed up and started snapping pictures, something Radetzky presumably had no control over. They hadn't hosted an embedded reporter since the Battle of Baghdad. Apparently their missions hadn't been media worthy since then. So much the better. The last embed had pissed off Sinclair. He was a know-it-all who kept trying to buddy up to them, as though they were all in this thing together. Fat chance. War correspondents were, by definition, nothing more than glorified pen pals.

To be fair, Sinclair hadn't given the guy much of a chance. He resented embedded reporters. They were a nagging reminder that Iraq was as much a media war as a military offensive. Half of the time, political types based their decisions on news clips more than official reports. As a result, half of their decisions were counterproductive. If they'd let the armed forces run the war, the notorious mission accomplished declaration would have been a fact rather than a gaffe.

"Got what you need?" Radetzky asked the embed.

"I could use a group shot."

"Over here," Radetzky said. He ordered his men to grab their weapons of choice for a photo op. McCarthy made an obscene noise, which he pretended not to hear. A commissioned officer, Radetzky was expected to facilitate what the Pentagon called strategic media coverage. Needless to say,

McCarthy called it propaganda. Semantics aside, it played an increasingly vital role in greasing the war machine. Seasoned members of the squad like Trapp were less critical of the press corps. Wounded in the Gulf War, he had spent some time in the VA hospital in Jackson. Vietnam vets there told him the government had learned its lesson at My Lai.

"Either you control the media or it controls you."

Trapp admitted that embedded reporters were a pain in the ass. But they were a necessary evil, not unlike rules of engagement. The American public was being bombarded with negative images of the war, compliments of Al Jazeera and other blatantly biased media outlets. Providing more impartial coverage was the only way to guarantee continued support of the military. Leftist complaints that embedded reporters lacked objectivity were ridiculous. The fact that they shadowed soldiers and even broke bread with them didn't mean they were really all in this thing together. Shooting pictures was a far cry from getting shot.

"Men, this is Earl Johnson," Radetzky said. "Associated Press correspondent."

Radetzky left it at that. Last time there had been an elaborate introduction, probably instigated by the embed himself. What a prima donna. Johnson was less intrusive. He nodded and went to work, setting up his tripod with no fanfare whatsoever. He was much older and infinitely less sycophantic than his predecessor. No wonder. Turns out he was a vet. He had almost made the US Marines his career, but opted out to salvage his marriage. It failed anyway. The military saves as many marriages as it destroys, thanks to the inescapable logic of emotional clichés. Absence makes the heart grow fonder. Women love men in uniform even more than they hate war.

Without thinking, the platoon congregated in rows. Guys upfront knelt on one knee. They didn't really pose. They fell in, taking their places in the endless ranks of photographs that shaped the collective consciousness of military men. Patriotism wasn't so much a sentiment as an image. Storming the beaches at Normandy. Planting the flag at Iwo Jima and Ground Zero. Uncles and fathers had shown them pictures of Korea and Nam. Sinclair's grandpa had been less forthcoming, not that it made any difference. Hunting through bookshelves and drawers, Sinclair found the inevitable black-and-white shots of men brandishing weapons, in this case the tommy guns and bazookas of World War II. Weaponry and landscapes changed over the years but never the soldiers themselves. Whether framed by Pacific palm trees or French vineyards, their faces always looked exactly the same. Blank. The unconscious imprint of these photographs inspired many a boy to dream of enlisting. The only way to solve the riddle of those enigmatic faces was to go to war.

"Must be anticipating civilian casualties," Trapp said. He was standing between Sinclair and McCarthy in the back row.

"Why's that?" Sinclair asked.

"They're deploying embeds."

"Spin doctors," McCarthy said. "All the news that's fit to print."

"Give or take a few body bags."

"Minor details."

"We make a mess. They clean it up."

Suddenly the airwaves were alive with logistical commands. Captain Phipps climbed out of his Stryker to consult with Lieutenant Radetzky. Tactical Operations barked orders into their headsets. Phipps looked excited. Radetzky looked like he always looked. Calm. In control.

"Confirm coordinates after every block," Captain Phipps said.

"Yessir," Lieutenant Radetzky said. He turned to his men. "Split into squads. Keep pace."

All along the perimeter of East Manhattan, captains gave the signal and companies slipped into Fallujah. Their stealth, in spite of all their gear, was remarkable. The Marine Corps's most cherished motto—swift, silent, and deadly—was particularly well suited to urban operations. They disappeared into the city, which seemed to lie in wait for them.

Radetzky's platoon was armed with a secret weapon. Sinclair headed up a sniper team tasked with covering maneuvers on the ground. Deploying snipers in search-and-destroy missions was highly unorthodox. Conventional wisdom said they slowed things down, leaving troops more vulnerable to ambushes. But conventional wisdom was as outdated in Iraq as conventional warfare. Perched on high, snipers could pick off insurgents moving from one bunker to the next. They were the eyes and ears of the platoon, providing security and intelligence in equal measure. Sinclair was in constant radio contact with Radetzky, who adjusted his strategies accordingly.

Sinclair's team snuck up the stairwell of an apartment complex overlooking several blocks of ritzy single-family homes. The rest of the platoon split up, preparing to clear a pair of compounds under his watchful eye. Lieutenant Radetzky led one squad, Wolf the other. McCarthy's bunk-mate Percy served double duty, backing up both squads with a shoulder-launched multipurpose assault weapon. SMAWs could level bunkers and smoke insurgents out of structures too well-fortified to storm. In theory, they were portable weapons systems. In practice, Percy was the only one strong enough to carry the damned thing. There were several other college football stars in the company. They looked like featherweight wrestlers next to Percy, who was posted behind a garden wall. Radetzky waited until everyone confirmed their positions. He never rushed their maneuvers. Slow is smooth, smooth is fast.

"Prepare to advance," Radetzky announced into his headset.

"I'm blind from eight o'clock to eleven," Percy said.

"You got that, Sinclair?" Radetzky said.

"Got it covered," Sinclair said.

"We're right behind you," Wolf said.

The two squads rushed single-file across the patios of adjacent compounds. Johnson followed Wolf's team, his camera at the ready. If a swift kick or two didn't pop the front door, they blew the lock. On extended campaigns, this tactic saved a lot of wear and tear on point men. Otherwise they had to batter down door after door, all because civilians lacked the common courtesy to welcome them into their homes. You tried to liberate a country, and they locked their doors in your face. Go figure.

Two men appeared on the roof of one of the compounds. Sinclair zeroed in on them, preparing to fire, and then relaxed his trigger finger. It was Trapp and McCarthy. They made a quick search of the area, checking for weapons caches, before disappearing back down the stairwell. Neither of them looked in Sinclair's direction for fear of giving away his position. But they could feel his eyes watching their backs. An umbilical cord of energy connected good snipers with their platoons.

The squads moved on to the next set of compounds. No one anticipated much resistance on the perimeter of the city, but you never knew. Unpredictability was the insurgency's most lethal weapon. The desert was wired with booby traps and IEDs. Urban combat was even more full of surprises. Every room in every single house was a potential jack-in-the-box. The sheer number bred boredom and complacency. Door after door popped open, hundreds and then thousands of them revealing nothing. Then out jumped Jack with an AK-47, and you'd opened your last door.

The platoon cleared three full blocks without encountering a living soul. Someone somewhere was trying to lull them into a false sense of security. Telltale signs told a different, more menacing story. Wolf, who had worked in construction before enlisting, was adept at identifying architectural anomalies. He and Evans carried crowbars, yet another secret weapon in unconventional warfare. They found a cache of grenades and Dragunov rifles in the pantry of an upscale house, hidden under a false floor.

"Where's Johnson?" Radetzky asked.

"Watcha got?"

"Exhibit A."

Johnson whistled. Wolf and Evans continued prying open the floorboards.

"Take five," Radetzky told the rest of the squad.

Everybody broke out cigarettes except McCarthy, the world's biggest mooch.

"How about a fag," McCarthy said.

"Looked in the mirror lately?" Trapp said, handing him a Camel.

The entire platoon knew McCarthy would hit them up, sooner or later, so they took turns plying him with cigarettes and chew. It was all part of the deal, the price he made them pay for the pleasure of his company. They stood smoking in the kitchen, flicking their butts into the sink. With the exception of designated lookouts, they instinctively avoided windows. Enemy snipers never took cigarette breaks.

Johnson went to work. This was just the kind of footage the Pentagon used to counteract the damage done by Al Jazeera newscasters. The minute coalition forces mounted an offensive, they started broadcasting graphic photographs of civilian casualties, portraying Americans as ruthless murderers of innocent bystanders. Air strikes on residential neighborhoods. Women and children sprawled across bloody bedroom floors. Sunni officials in the provisional government in Baghdad watched them. American officials in Washington watched them. The whole world witnessed them on the Internet. Dispassionate reports were far less compelling than Al Jazeera's version of what passed for the truth, complete with incendiary sound bites.

"Mosques Bombed by Coalition Forces in Anbar Province."

"American Marines Slaughter Civilians in Fallujah."

The fine line between news and entertainment had long since been crossed. To attract an audience, even Johnson's photographs would be hyped up with inflammatory captions. "Family Home or Terrorist Cell?" So much for the innocent bystander routine. Since when did housewives shelve grenades and rifles next to cleaning supplies and canned goods? The city was obviously armed to the teeth.

Radetzky radioed company headquarters, requesting a team of runners to transport the contraband weapons back to the base. Within minutes, a Humvee pulled up, and two marines hopped out. They were women, a private first class and a sergeant. Sinclair scoped their faces. One of them was pretty.

"Cover them," Radetzky ordered.

"Roger that," Sinclair said.

The arrival of women on the scene confirmed Sinclair's assumption that the platoon hadn't yet reached the skirmish line. Rear-echelon support teams stumbled into ambushes with alarming frequency. But the US military still tried to enforce rules of engagement forbidding women to perform combat duty. Technically the real action was on hold until they got the hell out of the way.

Radetzky advanced the men to the next block as the two women finished confiscating the weapons cache. Sinclair covered the Humvee until it finally sped off. By the time he turned his attention back to the squads, they were almost out of range. His team would have to relocate after the next set of houses. He would miss this perch. A convenient ledge allowed him to stretch full length to avoid muscle cramping. Comfort aside, the view was incomparable. There were very few apartment complexes in East Manhattan. Its seven stories towered over the posh homes huddled below. Snipers had a reputation for being notoriously cold-blooded. But it was hard not to get sentimental over such a well-appointed nest. Home sweet home.

The minute he got comfy, shit was bound to hit the fan. Murphy's Law. A gang of insurgents appeared in the alley bisecting the block. They ran, single file, hugging garden walls for cover. Enemy fighters were perpetually in transit, wary of being trapped and mortared in buildings. Mobility was their best defense against the superior firepower of coalition forces. Sinclair dialed the elevation and zoomed in.

"We've got company," Sinclair said. He spoke calmly into his headset, to avoid disturbing his aim.

Most of the men were wearing checkered kaffiyehs, the insurgency's unofficial uniform. They carried AK-47s and Dragunovs, the same vintage as the ones in the weapons cache. Their destination was unmistakable, a garden shed at the far end of the block, one of a handful of locations outside Sinclair's line of fire. Either they knew he was overhead or dumb luck was on their side. They had to sprint across an exposed driveway to get there. Sinclair squeezed the trigger. His first kill of the day.

"Location?" Radetzky said.

"West of Wolf's—"

Sinclair's warning was cut short by the sound of rocket-propelled grenades. Insurgents had set up their launchers behind the shed. They kept trying to lace RPGs through the windows of a freestanding compound. Wolf's men were trapped inside. Even when grenades missed the mark, random explosions blasted debris across the courtyard. The squad couldn't risk making a run for it. Machine gun muzzles appeared in the windows. Trapp and McCarthy ducked in and out, pummeling the shed with multiple rounds. An enemy RPG hit home and torched the bedroom right next to them. Close, but no cigar. Sinclair crept around the perimeter of his rooftop, trying to improve his angle. There was no way to nail the bastards without relocating.

Radetzky's squad was hamstrung in a neighboring compound. If they came to the rescue, they stood a good chance of getting blown away. Enemy gunners trained their sights on every conceivable escape route. The scope of Radetzky's strategic imagination had apparently eluded them. His men rappelled from unseen windows and stormed the shed. Most of the insurgents were picked off before they could even grab their gear. Gunners returned fire over their shoulders as they fled. One stampede of moving targets pursued the other down the smoke-filled alley.

When they reached the adjoining street, an insurgent managed to hurl a grenade before diving under a parked car for cover. It exploded well in advance of Radetzky's squad, but the concussion knocked a rookie off his feet. It was Sanchez, a new recruit from Tallahassee. Momentarily stationary and vulnerable, he was winged by enemy fire.

"Call a medic!" Radetzky shouted. "Let's get you out of here."

"It's a scratch," Sanchez yelled back. "I'm good to go."

Blood stained but didn't saturate the sleeve of Sanchez's uniform, evidence enough that he had plenty of fight left in him. The rest of the squad picked up the pace, determined to avenge his wound. But by the time they rounded the street corner, there was no one in sight.

"Enemy combatant under the car at three o'clock," Sinclair reported into his headset.

"Roger that," Radetzky said, motioning to three of his men.

They surrounded the vehicle. The insurgent pinned underneath fired wild shots to stave them off. Seeking cover, Radetzky decided to play it safe. He summoned Percy, who didn't even bother consulting his range finder. Positioning himself behind a nearby truck, he braced the SMAW against his shoulder and fired at almost point-blank range. The car exploded into flames. The squad exploded into laughter and applause.

"Bull's-eye," Sanchez said. He felt vindicated.

"All clear," Sinclair said.

The platoon reconnoitered in the alleyway. Wolf's squad high-fived the guys responsible for bailing them out. Sanchez's wound was superficial enough to be treated without wasting time waiting for a medic. Trapp did the honors. Growing up in Mississippi, he used to tag along on his father's rounds as a country doctor. Ailing farmers paid their bills with chickens and vegetables, if at all. He remembered playing endless games of Kick the Can with kids whose mothers had gone into labor. His father told him a woman's screams weren't important as long as her baby came out okay. But Trapp couldn't help thinking of his own mother, who had died in childbirth. He wondered if she had screamed so much.

Having been raised around illness and injury, Trapp eventually got used to it. His gore threshold was even higher than McCarthy's, which was saying a lot. Sharecroppers were accident prone or unlucky or both. They seemed to have an adversarial relationship with farm equipment. Grinders and thrashers made mincemeat out of hands and feet in the wrong place at the wrong time. Bandaging Sanchez's arm was child's play in comparison. Trapp dressed the wound like a matron changing a diaper. He treated severed limbs no differently than surface wounds. Gently and competently. Nothing fazed him.

Every company in the American armed forces was supposed to have its own medic. What was true in the army didn't always apply to the Marine Corps. Marines were used to doing more with less, making virtue out of necessity. Wolf's squad was proud of the fact that they'd spent their own money to equip themselves for Operation Iraqi Freedom. Government-issue equipment only went so far, covering necessities like arms, ammunition, and body armor. The rest was up to individual soldiers and platoons. Pooling their resources, Wolf's squad hit the sales at hardware stores. They mounted CB antenna, ammunition racks, and extra camouflage netting until their Humvees were battle ready. Radetzky's men took one look at the competition and went on their own shopping spree.

Back home, budget constraints starved VA hospitals, regardless of how many politicians promised to take care of wounded warriors. In the field, lieutenants took matters into their own hands. Radetzky made sure everyone was trained in first aid. They all carried blow out kits with bandages, tourniquets, QuikClot, and saline IV bags. The so-called company medic, Doc Olsen, trained them to doctor themselves when he was otherwise engaged. Technically he was always on call. Actually he was usually off ministering to the six other platoons under his jurisdiction. Trapp routinely tended to everything except evacuation cases. He finished dressing Sanchez's wound in half the time it would have taken to locate Doc Olsen, let alone fetch him.

"Sure you're okay?" Radetzky asked Sanchez.

"Never been better."

Sanchez wasn't just acting tough. Boot camp had taught him to believe that pain was weakness leaving the body, and he felt stronger than ever. Radetzky smacked his helmet for the first time since he'd joined the platoon. Sanchez felt like he'd been knighted.

"Move out, men."

The platoon split up again, clearing two houses at a time. Radetzky's demeanor reminded them not to let excitement impair their judgment. They worked methodically without taking unnecessary risks. It was just a matter of time before even the most pedestrian search-and-destroy mission hit the jackpot. Another platoon in the company had already stormed a compound crawling with feyadeen. If they were lucky, they'd flush out a terrorist cell, maybe even Abu Musab al-Zarqawi's hidey-hole. Then there'd be real fireworks—artillery, aerial strikes, the whole nine yards. The search half of the mission could be deadly boring.

Destroying what you found more than compensated for the tedium.

The squads were advancing so quickly, Sinclair's team had to relocate almost hourly. Their optimum position was one step ahead of the platoon, where they could anticipate resistance. Sinclair used his laser range finder to determine when to move. The squads were 748 yards away. He could manage 90 percent accuracy at that distance, provided wind wasn't a factor. The odds weren't good enough. They were all committed to giving 100 percent to each other. Sinclair started scouting out his next perch. He spied a rooftop with an imposing water cistern, perfectly situated. Usually cisterns were too exposed. This one had decorative embellishments wide enough to hide behind. It was love at first sight. The view would be drop-dead gorgeous, and there was plenty of cover.

"Range alert," Sinclair reported. "I need to advance."

"Can you wait till we secure the next compound?" Radetzky asked.

"Better not."

"Make it snappy. Things are starting to heat up down here."

Sinclair's team threaded its way through the neighborhood. They were able to move quickly in the wake of the platoon's maneuvers. His team was smaller than the other two squads, consisting of a single sniper and a couple of flankers tasked with rear security. The flankers cleared rooftops and then stationed themselves in windows or stairwells, depending on the layout of the building. To downplay their vulnerability, they referred to themselves as an escort service rather than a combat unit. Sinclair was their madam. Ordinarily he partnered with a spotter, an extra set of eyes behind the binoculars and scopes that magnified suspicious black specks into viable targets. But on search-and-destroy missions, Wolf's squad needed an extra gunner more than Sinclair needed extra eyes. Evans, his usual spotter, was in the thick of things down below. Sinclair envied him. It could get pretty lonely up there.

Sinclair was still unpacking his drag bag when a dozen or so insurgents converged to engage the platoon. They were better armed than usual, probably former Ba'athist militiamen. The leader of the pack was wearing what looked like an Iraqi police uniform, though Sinclair couldn't be sure with the naked eye. He grabbed his rifle and zoomed in. Sure enough, the point man was in uniform. He motioned and two groups of five fanned across a meticulously manicured garden. Sinclair confirmed the platoon's location. Wolf's squad was preparing to exit an adjacent compound. Radetzky's was still searching a cellar packed with suspicious crates. Either the home owner was a hoarder or he was hiding something.

"Heads up," Sinclair said, talking low and steady as he dialed his scope. "Enemy gunners knocking on Wolf's back door."

Sinclair centered his crosshairs on the official insignia on the man's chest. The police uniform gave him pause, but he was used to sorting out Iraqi disguises. The man had probably either stolen the jacket or deserted the force when he caught wind of Operation Vigilant Resolve. Or when his parents disowned him. Or when his wife was threatened one too many times by the Ba'athist underground. Sinclair squeezed the trigger and the man buckled into a flowering acacia. The pack dispersed, taking cover behind a stone wall. A hefty insurgent lugging a grenade launcher lagged behind. Sinclair picked him off, too.

"How many?" Radetzky asked.

"Nine left," Sinclair said.

Sinclair didn't think about the two dead men. Emotion of any kind compromised his concentration. McCarthy would have gloated over their deaths, hooting and hollering and slapping his buddies on the back. Sinclair wasn't fool enough to think his more restrained response made him a better soldier. If whooping it up steeled McCarthy's mettle, so be it. All that mattered was getting the job done, killing the enemy before they killed you. The decision to wage war was morally complex. But once you stepped foot on the battlefield, the only ethic was survival.

"Make that eight," Percy said. One of the insurgents had hightailed it straight into his SMAW nest. Dumb shit.

"Save some for us!" McCarthy yelled.

Wolf's squad exploded out the back door. Seconds later, Radetzky's men caught up with the action. They beat back the attack with superior firepower. This time, when they gave chase, an IED detonated in the alleyway. It was a classic bait and hook maneuver. The enemy must have thought it was worth sacrificing a few men to lure the platoon into the trap. Cowards. Their most effective strategies were almost always suicidal, completely at odds with American values. Real men never fought wars that way.

The platoon had learned to gauge the duration and range of IED explosions. The instant lethal debris settled, they rushed through dust and smoke to give chase. The remaining insurgents had covered a lot of ground, but Evans managed to mow down two more. The rest melted back into the malevolent city, seething with hate in the hot sun. Six down, five to go. Wolf wanted to track them down, but Radetzky was wary of friendly fire. They were verging dangerously close to the adjacent company's quadrant. It was time to get back to the business of clearing houses.

The minute the squads disappeared into the next set of compounds, a lone figure appeared at the gate of a nearby mosque. He paused at its arched entrance, as though waiting for a sign. Then he started walking across a tree-lined public square toward Sinclair's perch. Places of worship were strictly off-limits to fighters on both sides. Rules of engagement notwithstanding, minarets were often crawling with enemy snipers. Sinclair thought he detected a flash of light, what looked like a glinting gun barrel. But it could have been nothing more than a mosaic tile reflecting the midday sun. Fallujah's minarets pierced the heavens like so many sacred spires or dazzling daggers, depending on who inhabited the mosque that day. Huge speakers were mounted on muezzins' balconies. They were alternately used for prayer or ranting and raving, sometimes in the same breath. Sinclair's Arabic was rudimentary, at best. But he had heard phrases like *al mout li Amreeka* so many times even he understood them. Once the offensive was under way, the incessant racket of guns and grenades drowned out the sound of holy hate. Thank God for small mercies.

Even before scoping him, Sinclair could tell the man was unarmed. He walked slowly, with almost formal precision, toward the corpses in the alleyway. It was an old man, so frail he had difficulty dragging the abandoned bodies, one by one, onto the back porch of a modest house. At one point, pausing to catch his breath, he looked up at Sinclair. His expression was difficult to decipher. There was sadness, surely, but also pride and mute outrage. It was a look Sinclair had seen often in Fallujah, and never anywhere else.

Sinclair kept one eye on the platoon, the other on the old man. He might very well be a decoy, or worse, using age as a form of camouflage. Iraqis were never too young or too old to take up arms against Americans. But nothing suspicious transpired. The minaret glinted without exploding into gunfire. No one tried to recover the dead insurgents' rifles. They lay scattered, like so many tombstones, marking the spot where each shooter bit the dust. Apparently the old man's motives were purely devotional. He stopped and rested repeatedly, swatting flies off the corpses of young men much bigger and stronger than himself. Sinclair was always impressed by the bravery of everyday people, often women and even children, retrieving their loved ones in deference to their sacred duty. They walked fearlessly into combat zones, toiling slowly and deliberately, as though protected by a force field of grace.

Sinclair respected the enemy for venerating their dead. He even respected their dead in a general way. But they were all unknown soldiers to him. They didn't register as individual casualties caused by individual acts of war, let alone his actions. His response to his kills, to the extent that he had one, was qualified by the fact that they were technically insurgents, not soldiers. Maybe even terrorists. They didn't serve their country honorably the way he did. They didn't even have a country, though such dire dereliction was inconceivable to Sinclair, who loved America with a passion he scarcely understood and never questioned. There was no tomb of the unknown terrorist at Arlington National Cemetery or anywhere else. Yet they were treated with utmost respect by the women and children and old men who mourned them not as terrorists but as husbands and fathers and sons.

Sinclair's grandpa had taught him to respect death above all things. To revere the game you shot was to transform an act of violence into the ritual of the hunt. Animals weren't trophies to mount and display but noble partners in a primitive dance with death. In the same vein, if you didn't honor the men you killed in war, the act verged on murder. Were they not engaged in this very offensive because terrorists had desecrated bodies on Brooklyn Bridge? The Battle of Fallujah, if it ever merited the name, would be remembered as a crusade to safeguard the dignity of death itself, a man's right to an honorable burial. The old man's ministrations seemed to affirm that even insurgents maintained that right.

"A civilian is recovering the bodies," Sinclair reported into his headset. "He's dragging them into a house."

"Shit," Radetzky exclaimed. "They're not supposed to be here—"

"They were warned, Lieutenant." An imperious voice interrupted Radetzky. "Anyone who chose not to evacuate is a potential threat."

Periodically the tactical operations center listened in on their radio frequency, monitoring the platoon's advance. Captain Phipps seldom intervened. When he did, he expected results.

"Roger that, Captain," Radetzky confirmed.

"No pussyfooting around. Understood?"

"Yessir."

The whole platoon heard the order loud and clear. It didn't mean you had to shoot unarmed civilians. It did mean you fired first and asked questions later, if at all. Making the decision to spare the old man had been mercifully easy. But the boundary between civilians and insurgents was seldom so cut-and-dried in Fallujah. When in doubt, destroy. Delay and you get blown away.

With the exception of Lieutenant Radetzky, the platoon was energized by Captain Phipps's intervention. His blunt aggression fueled their bravado, something Radetzky discouraged in favor of a more measured tactical mindset. Sinclair noticed an immediate difference. They seemed to gather momentum, as though time were speeding up. Combat time, they called it. Even Sinclair experienced it, isolated from the accelerated action below. The first day or two of a campaign proceeded minute by minute like a regular clock. Then something clicked and whole days flashed by, punctuated not by hours but by how many close encounters they survived and how many corpses lay in the wake of their survival. Fatigue also messed with their internal clocks. They were lucky if they grabbed four hours of sleep a night. Even then, they kept one eye open, half an ear cocked, just in case.

Sinclair had gone days at a time without sleep during the Battle of Baghdad. The breakneck pace of shock and awe acted as a kind of amphetamine, real as opposed to synthetic speed. Talk about flying high. Fallujah was tame in comparison, a much more methodical offensive. At least so far. He had plenty of Provigil pills in his ruck, which he avoided taking as long as possible. The last thing the platoon needed was a jumpy sniper. He'd probably have no choice in the long run. Judging from Captain Phipps's impatience, nobody would be bedding down anytime soon.

Late in the day, Sinclair sighted a rifle team from a neighboring squad, cozy as can be on a penthouse balcony. They scoped each other and nodded gun barrels. Sinclair surfed his radio and found their frequency. The team was led by Lance Corporal Eddy, a sniper he'd met in basic training. They compared notes. The adjacent platoon had seen less action. But plenty of insurgents were retreating across their quadrant, just out of range. It was time to figure out where they were going.

"Spotted any Iraqi police uniforms?" Sinclair asked.

"One about three hours ago," Eddy said. "Leading a group of four or five thugs."

"Did you nail them?"

"They keep slipping through the cracks."

"Must have their own lookouts."

"Could be a cell nearby."

"That much traffic?"

"All in the same direction. South by southwest."

Sinclair reported these traffic patterns to Radetzky. Several other platoon lieutenants had fielded similar reports. Together they were able to map out a web of retreat routes converging on a sector just west of their location. Radetzky contacted Captain Phipps, requesting permission to temporarily suspend independent search-and-destroy missions. He proposed consolidating as many platoons as possible to execute a sting operation. Phipps passed the recommendation on to battalion headquarters.

"Permission granted," Colonel Denning said. "But you'd better make damn sure it's a cell and not a sewing circle."

"What's that supposed to mean?"

"Civilian casualties. Bad press. You name it, Phipps. We could use a clear-cut victory to silence the doves."

"Doves? I thought all the hawks in Washington were on the warpath."

"Just as many doves in Baghdad. Tell Radetzky to find that cell and make it snappy."

"Yessir."

"I've got tanks all dressed up with nowhere to go. Let's fill their dance cards."

Colonel Denning and Captain Phipps were divided over how to negotiate the persistent presence of civilians on the battlefield. It was up to Radetzky to figure out how to execute conflicting orders. Captain Phipps had all but told them to shoot everything that moved. The colonel's more prudent approach was more in line with Radetzky's own disposition. But the question remained whether he could protect civilians while at the same time safeguarding his men. Too often, prudence and safety were mutually exclusive.

Captain Phipps could only spare one other platoon. Its commander, Lieutenant Lloyd, had served with Radetzky in Afghanistan. Both had classical music collections. They bonded over the Ring Cycle. Though neither of them broadcast their love of opera, they were privately gratified when PSYOP units blasted "Ride of the Valkyries" to rally the troops. What their sound systems lacked in acoustics they made up for in volume.

The two lieutenants deployed five squads to form a circle around the suspected cell site. Radetzky attached Sinclair's team to Wolf's squad. The action might be too fast and furious to involve sharpshooting. But Sinclair could still act as the eyes and ears of the offensive, monitoring the results of feints designed to confirm the target location. Every time a squad advanced toward what Radetzky called the beehive, a team of enemy drones emerged to protect the queen. What had once been a luxurious townhouse was now a terrorist cell, the sinister version of what marines called tactical operations centers.

Once they advanced far enough into East Manhattan, American troops also commandeered family homes. They were instructed to treat them with respect. Heirlooms were neatly stacked in corners and covered with tarps to protect them from fallout. China closets were searched without breaking a single sugar bowl. This kind of fatuous politesse scandalized McCarthy. Taking time out for what he called tea parties jeopardized men's lives.

"We're marines, goddamnit. Not Avon ladies."

McCarthy was a disciple of General Sherman, an icon of the no-nonsense school of American military history. Declaring that war is hell was his way of acknowledging the brutality of battle. Pretending otherwise tended to exacerbate rather than ameliorate the devastation. One way or the other, precious cups and saucers were bound to suffer collateral damage. Alas. This time around, the platoon was authorized to dispense with gratuitous niceties. It was their first real chance to engage an actual enemy outpost, a welcome relief from the tedium of clearing houses. They were riding high because Sinclair had been instrumental in identifying the target. A little too high.

Wolf's squad was assigned to the southern arc of the offensive, closest to Phase Line Violet. Only a quarter of a mile separated them from the industrial sector, which had already been targeted by Battalion 1/5. Their position was crucial. If insurgents survived the initial attack, they would probably retreat in a southerly direction toward the area not yet cleared. Wolf's squad was tasked with cutting off their escape route. Plugging the hole was half the battle. Sometimes defense was the best offense.

"Secure a bunker," Radetzky ordered. "No telling how many hajjis will show up on your doorstep."

"We'll be ready for them."

Wolf chose the most imposing residence in the neighborhood, presumably the home of a Ba'athist bigwig. Percy and Sinclair staked out SMAW and sniper nests on the roof, a dynamic duo of brute strength and patient precision. Evans was tasked with backing them up. Out of habit, he stationed himself next to Sinclair. It felt right, fighting side-by-side again. Just like the good old days. The other gunners were posted at strategic windows in the compound below. Next thing they knew, tanks started rolling into the area. For good measure, a fleet of Bradleys was deployed to negotiate alleys too narrow to accommodate the big boys. Sacrificing stealth for firepower hadn't been Radetzky's idea, that's for sure. Colonel Denning's fingerprints were all over the op plan.

The grinding of tank treads on pavement must have alerted the cell. The whole block exploded as insurgents attempted to beat the big guns to the draw. Their survival depended on breaching the circle of squads before mounted artillery could finish them off. Lieutenant Lloyd's platoon dominated the firefight on the northern perimeter. Radetzky's men held their ground until Wolf's compound started taking heat from behind. The enemy had outflanked them. They were surrounded.

"Insurgents moving in from the south," Wolf reported into his headset.

"How many?" Radetzky demanded.

"Twenty. Thirty. A lot."

"Hang tough. We're on our way."

Sinclair stashed his sniper rifle and grabbed his automatic. Percy launched a series of rockets twice the size of the insurgents' best stuff. Evans was in his element, simulating an entire legion of marines. But there were only ten of them and untold numbers of enemy grenade launchers, difficult to locate in the smoky glare. If they were lucky, their assailants would overestimate the strength of their position based on the amount of ammunition the squad managed to pump out. Their only hope was to hold out until tanks crashed through the skirmish line.

"We're right behind you," Colonel Denning said. "Tanks are pounding the cell now. Then we'll roll those babies your way."

Even through the din of grenade explosions, they could hear and almost feel the tremendous concussion of tank bombardment in the distance. The main operation was proceeding according to plan. But Wolf's squad was beleaguered. Insurgents were making mad dashes toward their compound, zigzagging to avoid trampling the bodies of fallen comrades. Their eyes shone with conviction. Facing almost certain death in their attempt to storm the bunker, they sprinted toward Allah, guns blazing.

The gunners on the ground floor were calling for reinforcements. Wolf ordered Sinclair to back them up. For the first time during the offensive, he descended from his rooftop perch into the belly of the beast. Confronting the enemy at almost point-blank range triggered a sense memory. They looked like suicide bombers, fanatics intent on blowing themselves up for the glory of some random god. Sinclair's phobia gripped him. He focused on their torsos, not daring to look at their faces. It felt like their expressions alone could kill him. Bullets ripped their bodies apart midstride, and their faces just kept coming. He squeezed the trigger so hard his finger went numb. Let them all rush to meet their maker as long as they didn't take him along for the ride.

Wolf detected an almost imperceptible change in the squad's firepower. One of their guns had fallen silent. He ordered Trapp to investigate and man the position himself, if need be. The whole squad heard the exchange. The fact that Wolf sent Trapp didn't bode well. Their first and only priority under siege was engaging the enemy. Wounded men were expected to keep fighting until the threat was contained. But they all knew Trapp would bend the rules if the gunner in question urgently needed medical attention. He didn't.

Evans had been shot dead, a single bullet wound to the head. He fell as though hugging the barrel of his automatic. When Trapp pulled him aside to assume his position, he saw that his cheek had been branded by the smoldering muzzle. He wanted to compose the face, to succor the anguished expression before it froze forever in a death mask. But bullets were pinging helter-skelter, snapping Trapp back into action. In a rage over the loss of his buddy, he grabbed his gun and let loose. Whatever opening the enemy might have seized was slammed shut with a frenzied burst of rounds.

"Evans must have been hit," Wolf said.

Exceptional squad leaders can recognize the signature styles of their gunners. Trapp was at the wheel now, driving like a maniac.

"Let's get him off the roof!" Sinclair shouted.

"Maintain your position," Wolf ordered. "Trapp's got him covered."

Insurgents had given up on the idea of taking the compound by storm. Plan B evidently consisted of mounting an attack from several adjacent compounds. Wolf adjusted his strategy accordingly. His main objective was to prevent access to the only other three-story building within striking distance. If enemy grenade launchers managed to secure higher ground, the squad would be done for. He kept yelling into his headset, trying to contact the tactical operations center. Either the radio was dead or the blare of battle was drowning out their directives. Sequestering himself in a closet, he wrapped a pillow around his head as he strained to hear. Seconds later he rushed back out.

"Prepare to evacuate!" he hollered.

The order seemed incredible. The squad was surrounded. Outnumbered. They would be mowed down the minute they stepped foot outside the compound. But nothing justified second-guessing their commander. Sinclair obeyed instantaneously, without thinking. McCarthy was several steps behind him, swearing a blue streak as they raced down the hallway past a pair of gunners still cranking out rounds. The only conceivable explanation was that they hadn't heard the command.

"Evacuate the compound!" Sinclair bellowed.

"What?" they screamed back.

"Evacuate! Pronto!"

"Are you crazy?"

"Wolf's orders."

They grabbed their gear and joined the exodus. Wolf raced up the stairs to make sure the rest of the squad followed suit. On the roof, Trapp and Percy were equally incredulous, but they lowered their guns. Trapp started to prepare Evans's body for evacuation. Wolf intervened.

"Not now."

"It's okay," Trapp said, intending to hoist Evans onto his back. "I've got him."

"We'll be back," Wolf said. "I promise."

Wolf was responsible for protecting the living and honoring the dead, in that order. He knew full well Trapp would make the ultimate sacrifice, even for a lost cause. It was a Southern thing. In the midst of the melee, Trapp had removed Evans's flak jacket and spread it over his body, as though to protect him from fallout. He left a bandana folded under his bloodied head, cushioning his wounds. His Vietnam buddies swore by this ritual, a kind of good luck charm to protect life or, at the very least, limb. When the wounded recovered, they returned the bandana to its owner. Trapp always packed several in his ruck, hoping not to use them. Planning to get them back if he did. The platoon had never lost a man before.

Wolf led the way down the stairwell. Everybody else had congregated in the entrance hall of the compound. The attack still raged, unabated, AK-47 fire punctuated by RPG explosions just beyond the doorstep. If anything, the pace had picked up and the din was more deafening. Wolf radioed the tactical operations center again, confirming their readiness. Then he gave the signal, obeying his superiors with the same blind faith his squad mustered to obey him.

"Go!" Wolf shouted. "Straight ahead and just keep running!"

When they burst out the door, they saw a column of US Marines covering their flight with the legion of weapons they themselves had simulated during the shoot-out. In the distance they heard tanks grinding forward, already beginning to discharge missiles overhead. The enemy's feeble attempts to defend themselves melted in the ensuing conflagration. Their remains, if there were any, would be impossible to distinguish from the rubble. Trapp thought of Evans as he sprinted to safety, hanging on to Wolf's promise that they would return to honor his body.

The bombardment only lasted fifteen minutes. Even so, it was probably overkill. The squad watched from a safe zone three blocks north as smoke cleared and relative silence made their ears ring. A bird chirped outside the window of their refuge. Several men laughed at the innocent absurdity of the sound. They laughed because they were alive. Sinclair marveled at the resilience, or indifference, of nature. During Operation Iraqi Freedom, they had decimated one of the few desert towns that made the mistake of resisting the inevitable. As they prepared to move on to the next target, a pair of snakes slithered across their path. Apart from avoiding sticky pools of blood, they seemed oblivious to the death and destruction wrought by their human counterparts. Was their sphere so separate that the violence of war didn't register? Not that it mattered in the grand scheme of things. Survival compelled them all to carry on as though nothing had happened. To acknowledge the enormity of the carnage would be to die of fear alone.

A single building was left standing. Wolf and Trapp exchanged nods. There are times when the military actually becomes the well-oiled piece of machinery it aspires to be. Everything had worked perfectly. Scouts located the cell, the advance guard held the line, and tanks hit targets with the selective precision of snipers, leveling everything in sight without disturbing Evans's mausoleum. The various appendages of the battalion had communicated as one mighty soldier, preserving his body so that he, alone among the corpses strewn across the battlefield, could be honored.

Corpses. They avoided using this word in reference to America's fallen heroes. It was too impersonal. Too morbid. Men like Evans were exempt from the finality of death. Their bodies were shrines, not corpses, even when they were mangled beyond recognition. The tomb at Arlington Cemetery didn't honor the disembodied idea of an unknown soldier. Someone was actually buried there. No matter how nameless and faceless, his body was sacred. Enduring. A physical reminder that the bodies of lost warriors, wherever they were, were unforgotten. Patriotism wasn't just an abstraction. The nation was built on the flesh and blood of men willing to make the ultimate sacrifice for causes that never die.

Sinclair joined Wolf and Trapp at a bedroom window. They offered him a Camel. He dipped a chew of Skoal instead. They stood surveying the smoldering remains of the neighborhood until Trapp stubbed out his cigarette.

"I'm going back in," Trapp said.

"I'm coming with you," Sinclair said.

"There's no need," Wolf said. "A medevac team is on its way."

"It's Evans."

Wolf started to say something, then thought better of it. He stared at the building rising out of the rubble.

"You're right," Wolf finally said. "It's Evans."

Unstable wreckage kept collapsing under them, impeding their progress back to the bunker. The stretcher bearers were ill equipped to traverse the wasteland. They borrowed combat gloves to avoid cutting their hands on shattered glass. Eventually Sinclair and Wolf offered to carry the stretcher. At least their knee guards and body armor broke their falls. When they finally crossed the threshold of Evans's stronghold, Trapp asked the medics to wait while he and Sinclair retrieved the body. This request deviated from standard operating procedure, but they complied without question. Surely Evans deserved a moment alone with his buddies before beginning his long lonely journey back home.

Evans was right where they had left him, miraculously preserved. Gently, with deference to his undiminished right to privacy, Trapp started going through his personal effects. Official regulations assigned this task to medevac units, who were charged with bagging up belongings for bereaved families. But platoons had their own unofficial rites. Trapp knew exactly what Evans would have wanted his buddies to have and to hold. They had fought together for almost a year. They shared knowledge of what was truly important. He took a good luck charm from Evans's breast pocket, a fossil he had found in the al-Hajarah Desert. More than anything else, this talisman belonged to the platoon.

"If this bug can survive fifty million years," Evans always said, "we can survive this goddamn war."

Trapp turned to show Sinclair the fossil, to acknowledge their friend's thwarted will to live. He wasn't there. Still shaken from the squad's brush with death, Trapp thought Sinclair had been snatched from him by unseen enemies. The idea that insurgents could have survived the bombardment was irrational, and he knew it. Twelve straight hours of combat had taken its toll on his nerves. He started reciting the serenity prayer, a vestige of his brief encounter with twelve-step programs before the armed forces sobered him up. By the time he got to the part about accepting the things he couldn't change, he caught sight of Sinclair. His head was barely peeking out of the stairwell, staring wild-eyed at Evans.

Sinclair had witnessed untold numbers of enemy corpses. He had gathered up the severed limbs of fellow marines, piecing them back together in body bags. Nothing could have prepared him for the sight of Evans's fatal wound. All it took was a single bullet to the head. Another casualty on another continent besieged Sinclair, a flashback to something he'd never witnessed in the first place. The shot must have echoed through the forest, though no one was there to hear it. A single bullet through the roof of the mouth, angled just right. To do it to yourself, you have to pull the trigger with your toe. Jesus fucking Christ.

"Sinclair," Trapp said. "What's wrong, man?"

They heard the medevac unit on the stairs, ascending with the stretcher. At least Trapp did. Sinclair seemed deaf, dumb, everything but blind. He was obviously seeing far more than met the eye. Trapp intercepted the medics, drawing them to one side.

"We're going to need another minute here, boys," Trapp said.

"What's up?"

"Postmortem debriefing, if you know what I mean."

"Five more minutes is the best we can do."

Sinclair was usually a rock, a dogged fighter with just enough heart to be truly brave. The tougher the soldier, the harder he falls when he cracks up. The platoon would be swinging their battle axes again within the hour. They couldn't afford to leave a part of Sinclair frozen on that rooftop, staring at something no one else could see.

"What's going on, Sinclair?"

Trapp led him across the rooftop, as far away from Evans as possible. Sinclair craned to avoid losing sight of the body. Nothing registered except his head wound. Nothing else even existed. Trapp held Sinclair's face in his hands, forcing him to make eye contact.

"It's me. Trapp. Come back."

The urgency of Trapp's expression broke through, restoring a modicum of reality. Now Sinclair was in two places at once, in Montana and in Iraq. The past merged with the present. The platoon knew about Pete's death, but not the details of his suicide. The aspen grove. The self-inflicted head wound. Sinclair strained to see the body again. It still looked like Pete, not Evans.

"What's going on?" Trapp repeated. "What are you looking at?"

"Pete—"

"What about him?"

"He shot himself."

"Why'd he do it?"

"I don't know."

"Yes you do. He was your best friend."

He should have known all along, especially after the spectacle at the funeral. His sister, Candace, went berserk, crying and carrying on like it was all about her. She kept saying Sinclair needed to take responsibility for what happened. They all did. Somewhere deep down, Sinclair must have felt guilty as charged. He vaguely understood that this flashback meant that something was rising to the surface. Some terrible secret. He could either confront the truth or bury it again, this time with Evans.

When they were kids, he and Pete told each other everything. They dreamed the same dreams, even though one boy's father owned the ranch and the other's was just a broken-down bronco buster. Bonds like theirs were indissoluble, no matter what did or didn't happen on the road to manhood. If Sinclair's grandpa really forced them to attend college, they'd join the same fraternity and take the same classes. When they graduated, they'd run the ranch together.

"Equal partners," Sinclair said.

"We'll marry sisters and raise a whole passel of little cowboys and Indians," Pete said.

"You're kidding, right?"

The older they got, the more Pete called attention to the fact that he was Native American. Out of pride, Sinclair thought. Sometimes he wished he were Native American too, the real McCoy if ever there was one.

"You're nuts," Pete would say. "Like anybody really wants to be Indian."

Kids at school made stray redskin jokes. But they were all just part of the fun, like cracks about wetbacks and fags. It was a country school with one foot still in the bygone era of seasonal labor. Mexican students came and went with harvests. Ranchers' sons attended spottily during foaling season. Pete Swan was always absent the same days as Billy Sinclair. Teachers almost never demanded an excuse. When they did, Sinclair's grandpa wrote the note for both of them. Pete all but pretended he was an orphan. Being the son of a cliché embarrassed him.

Pete's father, Eugene, was still the best horse breaker in the county when he was sober, usually on Sundays. Liquor stores were closed and he invariably raided his own emergency stash sometime late Saturday night. Once he slept off the week's dissipation, he climbed on the bare back of the orneriest stallion in the paddock and bucked till it broke. Eugene only kept his job because the Swans had worked the Sunset Ranch since the Civil War. In the beginning, Sinclair's great-great-great-grandfather traded the horses Pete's great-great-great-grandfather bred from wild stock. They called them all great-grandfather for short, dissolving the distinction between generations and even families as they traced their ancestry back to the heyday of the Wild West.

There were several versions of the history of their founding fathers, all of them mythic. The one constant was that Samson Swan, Pete's distant progenitor, was the best dad-blamed breeder west of Kentucky. His partner's claim to fame was subject to debate. Great-grandfather Tyler Sinclair was alternately altruistic, shrewd, or downright disreputable, depending on the teller. He sold horses to the Confederacy or the Union, if not both armies, in which case he narrowly escaped swinging on the end of a rope. Sinclair's father, who was a confirmed skeptic, insisted that Tyler had deserted from the Confederate army, saving his skin by hiding in a hollow log to elude bloodhounds. As far as Sinclair was concerned, his father was a notoriously unreliable narrator, especially when the story involved military exploits. Vietnam had convinced his generation that war was just an excuse to open up foreign markets. If he'd been old enough for the draft, he would have slipped into Canada, especially since the Sunset Ranch was so conveniently located near the border.

"It runs in the family," Sinclair's father liked to say.

"What does?"

"Draft dodging."

"Knock it off, Dad," Sinclair said. "Just because you're a traitor doesn't mean great-grandfather Tyler was."

"Neither of us are traitors, Billy. What's the point of getting your butt blown off in a senseless war?"

"The Civil War wasn't a senseless war."

"It was if you knew damn good and well you were on the losing side."

"There was more at stake than just winning or losing."

"Like what?"

"Honor. The right to defend your land."

"A bunch of slave-holding rats clinging to a sinking ship doesn't make them honorable, Billy."

His father's relentless pragmatism offended the youthful idealism Sinclair had no intention of outgrowing. For him the central issue was patriotism itself, allegiance to a cause. The politics of the Confederacy were less important than the right to determine their own destiny. Democracy itself was at stake in the Civil War. When America fought wars, democracy was always at stake.

Grandpa's version of the story was much more circumspect. For one thing, he referred to Tyler's move to Montana as a migration rather than a desertion. Big Sky country beckoned and he went west with all the other young men. A hollow log and bloodhounds were involved. But the identity of the troops in pursuit was more nebulous.

"They could have been Yankees chasing a loyal Confederate soldier," Grandpa said.

"That sounds more like it," Sinclair said.

"If they'd been rebels tracking a traitor, they'd have nabbed him."

"Why's that?"

"Better bloodhounds. Used to tracking runaway slaves."

Grandpa's interpretation, cleansed of troubling nuances, appealed to the black-and-white clarity of Sinclair's moral universe. He simply couldn't comprehend anything that didn't fit into the scheme of good and evil. Right was right and wrong was wrong, and the measure of manhood was standing up for what you believed in. There was no question in Sinclair's mind that Tyler was a loyal patriot. But one troubling fact still dogged him. Horses with the Sunset Ranch brand—an "S" with a snake's head—had been registered in both Confederate and Union armies. The only possible explanation was that Yankees had commandeered the horses of fallen rebel heroes. Spoils of victory. Pete, whose imagination was less encumbered by moral certainties, offered a less exalted explanation. Tyler was a businessman, an entrepreneurial American dedicated to the belief that what was good for the goose was good for the gander. Whether this meant he was a traitor or not depended on your definition of the pursuit of happiness. One man's opportunism was another man's free enterprise. Pirates were notoriously hard to distinguish from patriots, especially during the Civil War.

Pete and Sinclair may have disagreed about the details of the illustrious history of the Sunset Ranch, but both boys blamed their fathers for its recent demise. Previous generations loomed in heroic relief against the immediate backdrop of alcoholism and cynicism. Whatever pride Pete took in his heritage had pretty much dissipated by the time he was a teenager. The Great Spirit had been distilled into a bottle, and the noble savage was a drunk. Sinclair's father's faults were more subtle, but no less egregious. The hired hands called him Mr. Sinclair, not without a hint of wicked western irony. All he ever did was sit at his desk, balancing books and delegating chores. He wore chinos and loafers and actually drank tea. With milk and sugar. Grandpa was the only real man left on the ranch, a throwback to the days when ranchers were still cowboys, not accountants. A lot can change in a single generation.

Grandpa was a living reminder of the unprecedented moral integrity of the Greatest Generation. His country sounded the alarm, and he mustered the quintessence of honor and altruism that transformed mere men into heroes. He rarely talked about how he came by the medals locked in his desk drawer. Humility was the better part of valor. But he liked to tell tales of his father's adventures in the war to end all wars, the nation's first brush with greatness. Times were hard in the hinterland. The ranch was struggling financially as the horse market adjusted to railroad monopolies in commercial transportation. The Sinclair boys picked up day labor when they could find it, especially in the off-season. Grandpa's father had been mining silver in the high country when he first heard the distant drums of war. A backward backwoodsman and proud of it, he wound up drinking champagne in the capitals of Europe. Needless to say, there was a fair amount of fighting somewhere in between the woods and the champagne. But no matter how much Sinclair probed, he always heard the same expurgated version of World War I.

"In the days when mountains still had veins of silver and whores had hearts of gold," Grandpa always said as he warmed to the telling.

Sinclair sat on Grandpa's lap until he was old enough to know what a whore was. Then he sat at his feet on a bear skin rug. There was always a fire flickering, if not on their hearth then somewhere near the front lines. Grandpa's voice seemed to travel great distances, spanning decades as well as continents.

"Without a moment's hesitation, he and his pals shipped off to see the world. Miners and ranchers and farm boys who'd never stepped foot outside Montana. Who'd never even heard of Archduke Ferdinand, much less the Young Bosnians. Just imagine."

Sinclair's imagination took wing. For every dyed-in-the-wool military man, there was a narrative archetype, a story that captured his fancy and held it hostage until he enlisted. In every war, the brutality of cold hard facts on the ground eventually gave way to the irresistible aura of heroism. No doubt Grandpa told his father's tale rather than his own because it sounded more mythic than real, at least until soldiers ended up shell-shocked or blinded by mustard gas. He willingly recounted fording the River Somme and breaking the stalemate at Château-Thierry. But when the Great War descended into the dank darkness of No Man's Land, something always came up. He had errands to run or it was high time Billy went to bed. The mere mention of his own tours of duty, three decades later in the same war-torn European fields and forests, sent him rushing off to nonexistent chores.

"Can't you see he doesn't want to talk about it?" Sinclair's father would say when Grandpa disappeared.

"He's modest, that's all," Sinclair said.

"He's trying to forget. Stop badgering him, Billy."

Sinclair's worldview was free of doubt and ambiguity. A family's military legacy was something to be proud of, plain and simple. If anything, Grandpa's reticence to reminisce about actual combat enhanced its mystique. Surely blood-soaked trenches epitomized the honor of sacrifice, not the futility of butchering a generation of young men for the sake of a few cubic feet of devastated land. Where his father had the gall to characterize fascism as the sinister side of nationalism, Sinclair revered the patriotic spirit that inspired the French to resist the Germans and the Americans to ride to the rescue, saving civilization from the barbarians at the gate.

"War itself is barbaric, Billy."

"You sound like Mom."

"Have you ever really listened to your grandpa's stories?"

"Of course I have."

"Something's been lost in translation."

By the time Sinclair was a junior in high school, he and his father stopped talking about politics. For one thing, the topic was forbidden at the dinner table. His mother was sick and tired of their endless wrangling. Besides, neither one of them wanted to hate the other, the inevitable outcome of continued discussion. They could maintain at least a semblance of filial devotion as long as they confined their conversations to sports.

The older Sinclair got, the more the armed forces appealed to his clear-cut sense of right and wrong. Another boy might have considered becoming a minister. But the Sinclairs were Sunday Christians. Too much religious zeal smacked of Mormonism and all those crazy sects in the deserts of southern Idaho. Pete accused him of being a zealot in his own right, worshipping at the altar of the gods of war. He was keenly aware of the fact that history had winners and losers, no less than military campaigns. Witness the fact that the Swan family name had mysteriously disappeared from legal documents verifying the ownership of the Sunset Ranch. For all its democratic high-mindedness,

Sinclair's patriotism was more a privilege than a right, the purview of the landed gentry.

"My great-grandfather couldn't have been a patriot if he tried," Pete said.

"Why not?" Sinclair asked.

"Didn't have a country, remember?"

"Give me a break. Indians are as American as apple pie."

"The American army didn't wipe out apple pie."

"Don't be ridiculous. Nobody wiped out anybody."

"Then where are they?"

"Where are who?"

"The Sioux."

"You're here, aren't you? You and your dad."

"Guess we slipped through the cracks."

One minute Pete couldn't stand being Native American, the next he wore it like a badge officially authorizing him to bash the government, especially the military. The idea that serving in the armed forces was a noble commitment to God and country was just pie in the sky. If half the country stood to gain, believing in that crap, the other half suffered for it. Or what was left of the other half.

It got to the point where Sinclair couldn't talk politics with either Pete or his father. He could have sworn they were in cahoots, conspiring to convince him that America's devotion to democracy was just an excuse to carry a big stick. But this would have required an unwonted spirit of cooperation. For whatever reason, Sinclair's dad never took a shine to Pete the way Grandpa did. He was proud of his own iconoclasm, a clear sign of intellectual maturity. When Pete expressed similar views, he got in trouble for being disrespectful. Mr. Sinclair had his own theories about the potential demise of the Sunset Ranch. He always pretended to know something nobody else knew about Pete Swan.

Sinclair and Pete never dwelled on their differences. They had better things to do, especially during hunting season. The deep hush of mountain forests put everything in perspective. Wild animals led them back to the source of what really mattered. Pete bagged his first ten-point buck the autumn of their junior year, the most thrilling event of both their lifetimes. A more sublime season was unimaginable. Then the weather took a permanent turn for the worse. It had never occurred to Sinclair that the simple joy of boyhood might not withstand the storm of adolescence. Pete was less naive, but equally devastated.

At first Sinclair blamed this girl Chelsea at school. He wasn't exactly dating her. The nearest movie theater was miles away, and neither of them was old enough to drive. There was a soda fountain in the village, the last vestige of Norman Rockwell's prophylactic idea of courtship. But they'd outgrown that kind of thing before they were born. When the snow thawed, they took walks along Bear Creek. Chelsea was fond of wildflowers. The fact that Sinclair knew all their names convinced her that he was a sensitive young man. He lost his virginity on a pine-needle bed.

Chelsea was surprisingly accommodating, bordering on promiscuous, according to Sinclair's strict codes. But he managed to quiet his scruples sufficiently to take full advantage of her lapses. Her parents were shockingly permissive, or just oblivious. He started sneaking in and out of her wing of their house with effortless, if guilty, ease. Sex was a lot more fun than he thought it would be, once he got the hang of it. But it took awhile. The first time Chelsea laughed in bed, he got defensive.

"What's so funny?"

"Nothing."

"You're laughing, aren't you?"

"I'm having fun." Chelsea grabbed the scruff of his cropped hair and yanked till he yelped. "Aren't you?"

He finally learned to let his hair down, as she put it. But there was still something vaguely unsettling about it all. The fact that he'd been watching livestock go at it for years probably didn't help. The whole business seemed starkly libidinal, even compulsive. He found himself sniffing around her house when he could have been off in the woods with Pete. What Chelsea called making love he called sex, though not to her face. They didn't love each other, no matter what she said. Sometimes it felt like he was at the mercy of a strange new force that threatened to sully the purest pleasures he had ever known.

He wasn't the swaggering type, though guys his age routinely compared notes with their buddies. Pete, on the other hand, was reluctant to talk about sex. At first Sinclair assumed he was just clueless, pretending to know the score when he was obviously still a virgin. And then, just as obviously, he wasn't. Not that he breathed a word about the big event. For some bizarre reason, he continued to avoid locker-room talk. Granted most of their friends were chivalric enough to refrain from divulging specifics. The identities of the girls themselves remained unspoken, if only to avoid fistfights. But Pete was downright secretive, even with Sinclair. It was the first real wedge in their friendship.

The spring of their senior year, it became painfully apparent that Pete wasn't the only one keeping secrets. Sinclair's entire family was on edge. His sister, Candace, started moping around in her room day and night, and his mother cried more often than usual. All the anxiety at home made him want to buddy up with Pete more than ever. But even when they went hunting, something wasn't right. Instead of being alone in the woods together, they were lonely. Sinclair sensed that Pete wanted to confide in him. Eventually he broke the cardinal rule of male friendship and tried to talk about what was wrong.

"What's up?"

"Nothing."

"You're so quiet."

"I'm always quiet."

"Not quiet like this."

"Lay off, will you? You wouldn't understand anyway."

At the time, Sinclair had been pissed off. It felt like Pete was being dishonest. Disloyal. But he may have been right after all. Three years later, staring at Evans's head wound, Sinclair still didn't understand. Otherwise he'd be mourning Evans rather than trying to resurrect Pete. Trapp kept asking him why Pete shot himself. If only he knew. If only he didn't know. Pete was barred from their house that summer. Sinclair and his sister went off to college without him that fall. His father and Grandpa practically came to blows over whether to throw the Swans off the property. And through it all, Sinclair had said nothing, neither defending nor denouncing the boy who was like a brother to him.

They said it was an accident. Even without studying the trajectory of the bullet through the roof of Pete's mouth, Sinclair knew that this was the first in a series of lies they would tell themselves about his death. Consummate hunters don't have accidents with guns. They wield them deliberately, with infinite respect for their capacity to kill at will. Sinclair made them show him the death certificate, signed and dated September 10, 2001. Cause of death: accidental gunshot wound. The fact that suicides couldn't be buried in sacred ground seemed to justify falsifying the document. The coroner obviously deferred to Grandpa, who had found the body. They must have thought they were protecting Pete's father, or Sinclair, or even Pete himself with their lies. God knows they were really protecting themselves. The pretense that Pete died accidentally let them all off the hook. It meant no one was responsible. It ameliorated the moral outrage they felt in the face of senseless death. Sinclair still felt it.

9/10/01. A date which will live in infamy. When the Twin Towers came crashing down the next day, the nation's tragedy seemed to echo Sinclair's personal loss, one cataclysm following the other in such rapid succession he was too numb to grieve. In self-defense, he made sense of all the senseless killing, constructing a narrative in which moral certainty filled the void left by Pete's suicide. The second calamity redeemed the first, giving Sinclair something to believe in again. As an act of terrorism against American ideals, 9/11 backfired. Life, liberty, and the pursuit of happiness rose out of the ashes, inspiring Evans and others to make the ultimate sacrifice. His death was not in vain.

"He did it because he thought there was nothing to believe in," Sinclair finally said.

"Why does that scare you so much?" Trapp asked.

"I was afraid he might be right."

Trapp could tell from the way Sinclair's eyes focused that he had snapped out of his flashback. They had witnessed their share of what civilians called PTSD, a ridiculous acronym. Nothing was post-traumatic about relentless trauma. Sinclair wasn't so much living in the past as unstuck in time. The only remedy was to keep grounding him in the palpable present. Trapp led him across the rooftop to Evans's body. One of the great paradoxes of combat was the solace of succoring fallen comrades. No matter what triggered PTSD, the root cause was more fear of dying than death itself. The dead are a kind of comfort, a reminder that there is repose at the end of that terrifying passage.

Together they laid out Evans's body, straightening his limbs to accommodate the stretcher. Sinclair retrieved the bandana Trapp had left behind. He wet it with canteen water and started wiping the blood off of Evans's face. His ears. His neck. He would have done the same for Pete if he'd had the chance. He knew Trapp was watching, making sure he was okay. As long as he focused on the task at hand, he would be fine. He pulled the chain around Evans's neck and his dog tags spilled out of his uniform. His fiancé would probably get to keep them, once he made his way back home. Trapp reached out and held them in the palm of his hand. EVANS, THOMAS C. 676-41-2625. O NEG. CATHOLIC. Their buddy.

The medevac unit was clamoring up the stairs again. This time Trapp waved them onto the rooftop. He and Sinclair relinquished the body but not Evans. He would always be part of the platoon. When the medics took his body away, Trapp and Sinclair stood for a minute surveying the wasteland surrounding them. Smoke still obscured the sky, but an orange glow low on the horizon confirmed that it was sunset. They rarely had time to contemplate the terrible beauty of combat zones, the apocalyptic wonder of it all. There was nothing more peaceful than the aftermath of war. The more in-depth conversation they might have had about Pete hung in the air. It would have to wait, especially now that Sinclair had recovered his equilibrium. Evans deserved the full force of their grief, tempered but not blunted by their compulsion to keep fighting. His death steeled their purpose to decimate the rest of the city. Nobody killed Americans with impunity.

"Evans was a brick," Trapp said. "Every inch a marine."

"He died a hero," Sinclair said.

"Amen to that."

Trapp took the desert fossil from his breast pocket and gave it to Sinclair.

"If this bug can survive fifty million years—"

Sinclair joined in on the chorus.

"—we can survive this goddamn war."

When Sinclair tried to hand Evans's talisman back, Trapp waved him off.

"You keep it. Something to believe in."

They turned and marched back down the stairs to rejoin the platoon. Radetzky had set up a makeshift base camp just south of the bombed-out quarter. The battalion had cleared everything from there to the feeder highway, and runners were able to deliver an actual cooked meal. Chicken à la king was gourmet compared to the MREs they'd been scarfing down all day. Blankets were spread across the floor. Half of the men were already conked out. A guard was posted at every window, more a formality than a necessity. As Wolf liked to say, employing one of his stock urban metaphors, the exterminator had made his rounds. The place was debugged.

"First-class accommodations," McCarthy said when Sinclair and Trapp showed up. It was the kind of snide comment McCarthy always made, and it comforted them. Everybody was relatively subdued, in unspoken deference to Evans. But they exchanged their usual flippancies to reassure themselves that life goes on, even in the combat zone. Radetzky approached them as they sat in actual chairs at an actual table, eating their dinner.

"Better grab some shut-eye while you can," Radetzky said. "We'll be moving out at 0200 hours."

Trapp checked his watch. "Four hours? I thought you said we'd take a break after we blew the cell."

"New game plan."

"Whose?"

"Centcom's."

"Where's the fire?"

"Pretty much everywhere. We've got to keep pace with the other battalions."

"Are they encountering as much resistance?"

"Apparently not. We're the lucky ones."

"Figures."

"2/1 has already secured the Jolan District."

They just kept eating. Even McCarthy was too exhausted to gloat over the news.

"And 1/5 expects to control the northern half of the industrial sector by morning," Radetzky said. "Colonel Denning says we've got to stop dillydallying around."

"I suppose they think Evans was killed dillydallying around," Trapp said under his breath. Radetzky pretended not to hear him.

They mobilized at 0145 hours, to leave time to tidy up after themselves. Blowing up a house was kosher, but not leaving dirty dishes in the sink. Marines were famous for upholding standards of decency that were either noble or nuts, depending on your perspective. Hygiene was a particularly irritating virtue. Not that grunts wouldn't have welcomed clean socks to stave off foot rot. But purely symbolic gestures, especially shaving, just pissed them off. Officers were forever ordering them to haul out their razors, even when they were in combat mode. If there were logical explanations for such random priorities, they had more to do with image than substance. Bearded, drug-infested insurgents were terrorists, not freedom fighters. Clean-cut marines were liberators, not infidel invaders. Never mind that facial hair was a sign of piety in Iraq.

The city was unnervingly quiet. Night-vision goggles transformed darkness into a spectral landscape of clarified shadows. Once in a while, particularly luminous objects startled them. Billowing curtains. A skittering cat catching the full rays of the moon. The neighborhood appeared to be deserted. Insurgents knew they were at a disadvantage in the dark. Some were probably hiding in underground tunnels, biding their time until daylight. Others had decamped entirely, slipping through security to spend the night in the desert. The platoon advanced three full blocks without firing a single shot.

The absence of actual fighters didn't necessarily diminish the threat. It felt like someone was leading them into a trap. Sinclair's team encountered a brick barrier blocking the rooftop of an apartment complex. Better luck next time. The stairs in a neighboring building had been ripped out, making it virtually impossible to access upper floors. They finally had to settle for a three-story home with good offensive visibility but an imperfect view to the south. Behind them, Fallujah smoldered in ruins. But there were still plenty of places to hide. Technically Iraqi troops were responsible for providing rearguard security. Patrolling cleared quadrants was as strategically necessary as clearing them in the first place.

Iraqi Security Forces had been deployed in previous high-profile offensives. Fighting side-by-side was the best way to promote the perception that the war was a joint operation, not an American occupation. Early on, Iraqi National Guardsmen seemed eager to get the job done. But when the insurgency terrorized Anbar Province, the feasibility of joint missions became increasingly tenuous. Iraqi soldiers expected the support of regional authorities, something US Marines had long since given up on. The coalition was fragile. When local sentiment shifted, it fell apart.

The Joint Task Force figured out ways to deploy the Iraqi National Guard without jeopardizing the success of the op plan. Tasking them with rearguard security duty was a prudent compromise. When the ING stuck to their guns, they significantly boosted the perceived legitimacy of the mission. When they didn't, American soldiers were less likely to pay the price. Controlling the optics of the coalition was half the battle, at least as far as the Pentagon was concerned. The official assessment of the role of Iraqi forces was unequivocal. They were indispensable. Unofficially their impact was negligible.

Marines were expected to commend their Iraqi counterparts, no matter what went down. This directive, which came straight from Centcom, was designed to make sure loudmouths like McCarthy shut their traps. It was like trying to plug a volcano with a wine cork. Whenever the press corps showed up, Wolf shuffled him off for a cigarette break. The last time McCarthy was interviewed, the entire platoon suffered for his indiscretion. The reporter was an investigative journalist for NPR, the type that snoops around trying to stir up trouble.

"A lot of folks back home wonder if Iraqi Security Forces are up to the job," the reporter observed.

"Good question," McCarthy said.

"What's it like, fighting with them?"

"Slightly better than fighting against them," McCarthy said. "On a good day."

McCarthy couldn't help himself. The platoon had almost lost a man when Iraqi Guardsmen failed to hold their ground during a firefight in Saqlawiyah. When Colonel Denning caught wind of the interview, he summoned Lieutenant Radetzky.

"Ever heard of a loose cannon, Radetzky?" Colonel Denning said.

"Sir?"

"One of your boys has been shooting his mouth off again."

"Yessir."

"Don't 'yes sir' me, Radetzky."

"It won't happen again, Colonel."

"Half the world is yip yapping about our strategic objectives. Unilateral this. Occupation that."

"Like it's any of their business, sir."

"The last thing we need is grunts bad-mouthing the coalition."

For once, Sinclair shared McCarthy's skepticism. Monitoring the Guard's movements in the wake of the platoon's advance, he noticed that their performance was spotty, at best. They kept hanging back, leaving gaps of three or four blocks between offensive positions and rearguard support. Insurgents could slip back into unoccupied areas at will.

"There's a defensive breach in the line," Sinclair reported into his headset.

"Where?" Radetzky asked.

"Pretty much everywhere. ING is lagging behind."

Radetzky passed Sinclair's warning on to Captain Phipps.

"Can you pick up the slack?" Captain Phipps asked.

"We're already spread too thin," Radetzky said.

"Offense is the best defense. Keep pushing forward."

The squads continued to clear compounds with unprecedented speed, almost without incident. There was nothing to report, nothing to shoot, nothing to do except anticipate the worst hiding behind the next closed door. Lack of resistance had become sinister, as though Fallujah were a monstrous house of horrors, a psychological as well as military threat. The platoon's anxiety wormed its way up to Sinclair's perch. He detected it in their maneuvers, which were uncharacteristically jumpy. They kept looking over their shoulders. Suspense alone prompted them to open fire.

The platoon's momentum gratified battalion headquarters. Paranoia, among other things, didn't register on their computer screens. Not that modern warfare was a glorified video game. Civilians were far more susceptible to the perils of simulation than military men. Officers in particular were trained to resist the numbing effects of technology. But training itself was a kind of virtual reality, once removed from actual combat. Battles were primarily conceptual unless you actually fought them, in which case you were never invited into the war room. Nothing would ever really bridge the gap between strategy and execution.

To a certain extent, commanders have always relegated war to the abstract realm of ideas. Even barbarian generals mapped their maneuvers with sticks in dirt. But historical comparisons were misleading. The degree of abstraction multiplied exponentially with each technological advancement, along with the speed and size of weaponry. As a result, the War on Terror was waged as much in cyberspace as in the real world. There was no there there, no need for real weapons of mass destruction when the idea alone catapulted the nation into war. Enemies were equally elusive, hailing from politically fabricated countries that appeared on maps one year and disappeared the next, if terrorism prevailed.

"Attention Kilo Company. TOC is modifying rear-echelon support."

Out of the blue, Colonel Denning's voice invaded the airwaves. Radetzky must have opened the tactical operations center frequency so the whole platoon could hear Colonel Denning's latest decree. He was like the Wizard of Oz, the man behind the curtain pulling levers attached to hundreds of men, thousands of weapons, with untold numbers of lives in the balance. Often as not, his orders seemed counterintuitive. The reality of war waged by boots on the ground seldom reflected the virtual reality of op plans. The gory details of actual combat were tragic, but not relevant.

"No more relay teams," Colonel Denning continued. "Just ammunition runners and medevac units, as needed."

"What about confiscating weapons caches?" Radetzky asked.

"Too risky. You're in the eye of the storm, whether you know it or not."

"Should we blow them or just keep moving?"

"Step on the gas, Radetzky. Floor it."

"What's the timetable?"

"Major Linville is expecting you at Phase Line Freddy by sundown tomorrow. You know how he gets when you're late."

The platoon had unwittingly crossed a strategic threshold. The fact that they hadn't encountered a single enemy outpost since the bombardment was immaterial. From then on, their contact with rear-echelon units would be limited to carrying ammunition in and wounded men out of kill zones. They were on their own, with the formidable exception of big-gun support. Bradleys and tanks lurked within striking distance. Cobras and F-15s could make the trip from desert airstrips to what was left of Fallujah in less than five minutes.

In global military circles, Americans were accused of hiding behind shields of technology and superior firepower. The quintessential example was Hiroshima, an act of unconditional cowardice. Whether justified or not, pushing buttons was a far cry from pulling triggers. Anti-coalition forces begrudgingly admitted that Operation Iraqi Freedom was less egregious than Desert Storm. At least the infantry made an appearance, if only to topple statues and plant flags. More than any other branch of the military, US Marines resented insinuations that they shied away from nitty-gritty combat. They still believed that wars were won by boots on the ground, not Pentagon generals clicking and dragging virtual troops across simulated battlefields. Bigwigs always overestimated the role big guns played in successful campaigns. Obsessing about weapons of mass destruction had prompted more than one disastrous invasion.

Whenever the topic of WMDs came up, McCarthy went ballistic. All the hype was yet another publicity stunt, a way to rally hawks and silence doves. At this rate, it would be déjà vu all over again, another stinking Cold War complete with paranoid politicians and prissy Pentagon brass who cared more about public opinion than winning battles.

"Since when was the decision to wage war a popularity contest?" McCarthy demanded.

"Since Vietnam," Trapp said.

"Apples and oranges," McCarthy said. "As long as there's no draft, public opinion is just background noise."

If Washington would just let the armed forces do what they were trained to do, the War on Terror would have a beginning, middle, and end instead of spanning the new millennium. The beginning had been 9/11, the middle was Iraq, and the end would be nigh when marines were finally let loose in the mountains of Afghanistan and Pakistan. Meanwhile everybody was pussyfooting around so-called weapons of mass destruction like they were the be-all and end-all of military might. When was the last time a WMD won a war? They were more like bogeymen than actual weapons. The very definition of the term was an affront to the infantry.

"What are we?" McCarthy said. "Chopped liver?"

Mass destruction was being perpetrated by American soldiers on a daily basis, thank you very much. Marines had toppled more than concrete facsimiles of Saddam and his Royal Guard. They had stormed his palace and brought Baghdad to its knees. They had flushed him and his Ba'athist rats out of thousands of desert holes, one by one. Insurrections in Ramadi and Mosul had been smashed by yours truly, and they would do the same in Fallujah. To date, the Marine Corps alone had killed tens of thousands of insurgents and leveled countless recalcitrant towns. The fact that United Nations inspectors couldn't find WMDs proved one thing beyond a shadow of a doubt. They couldn't tell their asses from their elbows.

Real weapons of mass destruction had human faces. They were swift, silent, and just as deadly as their nuclear and chemical counterparts. Not that McCarthy or anyone else thought US Marines occupied an exalted position in the pantheon of warriors. They were the ultimate grunts, and proud of it. In their version of military history, leathernecks were the first in and last out of every major campaign since Belleau Wood. Nations declared war. Platoons fought them. Without boots on the ground, the conflict played out in the press rather than on the battlefield. Virtually every marine motto attested to their dedication to the art and ethics of close combat. Real war, not virtual war.

"One shot, one kill."

"Gun control is hitting your target."

"Don't run, you'll just die tired."

"Never forget your weapon was made by the lowest bidder."

The Marine Corps's reputation for doing more with less was a badge of honor. They prided themselves in beating the odds when everyone else folded. This was precisely why Sinclair joined the marines rather than the army or the air force. He understood the necessity of artillery and air strikes in a pinch. Commanders couldn't afford to squander valuable human resources, especially in an all-volunteer infantry. But what he liked best was fighting face-to-face. No tanks or jets or white phosphorous, just rifles and automatics. Or better yet, knife against knife, the ultimate measure of courage. One man pitting his strength against another. No frills.

Snipers like Sinclair routinely scored more kills than gunners. But his relative distance from targets made him eager to join the action below. It was just a matter of time. Every block they cleared tightened the noose. The sheer density of fighters packed into smaller and smaller quadrants would eventually preclude long-distance sharpshooting. The sooner the better. House-to-house combat was always up close and personal. When they finally penetrated the heart of Fallujah, it would be downright intimate.

Colonel Denning proved to be right about their proximity to the eye of the storm. The platoon started encountering more and more munitions stockpiles, none of which they were authorized to confiscate. Their only option was to blow them to smithereens. If and when the Iraqi National Guard got their shit together, Radetzky would trust them to watch their backs. In the meantime, insurgents could easily reoccupy cleared areas, helping themselves to any weapons left behind. Not on his watch. He assembled both squads, to make damned sure everyone understood the game plan.

"You heard the colonel," Radetzky said. "Full speed ahead."

Having issued the official order, Radetzky switched off his headset. What Colonel Denning didn't know wouldn't hurt him. Letting speed take precedence over prudence would put his men at risk, something Radetzky only did when absolutely necessary. The bottom line was that they were expected to clear their way to Phase Line Freddy by sundown on the third day of the offensive. How they got there was their own business.

"While you're at it, destroy every single weapons cache you can find," Radetzky continued. "Our objective is two-fold. Get to Phase Line Freddy on time. Without getting our asses blown off."

The platoon breathed a collective sigh of relief. They were willing to follow Radetzky through the gates of hell because he never betrayed their trust. The squads peeled off again. They picked up the pace, working double-time to avoid falling behind. Whenever ordnance was discovered, they loaded it into abandoned cars and trucks. Everyone took cover while Percy did the honors, blowing the whole kit and caboodle sky high with his SMAW. It was nerve-racking work, especially for Sinclair. From a distance, Percy's controlled detonations sounded an awful lot like random IEDs, which squads were encountering with increasing frequency in abandoned compounds. Every time he heard a big bang, Sinclair held his breath until his buddies emerged unscathed.

Weapons caches told them a great deal about who was arming the insurgency. They were like miniature history lessons, documenting military conflicts spanning more than half a century. There were Cold War rifles from Czechoslovakia. Iranian FAL rifles. German Mausers and Heckler & Koch assault weapons. Soviet-era machine guns. Good old-fashioned hunting shotguns from local factories ranging from Pakistan to Afghanistan. Russian SVD sniper rifles no more than a year or two old. Even World War II Garand rifles manufactured in the United States. AK-47s were ubiquitous. International trade in weapons was a big business, with less official regulation than the manufacture and sale of children's toys.

The fact that East Manhattan was armed to the teeth should have precluded the persistent presence of civilians. But Fallujans were either inured to the risk of cross fire, or they had grossly miscalculated the scope and duration of Operation Vigilant Resolve. The platoon started confronting more and more women and children. The strategic net, designed to capture insurgents flushed out of other sectors, was also catching their families. Sinclair wondered why they hadn't slipped through the mesh. Every day they tarried would be more dangerous than the day before.

Time and again, squads kicked open front doors, and civilians rushed out the back. Women in burqas usually shepherded larger groups, traveling in teams with two or three families in tow. They moved calmly and quickly as though they had rehearsed their escape routes thousands of times over the years. Even the youngest children seemed preternaturally composed, seldom horsing around or making a fuss. There were a surprising number of babies. Sometimes they cried out, but the running and jostling soon pacified them. Sinclair scoped them all, visually frisking even children, who had been known to smuggle, if not wield weapons. They wound their way through streets and alleys, never bothering to take cover. Eventually they staked out another house or sought refuge in a mosque.

"The area is crawling with civilians," Sinclair reported to Radetzky.

"And insurgents," Radetzky responded. "We just nailed three in a laundry. Heads up."

"Roger that."

Sinclair felt left out. He hadn't even heard the kills over his headset. For the umpteenth time since deploying, he regretted being such a crackerjack shot. All morning long, he'd been stuck babysitting women and children, missing all the action behind closed doors. The only potential threats he identified were occasional teenage boys interspersed among families. One in particular looked like he might have a handgun tucked into his belt. He was disarmingly clean-cut and well dressed, almost preppy. The bulge could just as easily have been a cell phone. The fact that he had the same nose and deep-set eyes as the lead woman tipped the scales in his favor. He obviously wasn't masquerading as a family member to escape detection. This didn't necessarily guarantee his innocence. Even terrorists had mothers.

The other children were considerably younger, but the woman seemed most protective of her eldest son. She kept close to him, presumably shielding him from adulthood and its attendant dangers. The older the child, the more likely he would be targeted. Teenagers who might have vandalized cars in Iowa planted roadside bombs in Iraq. But this kid looked more like a bookworm than a punk. Sinclair scoped him until the family disappeared into a house the squads had not yet cleared. He probably should have taken him out anyway, to play it safe.

Maybe next time.

Then Sinclair knew he was in trouble. The word *maybe* didn't exist in military vocabulary. Never before had uncertainty reared its treacherous head in Iraq. He blamed the boy's mother. Talk about a lame excuse. He had learned to stanch his fear of IEDs and even suicide bombers. Surely he could withstand the sight of a woman without losing his nerve. His boot camp commander, Sergeant Troy, had warned them about the dangers of ambivalence. He hammered home his point with graphic examples, shouting at point-blank range to make sure it penetrated their thick skulls.

"Know what happens when you straddle the fence?"

"Sir!"

"You get your balls blown off. Know what happens to your buddies?"

"Sir!"

"They get their balls blown off."

"Yes, sir!"

"Want to live the rest of your stinking life with their blood on your hands?"

"No, sir!"

Sinclair vowed to shoot anyone carrying anything even vaguely resembling a gun. This was a war zone, not a kindergarten. Kids too young to drive were packing guns. Their mothers concealed grenades in their abayas. Not all of them. But it only took one to maim and mangle a body beyond recognition.

"Better theirs than yours," Sergeant Troy shouted.

"Yes, sir!"

A firefight erupted in a nearby compound, answered by the boom of a grenade. Two men dressed in black with checkered kaffiyehs jumped from second-story windows. Finally some action. They tumbled to break the impact and sprang up with the dexterity of either athletes or trained combatants. Sinclair hit the lead runner square in the chest, a clean shot. His fourth kill of the day tripped up the second man, who sprawled and skidded across the pavement behind a low wall. Sinclair dialed in the distance and bided his time. All those hours spent in hunting blinds had honed his patience as well as his aim. Sooner or later, kill number five would peek over the wall or make a run for it. Suddenly Trapp and McCarthy appeared at the back door of the compound.

"Watch the wall," Sinclair said into his headset. "One concealed insurgent."

"Got him," Trapp said.

Trapp motioned and Vasquez joined him at the door. They opened fire to cover McCarthy as he sprinted across the courtyard. The insurgent realized he was surrounded. Jumping to his feet, he dropped his rifle and raised his hands over his head in a single urgent motion. McCarthy emptied a round into the man's torso and then signaled to Sinclair, giving him a thumbs-up.

Sinclair didn't respond to this breach of protocol. Giving away a sniper's position was strictly taboo. McCarthy was obviously pretty pumped up, so much so he had just plugged a man in the act of surrendering. Sinclair refrained from scoping the corpse to check for the concealed weapon that would justify McCarthy's decision to fire. Second-guessing a fellow marine would have been another breach of protocol.

Wolf and the rest of the squad joined McCarthy's celebration in the courtyard. Like football players, they had been warned not to hotdog. Rubbing victory in your opponents' faces was especially bad form when the stakes were so high. But cameras were seldom around to enforce the ban. In any case, platoons could usually count on media discretion. Embeds had received their own warnings. They turned a blind eye to the spectacle of Americans dishonoring corpses. Conversely, footage of the enemy gloating over American bodies was worthy of prime time news. No one would ever forget the image of terrorists cheering the falling Towers. The image alone launched the War on Terror, allegedly justifying the eventual invasion of Iraq. Had Fallujans not been caught in the act of reveling on Brooklyn Bridge, Sinclair and his buddies would have been playing pinochle back at base camp rather than racking up kills in East Manhattan. The pictures, not the four charred bodies themselves, prompted Operation Vigilant Resolve.

Trapp high-fived Vasquez. McCarthy mimicked the dead insurgent, mincing around with his hands over his head.

"Don't shoot! I'm unarmed."

"Looked a fuck of a lot like an M16 to me," Vasquez said.

"He was on his way to the pawn shop," Trapp said. "To trade it in for a white flag."

The minute Radetzky's squad filed out of the adjacent compound, everybody sobered up. He had zero tolerance for anything except the mission at hand. Wolf started waving his men on to the next block of compounds, but Radetzky intervened. The closer they got to Highway 10, the less affluent the residents. Presumably Ba'athist fat cats disliked the sound of traffic as much as any other privileged faction. Houses in more modest neighborhoods were built practically on top of one another, close enough to facilitate jumping from one roof to the next. Radetzky ordered the platoon to mix things up, alternating street-level and rooftop points of entry whenever possible. The more varied their tactics, the less likely insurgents would anticipate their movements.

Ambushes were often conducted by lone gunmen stationed on living room couches. They were really more like suicide bombers, content to die as long as they took American soldiers along with them. Lounging around for days on end, they passed the time getting high on epinephrine and adrenaline. It's a wonder they managed to aim their weapons, given how high they were. Most of them never even bothered to stand up when coalition forces finally stormed their compounds. They just fired and took fire from prone positions until even the drugs stopped pumping through their veins. All that dope made them practically impervious to pain and death. The more syringes strewn across the floor, the more bullets their bodies absorbed before accomplishing their martyrdom.

Sinclair kept one step ahead of the platoon as they leapfrogged from one rooftop to another. He was perched high enough to see over the parapets of all but two target buildings, which were obscured by an apartment complex. He reported both blind spots to Radetzky, just in case. The squads modified their tactics accordingly, clearing these two compounds from down below. Their prudence paid off big time. Terrorists may not have had tanks and Bradleys, let alone Cobras and F-15s. But they had learned to make weapons out of almost anything. Trip-wired cars. Hijacked airplanes. Booby-trapped buildings. The roof of the second compound had disappeared into thin air. Artillery sometimes blew the tops off houses, but there was no evidence of bombardment. Telltale signs of demolition offered a more insidious explanation. Insurgents had destroyed the roof with sledgehammers, leaving a gaping hole that would have swallowed Wolf's entire squad. It was the biggest booby trap they'd ever seen.

"Holy Jesus," Wolf said.

Having worked in demolition before graduating to construction, Wolf appreciated the amount of muscle necessary to take down the roof. The entire top floor of the house was knee-deep in rubble.

"It's ingenious," Trapp said.

"It's cowardly," McCarthy said. "Like shadow boxing."

"Necessity is the mother of invention."

"Who said that?"

"Some stupid ass Arab dude. Too chickenshit to face the enemy."

"If it works, it isn't stupid."

"Guess what. It didn't work."

Volleys and grenade blasts erupted in a neighboring compound. Radetzky's squad had evidently hit the jackpot. Wolf regretted having to tear himself away from the pitfall. There was never enough time to marvel at the wonders of the combat zone. He ordered his men to descend and disperse across the courtyard below. If insurgents managed to elude the initial attack, they'd run right into Wolf's firing range. No such luck. Radetzky made short work of the compound, hoarding every last kill. Wolf's team felt cheated until they found out, much later, what they'd missed out on.

It wasn't that they were bloodthirsty. They had simply been trained to believe that the more they killed, the less likely they themselves would be killed. Not to mention the allure of heroism in the face of mortal danger. Sinclair in particular had been cursing his luck all day, feeling more like a spectator than a combatant. The fact that he'd just saved an entire squad from plummeting to their deaths provided some solace. Given his training, though, killing would have felt even more constructive than saving lives. He perked up when one of his gunners issued what sounded like a warning.

"We've got company."

In addition to watching Sinclair's back, the two other members of his team acted as spotters tasked with locating enemy fighters. Unless the threat was imminent, they let him do the honors. Stealth made them hold their fire. One clean shot from a sniper rifle was far less likely to give away their position than bursts of automatic rounds. Sinclair prepared to scope the target. False alarm. He heard footsteps and Johnson emerged from the stairwell.

"Mind if I shadow you for a while?" Johnson asked.

"Help yourself."

Johnson unhooked his camera straps and sat down. He seemed oblivious to the panoramic view of three US Marine battalions engaged in conquering a city. Maybe not Pulitzer Prize material, but pretty damned impressive. Even Sinclair, whose experience was limited to snapping pictures on his cell phone, appreciated the potential for dramatic photojournalism.

"I thought you guys liked to be in the thick of things," Sinclair said.

"There's nothing much to shoot down there."

"Sounds like Radetzky's squad is ripping through magazines at a pretty steady clip," Sinclair said. "What are they shooting? Mice?"

"I meant photographs," Johnson said. "Not a lot of good photo ops."

Sinclair no longer resented Johnson's presence in the platoon. They needed him now more than ever in the wake of the Australian camera crew debacle. Unauthorized Aussie reporters had secured a rooftop post in the Jolan District. They were shooting live, feeding footage directly to a CNN special report on terrorist cells in Fallujah. Aerial gunships were pummeling a middle-class neighborhood held hostage by Zarqawi's al-Qaeda militia. Several interrogation sites, where coalition sympathizers were tortured and even beheaded, had been targeted. Al Jazeera managed to hijack the footage, which they stripped of context and characterized as an unprovoked attack on innocent civilians. American reporters were expected to provide counterevidence of the insurgency's infiltration of so-called residential neighborhoods.

Sometimes it felt like they were waging war against Al Jazeera. Inflammatory photographs of the bridge mutilations had been largely responsible for launching Operation Vigilant Resolve in the first place. In retaliation, rogue media outlets were broadcasting inflated civilian casualty figures designed to make Americans look like terrorists rather than peacekeepers. The international community was horrified. More to the point, Fallujans were turning against them. There was a notable difference already, in spite of Baghdad's official support of the offensive. The insurgency was being aided and abetted by more and more former civilians every day.

"You never answered my question," Sinclair said.

"Which one?"

"The one about mice."

"You're right." Johnson tried to laugh it off. "Dead mice everywhere."

"Feisty little buggers. I could have sworn I heard grenades. And lots of cross fire."

Johnson was an ethical man. He believed in the power of journalism to safeguard the moral integrity of war. If someone had told him a week ago that he would cave under the pressure of propaganda, he would have decked them. The airwaves were swamped with images of leveled mosques and devastated neighborhoods. Nowhere, not even in the fine print, was there mention of insurgent snipers in minarets or terrorist cells in master bedrooms. The only thing more damning than footage of aerial strikes were photographs of civilian casualties. Johnson knew a booby trap when he saw one. Al Jazeera would have to get its own damned pictures of civilian casualties.

Johnson didn't know which was worse, the casualties themselves or his refusal to report them. Dozens of corpses were buried in his camera, most of which would stay there. Women. Several children. He couldn't stop shooting. Radetzky had finally pulled him aside to ask what the hell he thought he was doing. Surely one or two shots would have sufficed. There were kids in the hallway and mujahideen in a bedroom behind them, lobbing grenades over their heads. The squad tried to shoot around them. The women tried to protect them with their bare hands.

It felt like Vietnam all over again, back in the days when the war first started airing on television. Graphic shots of field hospitals. Villagers running from napalm. Kids on fire. Bleeding-heart liberals applauded the media, but the troops themselves felt betrayed. They put their asses on the line day in and day out. This was the thanks they got. But Johnson's perspective on the role of media had changed since Vietnam. He was on the other side of the lens now, far more aware of the big picture. On balance, news coverage protected rather than indicted soldiers. It kept governments honest, or more honest. Someone had to hold them accountable for the missions they masterminded. Atrocities could almost always be prevented on the drawing board, and almost never in the field.

"What's going on down there?" Sinclair persisted.

"Nothing much," Johnson said. "The usual."

Confiding in Sinclair would have been cathartic. He probably would have interpreted the decision to suppress the photographs as prudent rather than unethical, an embed's act of solidarity with his host platoon. Often as not in war, the very thing that made everyone feel better was exactly the wrong thing to do. Telling the truth would ultimately be bad for morale. Sinclair needed to be able to pull the trigger with a clear conscience. Killing was nerve-racking enough without having to worry whether your next bullet would end up lodged in some kid's gut. Snipers had a bad reputation for indiscriminate killing, yet another example of media hype. They were, in fact, the least likely of all soldiers to make mistakes.

Suppressing the photographs. Johnson tried to think of a less incriminating way to frame his decision. Given Al Jazeera's media stranglehold, the only way to combat trumped-up civilian casualty figures was to downplay them in the American press. Surely covering up something that wasn't true to begin with no longer qualified as a cover-up. At the same time, all this equivocation made him suspicious of his own motives. Shirking responsibility was always a crime against humanity. Civilians were killed. Photographs were not forthcoming. A fundamental truth remained behind closed doors, quite literally *in camera*. Wars waged in kitchens and bedrooms inevitably resulted in dead women and children. This was the kind of simple spatial calculation the architects of the War on Terror overlooked, pretending instead to protect family values at home and abroad. Making the world safe for democracy for yet another blood-soaked century, God willing. Johnson was no fool. Pretending that the ethics of journalism were complicated didn't change the stark clarity of facts on the ground. Erasing evidence didn't erase accountability.

It wasn't the first time the specter of censorship had come back to haunt him. He remembered hearing one of those cultural critics interviewed on NPR, so far to the left he claimed the invasion of Iraq violated international law. If the guy hadn't gotten tenure at some fancy university, he'd have ended up in jail for treason. Johnson listened to liberal stations for a laugh, just to see how outrageous their pundits could be. But professor so-and-so made a point that defied political classification. He could have been Republican or Democrat, even Sunni or Shia for that matter. They were talking about the proliferation of forensics shows on television. *Cold Case. CSI. Without a Trace.* In 2001 there was one. In 2006 there were eight, two of them Emmy winners.

Something beyond the public's perennial thirst for blood and gore must have accounted for this exponential leap.

"Body bags," the professor said cryptically.

His attempt to simulate lecture-hall dramatics fell flat on the radio. The talk show host blathered on to break the silence. If Johnson hadn't been a Vietnam vet, he would have changed the channel. He had his own unresolved issues with body bags. Peaceniks had trafficked in images of dead soldiers to advance their cause. Typical sixties hippie hype. So much for valor and heroism. Casualties were depicted as victims, not warriors. The more mutilated the bodies, the more college students protested and congressmen wagged their heads. Peace was brokered by trivializing the ultimate sacrifice.

This time around the problem was the absence rather than presence of body bags in the media. Either the Vietnam War had saturated the American public's capacity to process graphic facts, or journalists had succumbed to political pressure to suppress images that had formerly fueled antiwar demonstrations. One way or the other, dead soldiers remained out of sight, if not out of mind. A running count of casualties in Iraq was considered adequate coverage of the carnage.

"What happens to all those dead bodies?"

"Get to the point, goddamnit," Johnson said aloud, glaring at his car radio.

Rhetorical questions pissed him off. They were forbidden in journalism, for good reason. Reporters were trained to track down facts. They followed leads instead of asking leading questions. If professor so-and-so really gave a shit, he'd focus on the fate of the bodies themselves, not his own academic abstractions, how fallen heroes were transported home on commercial airliners without adequate provision for the military pomp and circumstance they deserved. Anything to save a buck. When they finally touched down on

American soil, their bodies were unloaded like so much baggage. It was a disgrace.

"They disappear into thin air," the professor said. He paused to underscore his punch line. "And reappear in the guise of the dead bodies on forensics shows."

At first Johnson had scoffed at the gratuitous ingeniousness of this hypothesis. Then something shifted in his mind, altering the locus of reality itself. In their absence, the bodies had become a larger-than-life media presence, the virtual stars of forensics shows. Their spectral role in America's collective unconscious too closely resembled the simulacrum of weapons of mass destruction. Though nothing more than figments of the political imagination, they had allegedly justified the Iraq War. Saying it made it so.

The fact that the first primetime forensics show aired in 2001 implicated 9/11. An inconceivable 2,753 bodies disappeared into thin air on that glorious September morning. A sky that blue was impossible to reconcile with a day that dark. Cognitive dissonance. Emergency medical facilities were put on red alert. Day after day they waited for bodies that were not forthcoming. A few passersby injured in the fallout were treated, but not a single one of the 2,753. From dust to dust.

"The good news is that the American imagination won't tolerate the disappearance of all these bodies."

"I'm assuming there's a downside." Even the talk show host was getting impatient.

"The bad news is—"

Johnson had switched off the radio. He wasn't ready to hear that facts were obsolete in the new millennium. Violence was a spectacle, not an actual phenomenon, something you turned on and off at will on Netflix. YouTube. On Demand. News and entertainment were indistinguishable. Blogs replaced investigative journalism. Pundits jousted windmills rather than exposing the truth. Accountability evaporated into cyberspace. Johnson had always prided himself on being tough and ethical, and tough enough to be ethical. Age or Iraq must have worn him down. He was no longer idealistic enough to do his job.

Sometimes he thought that carrying a camera was more perilous than carrying a gun, psychologically if not physically. In the US Marines, you lived and breathed and fought as a team, shielded from doubt by the powerful force of *Semper Fidelis*. Journalists were a breed apart. The troops were great once you gained their trust. But even embeds ultimately worked alone. There were times when he felt almost like one of the men themselves, and then there were times like this.

Sinclair kept his sights trained on potential targets below. He welcomed the excuse not to look at Johnson. Guys needed privacy when they cracked up. He knew that if Trapp were there, he'd make Johnson tell him what was wrong. Trapp was a great believer in words, as though sucking it up were a problem rather than a solution. Sinclair assumed it was a Southern thing, a regional tendency to wear their hearts on their sleeves. A classic Westerner, Sinclair had about as much faith in words as in shrinks and their talking cures. They were a kind of last resort, a way to communicate things that didn't really matter much anyway. Geography often determined how language was used or not used, as the case may be. New Yorkers talked a mile a minute. New Englanders talked down to you. People from sparsely populated areas tended to use language sparingly, communing more with nature than with each other. Sinclair's inclination to remain silent accounted for the fact that Johnson was there in the first place, grappling with the ethical implications of his professional decision to remain silent.

Out of nowhere, two police cars roared around a corner into an alleyway. Sinclair zoomed in on them. The fact that the drivers wore official uniforms gave him very little pause. The majority of the police force had already joined the insurgency. Plainclothes passengers in the backseat were either civilians or mercenaries, depending on whether the things they carried were lethal or not. The cars screeched to a stop, disgorging a dozen men toting AK-47s. Enemy snipers must have pinpointed the platoon's location. Sinclair was expecting Wolf's team to emerge from a nearby compound any minute, with Radetzky's not far behind next door.

"The alley is armed," Sinclair said calmly into his headset.

The more menacing the threat, the more measured he spoke. Sinclair's buddies had learned to heed his composure as much as his words.

"A full squad."

Sinclair's training kicked in. He automatically referred to the enemy as a squad of soldiers rather than a gang of insurgents. The War on Terror used archaic language dating from the good old days when battles were waged by men authorized by their governments to bear arms and wear uniforms. He hardly knew what to call the targets in his crosshairs. Jihadis, feyadeen, muj fighters. They might have been terrorists imported from Syria or Pakistan. Chechen snipers, Filipino gunners, Afghan mortar men, Pakistani suicide bombers, Saudi arms runners. Their nationalities affected their maneuvers. It was like fighting a dozen armies on a single battlefield. Just when you thought you understood the tactical mentality of one faction, another one joined the insurgency.

Sinclair managed to pick off one of the uniformed fighters before the rest took cover. For good measure, he blew his brains out. Insurgents had been known to commandeer bullet-proof vests along with uniforms. The target was smaller, but Sinclair felt confident enough to scope the head instead of the body. Some days were like that. He was in the zone and could afford to take tough shots.

McCarthy and Trapp reappeared on the roof of a cleared compound. They lobbed grenades over the edge of the parapet. At least one hit home. The screams were so unrelenting it might have been two. Radetzky's squad took advantage of the smoke screen, fanning across the courtyard under cover of Wolf's team. Vasquez managed to flush out three gunners. He nailed one himself. Sinclair picked off the other two without even having to move the barrel of his rifle. They ran right into his sights. If only it were always that easy.

The enemy's lack of training kicked in. They panicked. The second uniformed driver sprinted back to his patrol car. One of his passengers managed to pile back in before he screeched off. The dead driver had left keys in the ignition of the other car. A frantic insurgent managed to climb behind the wheel without getting gunned down. The car sped off, leaving the rest stranded. Radetzky's squad mowed down every last one of them before they had a chance to regroup. Nine kills scored without suffering a scratch. When the platoon was fighting as one, they were almost invincible.

Sinclair was appalled not by the carnage but by the cowardice. A marine would rather die ten times over than desert one of his own on the battlefield. Valor and heroism all stemmed from one fundamental martial virtue. Loyalty. Dishonorable discharges always resulted from one unthinkable vice. Betrayal. They had all sworn to uphold a code of ethics, to be sure. But loyalty to your buddies was all that really mattered. The rest was just window dressing.

Sinclair had always had a horror of betrayal. He was slow to learn that what you hate and fear will never let you rest in peace. Grandpa always said that everyone was predisposed to be their own worst enemy, something Sinclair never understood until he got to Iraq. Call it fate or a psychological complex, your nemesis ultimately tracks you down. His first run-in with the idea of betrayal was in church, of all places. His mother used to force them to attend services to commemorate Christ's birth and death. Judging from her lax approach to the rest of the ecclesiastical calendar, she was far less interested in the savior's actual life. Christmas was torture, an unmitigated bore from start to finish. At least Easter had plenty of gruesome stories to spice things up. Gethsemane and Golgotha were worth the price of admission, no doubt about that. But all that crap about cocks crowing three times was infuriating. Sinclair would have stormed right out of church if his mother hadn't told him, in so many words, to keep his butt glued to the pew, or else.

First of all, cocks didn't crow on cue. They crowed when they were damned good and ready, usually when you were trying to sleep in. Sinclair was willing to forgive incidental factual errors here and there. Even Grandpa had been known to stretch things a little for the sake of a good story. But the betrayal itself was unfathomable, not to mention out of character. Judas was a born liar and Christ never should have trusted him to begin with. But Peter was his right-hand man. They fished together and would have gone hunting, too, if there'd been animals in that godforsaken desert. When they were alone, Jesus probably called him Pete, the loyalest name on the planet. The rock. There was no way Peter ever made those lousy cocks crow. Not once, not three times, not ever. He'd have crucified himself, pounded the nails into his own wrists and feet, before he'd betray a fellow apostle, let alone Christ.

Loyalty was unconditional, like love only much less fickle. You could conceivably be loyal to more than one person at a time, provided conflicts of interest didn't intervene. Platoons were like that, aggregates of the kind of pure, unwavering devotion Sinclair shared with Pete from day one, or at the very least day six. They were born within a week of one another, pulled by the same midwife into what Sinclair always assumed would be parallel lives. Till death do us part. Everybody blamed everybody else for Pete's suicide. The last letter Sinclair's sister ever wrote to him was one long outrageous accusation. She said he'd let

Pete down. Truth be told, it was the other way around. Suicide was the ultimate betrayal.

If there were warning signs, they were miniscule in comparison with the magnitude of the crime. Being moody hardly qualified as a red flag. Sinclair assumed Pete was just itching to graduate. They both were. But the only thing that improved over the course of the summer was the weather. For some reason, Pete decided to hire himself out rather than work on the ranch. He was juggling several jobs, thinning fruit and baling hay on neighboring farms. By the time he got home, it was too late to even go fishing, not that he seemed to care. When Sinclair asked why he was wasting his time for chump change, Pete said he should ask his father.

"I'm asking you."

"I'm not at liberty to talk about it."

"Cut the crap, Pete. You sound like a TV show."

"I'm quoting somebody. Take a wild guess who."

"Somebody I'd rather not drag into this."

"If you don't want to ask your dad, ask your grandpa."

Grandpa, who was the self-proclaimed straightest talker west of the Mississippi, said he wasn't at liberty to talk about it either.

"Ask your father."

The whole line of questioning obviously made Grandpa angry. Sinclair couldn't tell if he was mad at his father or Pete or both. Everyone seemed privy to some big secret except him. Enough was enough.

His father was in the study with his foreman, Nick. He was ordering him around, as usual, even though the foreman knew a hell of a lot more about ranching than he did. Nick looked happier to see Pete than his dad did. The feeling was mutual.

"I was just leaving," Nick said, getting up.

"Don't forget what I told you about those inseminators," Mr. Sinclair said.

Nick winked at Sinclair on his way out, having already forgotten what he had been told about those inseminators. It was the only way a cowboy like him could tolerate working for a white-collar rancher like Mr. Sinclair.

"Have a seat, Billy."

"No, thanks," Sinclair said. "I just want to ask you a quick question."

"If it's about that saddle, the answer is still no."

"It's about Pete."

"I seem to recall discussing this already. Several times."

"You told me he's not welcome here anymore. But you never told me why."

His father made a show of checking his watch.

"Got all afternoon? Or should I just list the top ten reasons so we can both get back to work?"

"One good reason will do."

"I can't trust him anymore."

"What did he do?"

His father fingered the railroad spike he used as a paperweight. He started to say something but decided against it.

"Come on, Dad. What's going on?"

"Let's put it this way, Billy. I've been around hen houses long enough to know when there's a fox snooping around."

That's all he could get out of him. A conspiracy of silence kept Sinclair in the dark. The whole family was in on it, even Candace. She was such a blabbermouth he probably could have coaxed it out of her. But that would have involved acknowledging that she knew something he didn't know about Pete. There was nothing Sinclair hated more than his sister horning in on their friendship. She had scads of friends, one for every day of the month. He had one. She ought to respect that.

He had no desire to broach the subject again with Pete. The beauty of their friendship was its simple, quiet clarity. Talking, for what it was worth, just complicated things. Candace liked to make fun of them. She'd mimic their conversations, making grunting noises and clearing her throat a few times. She said it was a guy thing, as though that made it shallow. Damn right it was a guy thing. It was a refuge and a comfort. But even their silences were invaded this time. They were fraught and depressing.

Sinclair was initially relieved when Pete finally reached out, as Candace put it. It was such a girlie way of describing what happened in the aspen grove. The idea that he had rebuffed Pete's so-called cry for help was pure Candace, straight from all the self-help books she was reading when she wrote that goddamned letter. She had a whole shelf of them. Somebody was making good money off people trying to cope with loss. There was a big market for bereavement in the wake of 9/11.

Candace was right about one thing. Pete had an awful lot on his mind that day. It was their last weekend together before Sinclair left for college. They were supposed to go grouse hunting, but Pete said he wasn't in the mood to kill anything. That should have been a tip-off that something was terribly wrong. A hike was proposed. They set out without a destination, knowing full well where they'd end up. They loved every inch of the forest, especially the aspen grove. It was their real home, not the four walls where they played house with their families. Neither of them ever made the pilgrimage there alone.

The grove was a living shrine to the animals they hunted and killed over the years. They had mounted antlers on the trunks of trees, taking care to replicate the exact height of the animals, which they measured in hands before skinning them. As the trees grew, the antlers seemed to rise higher and higher, totem souls unencumbered by bodies. The most imposing was a moose rack, a gigantic beast Sinclair bagged just east of Yellowstone Park. At sunset its shadow stretched halfway across the grove, a looming apparition that spooked them as boys and humbled them as men.

They liked to pretend nobody else knew about the grove. It may have been true. The terrain was steep and there was no trail. The only other evidence of visitations was deer and bobcat tracks, and holes left by bear digging roots. There was a streambed nearby, almost always dry in summer and raging with runoff every spring. In September, they gathered pebbles, which they carried in their pockets to protect them from teachers and other civilizing threats. In May they put them back where they had found them. Up there it was never hot and bothered the way it was on the valley floor. There was always a breeze, uphill in the morning, downhill at night. Aspen leaves were forever quaking, a hushing sound that made the two of them even quieter than usual.

Neither of them said a word until they crested the ridge. They dropped over into the Eagle Mountain watershed, much wetter and wilder than the grazing land below. In the distance, a bright white line traced the blue ridge of the northern Rockies. They had been hiking for two hours, long enough to hit their stride and settle into one another's company. Sinclair was surprised when Pete broke the silence.

"Did you talk to your father?"

"Yup."

"What did he say?"

"Something about a fox in a henhouse."

"Whatever that means."

"You tell me."

"Did he mention a girl?"

"Nope."

"Then he lied."

"Wouldn't be the first time."

Trashing one of their fathers was usually a surefire way of bonding. But the gesture felt empty. The fact that Mr. Sinclair was an asshole wasn't enough to repair the damage their friendship had suffered over the past few months. Sinclair assumed it had something to do with the fact that he was on the verge of leaving for college, separation anxiety or whatever Candace's self-help books would have called it. The last thing he expected to come out of Pete's mouth was reference to a girl. They could see the tops of the aspen trees below, shimmering silver against a backdrop of dark pines. Sinclair was determined to finish the conversation as quickly as possible. There'd be hell to pay if anyone talked about girls once they reached the grove.

"A girl."

"Yup."

"What a relief."

"I'm glad you think so."

"I thought it was something serious."

"It is serious."

"You got her knocked up?"

"I never said that."

A red-tail hawk was hovering over the grove. Sinclair couldn't reconcile the pure serenity of its flight with the garbage pouring out of Pete's mouth. This was the kind of conversation other men had in smoke-filled bars, half drunk on tequila. Anywhere but here. Anyone but him and Pete, who steered clear of tequila.

"Are you sure it's yours?" Sinclair said.

"It's not about that."

"It's never about that. But it happens."

"Shit happens, that's for sure."

Sinclair could feel Pete looking at him. He pretended not to notice. They were traversing the last escarpment descending into the grove. He slowed down, letting Pete take the lead so he wouldn't have to make eye contact.

"I was hoping you'd talk to the girl's father," Pete said.

"It's your mess. You talk to him."

"He doesn't like me."

"And I'm supposed to tell him what a great guy you are."

"Something like that."

"So you can marry some girl you got knocked up."

"Forget it, Billy. I'm sorry I even brought it up."

Pete peeled off and headed straight down the hillside. They never went that way. He slipped on some shale and cussed it out. Sinclair stuck to the game trail. By the time he reached the grove, Pete was already sitting under the moose rack. He wanted to sit down next to him. He wanted a lot of things he was pretty sure he could no longer have.

"You've known this girl for what? Six months?"

"Years."

"First I ever heard about it."

"You get ornery when I bring up girls."

"She's got you where she wants you, that's for sure."

"I love her, Billy. Can't you understand that?"

If he hadn't said that one word, things might have worked out differently. *Love.* Their intimacy was predicated on never betraying each other with language. Sinclair had always known they would both eventually marry and have children. That was part of being a man, too. But their families would complement, not replace, their bond. Let women use words with careless abandon, emptying things of their intrinsic value. Let them wax poetic about romance and crushes and even passion as long as they shut the fuck up about love.

Sinclair recoiled from the word as if from a blow. Punching Pete in self-defense seemed the most appropriate response. Instead he marched to the other side of the grove. He and a mule-deer rack watched the sun sink in the western sky. He was careful to think about nothing, the only real way to keep language at bay. Pete was watching the moose shadow spread across the grove. When it reached Sinclair, he got up and started climbing back up the hillside.

Sinclair often wondered whether he would have run after Pete if he'd known he was suicidal. Incompatible emotions blocked his grief, equal parts guilt and anger. No matter how many times he rehearsed their final conversation, he couldn't envision a better outcome. The cardinal rule of friendship was that men never allowed women to come between them. Pete had offered him a false choice. Sinclair could have either betrayed their friendship by helping him or by refusing to help him. Catch-22.

The military was as close to an ideal masculine community as you could get. But nothing, not even the US Marines, was a safe haven. The threat was ubiquitous. The sight of mothers in combat zones. Letters from home fraught with worry. He had seen his buddies break down crying reading them. But love of wives and children never compromised their blood brotherhood. When duty called, they answered with unflinching loyalty. Even Trapp, the most devoted husband in the whole platoon, had his priorities straight. His wife had threatened to divorce him if he redeployed to Iraq. He had done it anyway. She eventually came around, of course. Deep down, women want to be married to men, not cowards. They try to domesticate you, fully expecting you to resist. Pete should have resisted.

Semper Fidelis wasn't just a martial ethic. Without being faithful to one another, men couldn't be faithful to anyone else. They couldn't even be men. Compromising this fidelity was hazardous for everyone concerned. Sinclair had witnessed the devastating results both on and off the battlefield. Pete was dead. Nine enemy corpses littered the courtyard below. Different contexts masked the same tragic flaw. Men self-destructed when they betrayed what they held most dear. Each other.

Wolf's squad was stripping weapons and ammunition off the dead insurgents. The one in the police uniform was clutching an M16. He had obviously had more luck in previous encounters with coalition forces. American rifles were the ultimate status symbol, proof of having killed an infidel invader. Like scalps, only much more useful. Radetzky intervened, waving the squads on to the next set of compounds. Colonel Denning had issued another blanket order.

Every company in the battalion was expected to reach Phase Line Freddy a full six hours ahead of the original timetable. Defensive measures, including destroying enemy ordnance, were too time-consuming to accommodate the accelerated pace. Radetzky knew that every weapon left behind could be salvaged by insurgents, eventually killing one of his men. The Iraqi National Guard was officially AWOL.

"Who's going to watch our backs?"

"Yours truly," Sinclair said.

"Not unless you've got two sets of eyes," Radetzky said. "We need you out front."

"Meanwhile our asses are hanging out to dry," Wolf said.

"Offense is the best defense."

"You keep saying that. Like you're trying to convince yourself."

"They can't shoot what they can't catch," McCarthy said.

"You heard the man," Logan said.

"Get the lead out!"

Everyone understood the dangers involved in abandoning armed corpses. They forged ahead because they were trained to follow orders. With the exception of Wolf and Radetzky, who felt responsible for their squads, they obeyed with alacrity. An accelerated campaign was a double-edged sword, but the excitement outweighed the risk. At this rate, barring unforeseen resistance, the city would be theirs by the end of the week. Sinclair felt proud to be a part of what promised to be a crowning victory in Iraq, second only to the blitz on Baghdad.

This section of East Manhattan, bordering on the industrial sector, was like a massive smoking gun. Evidence of recent occupation by enemy units was everywhere. Syringes. Dirty dishes. Trashed bathrooms. They kept alternating roof-top and street-level entries whenever possible. Walled-up staircases and other makeshift fortifications tapered off. There were still plenty of booby traps, but most of them had been wired too hastily to pose much of a threat. Unlocked doors were a dead giveaway. Welcome mats were sinister reminders that hospitality had become lethal. The pace imposed by Colonel Denning technically forbade taking time to search for traps. But Radetzky slowed down just enough to test the waters. When in doubt, they fragged the joint with grenades before diving in.

If everything went according to plan, the Thundering Third would dovetail with Battalion 1/5, forming a mile-wide offensive. Pivoting west as 2/1 moved east out of the Jolan District, they would squeeze the life out of remaining insurgency strongholds. The prevailing mood was grimly exuberant. Then their momentum was unexpectedly derailed. The other half of the company was taking continuous fire from a mosque a quarter of a mile from Sinclair's position. He had first noticed its mosaic minaret at high noon, glinting in the blindingly blue sky. Failure to distinguish between light refracting off of mosaic tiles and gun barrels would put the entire platoon at risk. Any doubts about the source of all that glinting were dispelled when the mosque's imam started broadcasting double-barrel prayers, amplified to high heaven by mammoth loudspeakers mounted on the dome. His ranting and raving sounded anything but pious to Sinclair. The fact that mosques maintained their status as neutral zones made him all the more wary of their veiled threat.

Even before the attack, radical clerics had broadcast holy hatred five times a day, seven days a week. On patrol, the platoon tried to tune out the call to jihad while meeting and greeting the Iraqi people. This ideological disjuncture took its toll on soldiers and civilians alike. Even their most successful peacekeeping missions were accompanied by ominous undertones. A handful of Fallujan imams cooperated, allowing patrols to search their mosques for weapons caches and bunkers. They were vastly outnumbered by collaborators inciting people to arm themselves against Christian crusaders. The call to arms wasn't exclusive to the militia.

Al-jihad fi sabil Allah!
Fard al-kifayah!

All who believed were commanded to fight in the cause of Allah. Women and even children were enjoined to do their communal duty. No wonder families were still embedded within the insurgency in East Manhattan. Minaret broadcasts had drowned out coalition injunctions to evacuate the city. The fact that this particular imam was still preaching confirmed that Sinclair's company was approaching occupied territory.

Radetzky decided to duplicate the strategy that had led to the destruction of the cell the day before. Colonel Denning tentatively authorized the plan, pending the findings of exploratory feints. Five platoons in the vicinity of the mosque were ordered to suspend search-and-destroy missions in order to surround the target. Extra rooftop coverage was dispatched to act as the eyes and ears of the offensive. Sinclair and Logan were stationed together atop a compound with a clear view of the mosque's palatial entrance. Even when its speakers were silent, its imposing architecture broadcast an unmistakable message. Imams were the keepers of the keys to the city. No one dared challenge the authority of Fallujah's spiritual leaders.

After the grueling pace of the past two days, it was a relief to be ordered to hold one position. With just the two of them on the roof, it was like being back at the base. They lapsed into their almost domestic relationship, enjoying the familiarity of one another's company. Logan scanned the area with binoculars, and Sinclair probed suspicious nooks and crannies with his rifle scope. Orphaned cats and dogs prowled alleyways, looking for something to eat. They could hear them pawing through overturned garbage cans, fighting over scraps. Otherwise the neighborhood was conspicuously quiet, not so much abandoned as holding its breath. Even the mosque had fallen silent. Then Radetzky started mobilizing exploratory feints, testing the waters to see what they were up against. Every time a decoy unit of marines advanced, it was bombarded with unprecedented firepower, including missiles and mortars.

"They've stockpiled some big babies in there," Sinclair said.

"Time to roll in the tanks."

What seemed like an obvious game plan wasn't forthcoming. The delay seemed inexplicable given the rush to reach the phase line.

"I smell a rat," Logan said.

"Baghdad?"

"The CPA."

"Better known as Confused Political Assholes."

Every time Centcom authorized a mosque attack, the Coalition Provisional Authority tried to pull the plug. They were provisional in more ways than one, allies only insofar as they needed Americans to enforce their newfound authority over sectarian insurgencies. Even then, mosques were sacrosanct, a perennial reminder that Allah was the true authority in the region. Radetzky refused to confirm or deny Logan's conjectures that the CPA was obstructing the offensive. Even more tightlipped than usual, he ordered his men to hang tight. Sinclair still had faith in the coalition. He offered a more humane explanation.

"Must be evacuating civilians before we launch the attack," Sinclair said.

They watched the mosque for almost an hour, and not a soul entered or exited the main gate. Like a castle, its drawbridge was already raised for battle.

The militaristic impregnability of the structure impressed Sinclair the soldier but offended Sinclair the American citizen. He had been raised to respect the separation of church and state. The rhetoric of the Axis of Evil notwithstanding, he continued to believe that the United States exemplified this fundamental democratic principle. In Iraq, the conflation of politics and religion constituted yet another permeable boundary that confounded his understanding of an ethical universe of mutually exclusive forces. Good and evil. Democracy and radical Islam. Separation of church and state was right, and everything else was wrong. Occupying a mosque violated more than just rules of engagement. A more flagrantly sacrilegious military strategy was almost inconceivable. Almost. Snipers were notoriously susceptible to the seductions of minarets, whose shooting angles were incomparable.

"How would you say churches compare with mosques?" Sinclair asked Logan.

"I'm not following you."

"If you had to hunker down in a mosque or a church, which would you choose?"

"A mosque. Just look at that minaret."

"Churches have spires."

"Purely symbolic. Churches are never used for military purposes."

"What about the Crusades?"

"That was a long time ago. And they were Catholics, not Christians."

"Very funny."

"I wasn't trying to be funny."

"Sorry."

Sinclair had trouble negotiating Logan's born-again distinctions. They seemed unnecessarily elaborate or alarmingly loose, depending on the context. For starters, the difference between Christians in general and born-agains in particular eluded him. Logan said the determining factor was the believer's relationship with the word of God.

"You mean the Bible?" Sinclair asked.

"What else would I mean?"

"Catholics read the Bible."

"Correction. Catholics have their own liturgy. Loosely based on scripture."

"What about Methodists? And Lutherans?"

"Sunday Christians."

"But Christians all the same."

"God will separate the wheat from the chaff on the last day."

"Meaning?"

"You're either born again or you're not."

To Sinclair it seemed more a question of degree than anything else. As far as he could tell, garden variety Christians talked the same talk, but practiced what they preached less vehemently. He knew better than to say this to Logan, who was virulently opposed to radicalism of any kind. Just look at jihadis, murdering innocent people throughout the region. Even Israel, the holiest of lands, wasn't exempt from their violence.

"Don't get me started," Logan would say.

It didn't take much. The mere mention of Palestinians elicited tirades about the audacity of Arabs staking claims on the birthplace of Christ. As far as Logan was concerned, their demands defied historical record. Virtually every reliable source confirmed that Jews were the chosen people, the true heirs of the holy land. Jesus was a Jew, after all. The first great convert. Logan sincerely regretted that Jews wouldn't be saved on the last day unless they accepted Christ as their personal savior. And why not? Technically, they were just unconverted Christians.

When voting in national elections, Logan chose candidates based on their commitment to unconditional military support of the Israeli army. His decision to enlist in the Marine Corps was based largely on the belief that victory in Iraq would help safeguard the state of Israel. Fallujah's imams apparently agreed, albeit for radically different reasons. Another of their favorite rants, broadcast in the same breath as evening prayers, characterized the American occupation as a conspiracy designed to aid and abet Jews intent on stealing Iraqi oil. Divested of regional propaganda and dogma, the insurgency's insistence on the intertwined fates of Israel and Iraq was a mirror image of Logan's viewpoint. Sinclair took this bizarre concurrence as yet another example of the dangers of mixing religion and politics.

Though Logan was highly sensitive to distinctions among Catholics, Protestants, and born-agains, he lumped al-Qaeda, Hamas, Fatah, and Hezbollah into a single monumental terrorist bogeyman, intent on destroying Western civilization. Even Sinclair tended to agree that ideological and sectarian differences changed nothing on the ground. From a purely militaristic point of view, the United States of America was the world's supercop, cracking down on the latest wave of international crime. Globalism had upped the ante. Twentieth-century fascism and communism had morphed into an even more insidious threat. New-millennial terrorism.

Sinclair was equally committed to taking the fight to the enemy. Skeptics like his father said the conflict in the Middle East was all about oil. The few pinkos left in the world blamed capitalism, as usual. Radicals of all stripes said it was a religious war. But Sinclair knew they were fighting to safeguard freedom at home and abroad—freedom of speech, freedom from want, freedom from religious persecution, the freedom to vote according to the dictates of your conscience—everything his military uniform represented. His war was ethical, not religious. Had Americans all been fighting the same battles, they might have already prevailed.

Logan was all for freedom as long as it didn't affect prayer in schools. The First Amendment made him a little edgy. It was prone to falling into the wrong hands. The sixties had inspired Congress to outlaw flag burning, among other un-American activities. But the debate over whether the Pledge of Allegiance should include reference to one nation under God still reared its ugly head. When one of Logan's college history professors claimed the phrase had only been added in 1954, he dropped the class. He made the mistake of recounting this story during one of the platoon's late-night gabfests. Wolf pounced on every opportunity to alleviate combat anxiety with comic relief. The more humorless the target, the better.

"You're saying America is a Christian country?" Wolf asked.

"I'm saying we're one nation under God, and the God in question has a long white beard—"

"Kind of like imams?"

"You didn't let me finish. And nothing on his head. Not a turban or towel in sight. Just more of that lily white hair."

"Not even a yarmulke? I thought your God was Jewish."

In self-defense, Logan eventually adopted the platoon's don't-ask-don't-tell policy regarding religious convictions. But not before everyone understood that his patriotism was an act of faith. There was only room for one God in Iraq. His. Logan's condemnation of sectarian militias didn't undermine his belief that the United States was authorized to wage war in the name of Jesus Christ. After all, double standards were standard fare in religious wars. Mirror images of monotheism were embattled in the Middle East, not that either side recognized their reflection. Sinclair stopped short of equating Logan's fervor with the fanaticism of the insurgents in the mosque. A lone born-again marine could hardly be held responsible for the apocalyptic tenor of this war. Besides he was very fond of Logan. They had been through a lot together.

They cracked open a couple of MREs, more to stay awake than to stave off hunger. As usual, they swapped food groups. Logan was crazy about chips. When they had access to unlimited ready meals, he opened one after another and scarfed down bag after bag. Sinclair was perfectly willing to trade chips for fruits and vegetables, presumably because his mother had never allowed her children to eat junk food growing up. This was one of several private rituals, nobody's business but their own. Around the other guys, Sinclair forfeited extra vegetables to avoid being teased. Logan wasn't the only brunt of Wolf's goody-two-shoes jokes. In the middle of his second bag of chips, Logan raised a finger as though testing the wind.

"Hear that?"

They both stopped chewing and listened to the distant grind of approaching tanks.

"Fasten your seatbelts, ladies and gentlemen."

But still nothing happened. The tanks stopped, just out of artillery range, and even the Cobras patrolling overhead disappeared. Then Radetzky radioed an inexplicable order.

"Retreat two blocks. Reconnoiter in the last cleared compound."

They had expected to hold their positions to pick off insurgents escaping the mosque bombardment. As many could be killed in flight as were incinerated inside by mortar explosions. This flush-and-plug strategy had been employed to great advantage in Baghdad, where heavy artillery was the backbone of almost every operation. It reminded Sinclair of shooting galleries at good old-fashioned county fairs, minus the Kewpie doll prizes. Logan thought of it more like a computer game with rapid-fire targets. He was disappointed when the plan fell through. Gunners rarely had the opportunity to practice sharpshooting.

"What's up with that?" Logan said.

"Maybe they're holding hostages inside."

"Then turn up the heat. Smoke 'em out."

"Don't worry. Radetzky knows what he's doing."

They hustled back to the designated compound, anxious to find out their next move. No one admired Radetzky more than Sinclair. With the foresight that separates officers from their men, he had no doubt devised another brilliant plan. Sinclair studied Radetzky's maneuvers with an eye to emulating them some day. He had originally enlisted because of 9/11, but the longer he served in the Marine Corps the more he considered making a career of it. One in a hundred grunts were officer material. Sinclair certainly had the right attitude. Time would tell if he had the right stuff.

Reunited with the platoon, Sinclair noticed that Radetzky seemed distracted. He ordered his men to lie low until daybreak. All but the most die-hard gunners welcomed the chance to bed down. Insomniacs spent their time cleaning weapons and muttering questions, none of which had answers. The usual flurry of radio transmissions from Tactical Operations was suspended. Periodically Radetzky checked in with the battalion commander. Otherwise he sat brooding, not even consulting his beloved aerial map of the city. Sinclair echoed his mood. They were far more on edge sitting around than they would have been gearing up for battle.

Half of the company was crammed into a single compound. The floors were so jammed with prone bodies you couldn't walk from one room to another. Snoring competed with the noise of dueling broadcasts outside. A psychological operations team tasked with bolstering morale was stationed nearby. Their loudspeakers sounded like they were inside the room, if not inside Sinclair's head. Trying to drown out harangues from the mosque necessitated turning the volume up a notch every other minute. As usual, PSYOP's choice of material was predominantly gothic, as though they had all watched *Psycho* one too many times as kids. They were forever splicing together audio clips from slasher films. The target audience was ambiguous. They were either terrorizing terrorists or trying to pump up guys like McCarthy who reveled in gore.

Sinclair honestly didn't know which was worse, the imam's fanatic denunciations or the accompanying maniacal laughter, which sounded like the Joker in *Batman*. Both sides were screaming amplified bloody murder punctuated by the bone-rattling percussion of heavy-metal songs. Dead on Arrival's "Attack of the Peacekeepers." "Killing an Arab," courtesy of The Cure. The War on Terror was the first war with an official soundtrack. The fact that it sounded more like a horror film than a military operation said a lot about the new millennium, none of it good. Guys like Sinclair would have preferred something a little more patriotic, maybe "The Battle Hymn of the Republic," to remind them of what they were really fighting for. Guys like him were in the minority.

Around 0400 hours a commotion next door roused the platoon. They took turns peering out of bedroom windows, trying to catch a glimpse of a bedraggled group of Iraqi National Guardsmen in an adjacent compound. Rumor had it they'd been flown in from Kurdistan to make a cameo appearance at the mosque attack. Everyone knew this was highly unlikely, but it made for a good story. Until recently, most of the INGs in Anbar Province hailed from CAP India, a Combined Action Platoon trained by veteran US Army and Marine Corps officers. They were virtually all Shiites whose desire to avenge themselves on Ba'athist Sunnis outweighed every other consideration, including death threats. Then the insurgency devised an even more compelling deterrent. They claimed the coalition was pitting Shiites against Sunnis to facilitate foreign domination of the region. Sectarian squabbles were momentarily eclipsed by a new species of Iraqi nationalism, united against the United States.

Kurdish freedom fighters hated both factions. Near genocide convinced them that sectarian problems continued to demand sectarian solutions. If Shiites and Sunnis decided to resist American intervention, Kurds would embrace it. Their enemy's enemy was their friend. Centcom was perfectly willing to adopt Middle Eastern mottos and motivations when they came in handy. Shiite Guardsmen were defecting, and the coalition had to take what it could get. Kurds stepped in to replace them.

This particular unit looked more like whipped Shiites than Kurdish freedom fighters. Uniforms were mismatched. Their weapons wouldn't have passed even a cursory inspection. They had the haunted expressions of traitors, not mercenaries, tricked into pitting themselves against their own regional interests. At the crack of dawn, they rallied for morning prayers. What they may have lacked in military discipline they made up for in spiritual conviction.

Inside the mosque, insurgents prostrated themselves to the same God, enemy camps united in spirit to Allah. Politics were a Western invention, a mere blemish on a region whose deep structure was profoundly religious. Not to worry. Their prayers were part of Washington's strategic plan. INGs were really only there to justify, not carry out, the mosque attack. The more devout they were, the better. As long as they showed up for photo ops, no one could claim American infidels were wantonly destroying sacred property. Headlines and captions would encapsulate the apparent truth.

"Insurgents Attack Coalition Forces in Fallujah."

"Muslim INGs Liberate Occupied Mosques."

The offensive was scheduled to begin at dawn, but Radetzky was still brooding at the kitchen table at 0630 hours. Sinclair must have finally managed to doze off. There seemed to be no other way to account for the unmistakable sound of an airstrike, which he assumed was part of a recurring nightmare that had plagued him since the Battle of Baghdad. Rules of engagement forbade air attacks on mosques, if only to thwart the insurgency's most effective recruiting tool. Nothing inspired jihad like the specter of burning Qurans. It turns out Sinclair wasn't dreaming. The rule had been waived in light of what the CIA called incontrovertible evidence of the mosque's strategic violation of Appendix D, No. 3-7. As far as McCarthy was concerned, they could call it whatever they liked as long as it authorized them to kick ass. Judging from the whining pitch and trajectory of laser-guided missiles, F-16 Vipers were targeting the mosque. The strike only lasted a couple of minutes, which was typical of aerial attacks. It didn't take long to do the job using 500-pound explosives.

"No wonder they didn't bother backing up the offensive," Sinclair said.

"Even cockroaches can't survive bombs that big," McCarthy said.

"This is East Manhattan, remember?" Wolf said. "If these roaches are anything like their cousins back home, nothing can kill them. Not even nukes."

They waited almost an hour before going in to mop up. The platoon was growing accustomed to inexplicable delays. The same couldn't be said for the gang of CNN reporters that suddenly showed up, eager to start documenting evidence to justify the strike. Whenever a holy site was targeted, reinforcements were sent in for the sake of media damage control. Nothing was more damning than Al Jazeera's coverage of mosque attacks. There was never any mention of grenades dropping like manna from minarets. Or weapons caches concealed behind qiblah walls. They featured pictures of domes with what looked like gaping holes ripped open by what was characterized as indiscriminate bombing. The extent of the damage was actually miniscule in proportion to the scale of the threat. Laser-guided bombs guaranteed an unprecedented level of precision. Under the rules of engagement of virtually any other war, the buildings would have been leveled.

Johnson was convinced imams hired their own version of embedded reporters, providing front row seats to anyone willing to conceal evidence of military operations in their mosques. Hospitals did the same thing, giving Al Jazeera photographers access to emergency rooms. Or so they said. The footage could have been bogus for all anyone knew, dating from Saddam's genocides or the war with Iran. Heart-wrenching photographs of wounded children and stricken parents. Burn victims. Amputees. American reporters were too intimidated to follow up on these reports. More than one had already been kidnapped, even killed. They were only safe when embedded with the military.

Radical Arab networks funded out of Saudi Arabia and Qatar established what amounted to a global media monopoly. Coalition news outlets could either screen their footage or none at all. Washington decried Al Jazeera's smear campaigns. But the Iraqi provisional government refused to shut down its television studio in Baghdad. More embedded reporters showed up. Axis of Evil rhetoric was ratcheted up a notch. Tit for tat. Johnson seemed genuinely upset that both sides were more concerned with hype than documentation. He wasn't naive enough to think that absolute objectivity was possible, but you didn't have to spin news like a disc jockey. The guys from CNN were practically frothing at the mouth, they were so excited at the prospect of carnage. Vietnam had cured him of what he called ambulance-chasing journalism.

"They act like war is a blood sport," Johnson said.

"It is," McCarthy said.

"It's a blood ritual," Sinclair said.

"Same difference."

"Hardly," Johnson said. "One of them plays to an audience."

"So much the better," McCarthy said. "Guess what happens when the public isn't rooting for the home team? You were in Nam. You know goddamn good and well what happens."

"This isn't Nam."

"Not yet anyway."

Sinclair's respect for Johnson grew with every passing day of the offensive. No doubt his military training bolstered his professional ethics. He was there to report what was really happening, not some trumped-up version of what this or that government wanted people to believe. Sinclair thought all embedded reporters should be veterans of the armed forces, preferably US Marines. Never mind the fact that even marines had dirty little secrets. Or not so little, as the case may be. Pictures of civilian casualties still lurked in Johnson's camera, destined never to see the light of day. He wondered if what they were about to witness in the mosque would change his mind about publishing them. The free press commitment to all the news that's fit to print implied that something somewhere was off-limits. Johnson wanted to believe that fairness rather than censorship was the determining factor. Under the circumstances, the likelihood of maintaining his ethical integrity was roughly equivalent to one of McCarthy's milder invectives. When pigs fly.

By the time they gained access to the mosque, there was nothing left to photograph. Unidentified muckety-mucks, probably Sunni clerics, were pulling strings behind the scenes. All the weapons, all the wounded, all the dead had vanished. CNN reporters had to content themselves with shots of Iraqi National Guardsmen, rifles at the ready, fending off the bloodstained rubble. The dome held up to the bombardment, but the minaret had fallen and crashed into a public square, where its mosaic shattered like a broken mirror, still glimmering in shards. Scouring the premises for nonexistent weapons caches, Sinclair and Logan discovered a gate in back that hadn't been visible from their surveillance perch.

"They must have evacuated civilians through here," Sinclair said. "Before the strike."

"I'm sure they did," Logan said.

Times like this, Sinclair and Logan were relieved to be fighting side-by-side. Articulating what they would have done to avoid collateral damage spared them from imagining what might not have been done in the heat of battle. Sinclair was as devoutly patriotic as Logan was evangelical, an increasingly common coalition that distinguished the Iraq War from previous conflicts. The assumption was that ideological purity would trickle down into actual op plans. Distinguishing between civilians and enemy combatants was difficult, but not impossible. It's what the American military did and terrorists didn't do. It's why God was on our side, not theirs.

The mosque had been a symbolic as well as military stronghold. When afternoon prayer time rolled around again, imams would no longer broadcast divinely authorized resistance, at least not in this neighborhood. Insurgents were on their own now, engaged one-on-one with coalition forces, not infidels. Sinclair was alternately relieved and disturbed. He certainly wouldn't miss hearing clerical calls to arms, reverberating from Pakistan to Turkey in the universal language of jihad. But destroying mosques was one hell of a way to shut them up.

The platoon dispersed and fanned back out across the advancing skirmish line. Banking on the probability that the air strike had flushed resistance out of a wide radius, they moved quickly to make up lost time. Sinclair's sniper team had to find new perches almost every half hour, just to keep up. Their third nest was a real beauty, commanding a view of the entire city. Tanks and Strykers were lined up on Highway 10, poised and ready for the second half of the offensive. Battalion 1/5 was advancing from the northern front, right on schedule. To the west, smoke billowed from the Jolan Cemetery. Apparently the mosque wasn't the only aerial target, rules of engagement notwithstanding. Battalion 2/1 must have summoned the Vipers before they even had time to touch down for refueling.

Sinclair wrenched his attention away from the awesome sight of F-16s pounding the cemetery. Without buildings to absorb the initial impact, guided missiles cratered the killing fields. The temptation to zoom in was almost overwhelming, but the squads below were relying on his vigilance.

He had to content himself with imagining the devastation. Bodies in various stages of decay blown from their final resting places, lying side by side with fresh casualties. Wasted generations of a city constantly under siege. There would be hell to pay for bombing a graveyard. Insurgents were playing Russian roulette with public sentiment. Even when they lost battles, they forced American troops to attack targets that threatened to compromise their moral integrity. Mosques. Cemeteries. Home after home after home.

Radetzky's squad emerged from a four-story apartment complex. Wolf's team was spending an inordinate amount of time clearing a single-family house. Sinclair wanted to radio Wolf, to find out what was going on. But Radetzky forbade nonessential chatter in his platoon. Something fluttered in Sinclair's peripheral vision. Without moving his sights he scanned across a courtyard with the naked eye. A white flag poked through the back door of a neighboring compound. Then a head appeared. Sinclair swung his rifle around. A man emerged and walked tentatively onto a patio. Sinclair sighted him and dialed the distance into his scope. He was accompanied by three other men, all dressed in dishdashas. The leader waved the flag back and forth. The rest followed in single file, heads down with hands raised over their heads.

"Alert," Sinclair said into his headset. "Insurgents signaling surrender. Just south of Wolf's location."

"How many?" barked Radetzky.

"Four."

White flags were a notoriously dangerous weapon, especially in Iraq. Not unlike suicide bombers, sectarian militias were trained to use the act of surrendering as a decoy. Why save your ass when getting it blown off was a ticket to heaven? Radetzky's first priority was to defend his men against potential attacks waiting in the wings. His squad was at risk, midway between two compounds with nothing but a garden shed for cover. He scanned the immediate vicinity, searching for more viable defensive positions. Their only real option was the building they had just vacated. Within seconds, several members of his squad regained access to windows overlooking the patio. Their gun barrels kept emerging and withdrawing, trying to get a bead on the clowns with the white flag. Sinclair could see that their angle was hopeless.

"Don't worry," Sinclair said. "I've got them."

"Where's the terp?" Radetzky asked.

The question surprised Sinclair. As far as he was concerned, interpreters were a waste of time. Body language was far more reliable than Arabic, which tended to conceal more than it revealed. Sinclair had learned to trust his instincts. Something about the leader's demeanor didn't ring true, like he was spoiling for a fight rather than trying to avoid one. Whether Radetzky agreed with this assessment of the immediate threat was irrelevant. His job as an officer was to keep one eye on his men, the other on the objectives of the overall mission. Centcom insisted on gathering intelligence even in accelerated combat mode. Interrogating prisoners of war could yield the kind of information they needed to pinpoint enemy cells. The trick was distinguishing between ringleaders and lackeys who had nothing to hide.

The interpreter was usually readily available. Very few platoons had the grit and discipline necessary to produce prisoners. It was much safer and expeditious to produce corpses. Their latest interpreter, Sajad, had been embedded in the company for almost three months, an unprecedented length of time in Anbar Province. Terps usually only hired themselves out as a last resort. The war had crippled local economies, and their families risked starving to death if they didn't join forces with Americans. Sooner or later, death threats altered the calculus of survival. Their families risked being murdered in their beds if they continued to collaborate with infidel invaders. Choose your poison.

Sajad publicly attributed his resilience to bravery and commitment to the coalition cause. Much more to the point, he had nothing left to lose. His mother and seven siblings had fled to Syria when Saddam executed his father, forcing the family to cover the cost of the bullet lodged in his skull. Sajad was the eldest son. Someone had to stay behind to even the score.

Sajad's facility with languages was astonishing. He mimicked idiomatic phrases and even gestures with far more nuance than previous interpreters. He had a wonderful sense of humor in five out of his six languages, a sure sign that he negotiated cultural differences with a sharp tongue. The English language's penchant for euphemisms never ceased to amuse him. He made liberal use of air quotations to underscore his mastery of evasive terminology.

"As you know, I am particularly eager to interrogate Ba'athist officials," Sajad liked to say, flourishing his forefingers around the word *interrogate*.

Joking aside, Sajad heartily approved of enhanced interrogation techniques, especially in Sunni regions. They dovetailed with his vendetta. His best friend worked as a security guard at Abu Ghraib. This was his dream job. Getting paid to waterboard Saddam's cronies was almost too good to be true, the best possible way to avenge his father. Harassing dethroned Ba'athists was a close second.

Sajad was due to arrive in five minutes, accompanied by an armed escort. In the meantime, Wolf's squad was ordered to intercept the white flag, which was still cautiously traversing the patio. Trapp's pidgin Arabic would have to suffice until the terp showed up. He kept his distance, flanked by Wolf, Logan, and McCarthy. Their four guns were trained on the four insurgents, who stopped dead in their tracks, frantically pointing at what looked like a kitchen towel fastened to a broomstick.

"Marines, we're not armed," the leader said in broken English.

"Stay where you are," Trapp said in Arabic.

"It is safe," the leader said. "Let us talk."

"Raise your hands over your heads," Trapp shouted.

Everyone except the leader obeyed.

"Idiot," Trapp said under his breath. "Drop the flag and put your hands up," he shouted in English. His dictionary of stock military phrases had failed to mention anything about dropping flags.

"Cuff them," Wolf ordered. "He can't shoot while he's showing off his dirty laundry."

Wolf and Logan covered while Trapp and McCarthy advanced. Sinclair was poised and ready to open fire at the slightest provocation. Everyone was annoyed. Taking prisoners was more trouble than it was worth. For one thing, you had to waste personnel guarding them until shuttle teams took them off your hands. The platoon had processed their fair share of detainees en route to Baghdad. During the first few days of Operation Iraqi Freedom, the desert looked more like a refugee camp than a battlefield. They had been warned to be on the alert for ambushes masquerading as surrenders. But everyone except Saddam's Republican Guard was intimidated. Disappointingly so. Nothing was more depressing than the sight of soldiers too demoralized to put up a fight.

A sudden barrage of AK-47 fire propelled Trapp's team into the dirt. Sinclair saw tracers streaming from the windows of an adjacent compound. Wolf must have spotted them even before they opened fire. He and Logan let loose. Their M249s overpowered the 47s, forcing the enemy gunners to duck back out of range. Trapp's men scrambled for cover. It was impossible to tell whether the four surrendering men were in cahoots with the gunners. Then one of them lifted the hem of his robe. Sinclair waited until he saw the barrel of a rifle and then squeezed his trigger. Bingo.

The impact sent the rifle skittering across the courtyard. The leader was still waving the flag. Shooting unarmed men was against the rules of engagement. Logan plugged him without bothering to confirm malicious intent. Delay and you get blown away. McCarthy picked off the remaining two men while Sinclair was still scoping the folds of their robes.

Sinclair turned his attention to the gunners pinned behind the window frames. He measured the distance and dialed it in. The angle was possible but not probable. RPGs had a far better chance of breaking up the ambush. Wolf and Logan sprayed the windows with automatic fire while the others tried to thread the needle with grenades. Most of them bounced off the walls and detonated in the courtyard below. When one of them laced through a window, the squad cheered. Resistance tapered off and then stopped altogether.

A less seasoned squad might have assumed the enemy had been dispatched. There was no telling how many were left or where they might be hiding. The fact that nobody was seen evacuating the building didn't mean they were still trapped inside. Underground tunnels were especially common in Ba'athist neighborhoods, where party officials had been prepared for the worst since the Iran-Iraq War. Wolf suspected they were actually playing possum. The only sure way to find out was to rush the compound. It was the kind of last resort the insurgency counted on to nullify superior American firepower.

Radetzky was an aggressive but prudent commander. He virtually never forced his platoon to resort to the last resort. Several of his men appeared on the roof of a neighboring compound, carrying a metal ladder. He had already determined that the distance between the two concrete structures was too wide to jump. The ladder was just long enough to bridge the gap. One by one his squad crossed, arms slicing the air as they struggled to keep their balance.

Radetzky hurled his automatic to a spotter to avoid falling. He ended up crawling, rung by rung, to the other side. The squad tried not to laugh until Radetzky himself cracked up.

"So much for officer training."

Radetzky knew the break in decorum would loosen them up. Like ballplayers, they performed best when oblivious to pressure. Jokes at his own expense were particularly hilarious, a surefire way to bond with his men. It was a delicate balance, being one of them without compromising his authority. He was well aware that his success as a commanding officer relied on loyalty, not just obedience, their willingness to go above and beyond the call of duty. By the time the spotter returned his automatic, Radetzky was back to business as usual. Focused and in control. They followed him down the stairwell, weapons at the ready.

Within a minute it was all over. A handful of enemy fighters hadn't decamped after all. They were lying low, waiting for Wolf's team to make the fatal mistake of storming the front door. All but one never knew what hit them, a ballistic testament to Radetzky's superior strategy. Swift, silent, and deadly. The last of the six was hiding under a bed. He was technically unarmed, having left his rifle at his post in the window. Details, details. Telltale evidence indicated that the compound had been crawling with insurgents. The rest had, in fact, escaped through tunnels.

The two squads converged in the courtyard. Radetzky barked orders, already mentally engaged in the next attack. Wolf spit on the blood-spattered white flag, an emblem of the unworthiness of their enemy. He usually left fist pumping and foul-mouthed bravado to men like McCarthy. But when things got too psychologically complicated to express in four-letter words, Wolf stepped in to provide the catharsis everyone needed to keep PTSD at bay. Radetzky, who trusted him implicitly, turned a blind eye. Commissioned officers were required to make dispassionate decisions, calculating risk and reward with unflinching resolve.

Noncommissioned officers picked up the emotional slack. Radetzky was the head, Wolf the heart of the platoon. They were a perfect team.

Wolf spit on dirty towels fastened to the ends of broomsticks, to restore the sanctity of real white flags protecting real civilians. He flipped the bird behind the backs of imperious commanders so his men wouldn't have to. When rules of engagement endangered the platoon, he broke them. Once he had even shot a dead insurgent in the groin. Desecrating enemy corpses was strictly forbidden. But the bastard had simulated death until Lance Corporal Rodriguez was close enough to get his balls blown off. Trapp tried to stanch the wound, but Roddy died before the evac unit showed up. It was the company's first casualty in Iraq, a specter of their most visceral anxieties. Killing Roddy's murderer wasn't good enough. They needed a graphic illustration that nobody mutilated marines with impunity, and they got one. Everyone felt better after Wolf wasted the prick's crotch. When he used up one magazine, he loaded another.

Word of the white flag slaughter must have spread through the neighborhood. Foreign fighters, especially Pakistanis, were equipped with state-of-the-art communication devices. This level of technological sophistication debunked claims that Fallujans were mounting a homegrown insurgency. They were caught in the crosshairs of jihad, a global army that transformed guerilla warfare into terrorism. This kind of conflict had no boundaries, national or otherwise, no front lines or even combat zones. The fact that the platoon cleared two blocks without firing a shot didn't mean the enemy had been vanquished. They were biding their time, playing the long game. Having less powerful weaponry didn't guarantee that they were at a disadvantage. They just had to be more unpredictable, equal parts moving target and booby trap, masters of the unfair fight.

Radetzky was eager to give chase. The sooner the platoon tracked them down, the less time the enemy would have to regroup in the wake of the white flag debacle. A West Point-trained officer, he never let his training get in the way of adapting to conditions on the ground. At the same time, he never tried to beat jihadis at their own game. The only way to prevail against terrorists was to force them to engage in more conventional forms of warfare, the kind American troops were trained to win. Neighboring platoons were also encountering less resistance, corroborating his theory that a trap was imminent. He radioed Colonel Denning, requesting permission to launch another coordinated offensive. Almost unbelievably, they were ordered to retreat.

"We're on a roll," Radetzky told Colonel Denning.

"You're about to roll right into a mortar field. Salinger's platoon just got hammered."

"They're two quadrants to the south."

"It's that big, Radetzky. We're mounting another air strike."

They were ordered to fall back three full blocks. Battalion headquarters had tremendous faith in the accuracy of laser-guided missiles. Radetzky prided himself on never having lost a man to friendly fire. He pushed the platoon back even farther. Covering the same terrain in reverse was demoralizing. They had risked their lives every step of the way. Insurgents they had killed that morning were bloated and stinking in the heat. Entire limbs had been gnawed off by dogs wandering in packs, already feral with starvation. One of Sinclair's kills was unrecognizable as a human being. Location was its only identifying characteristic. Another was almost completely intact. Its lips alone had been chewed off, probably by cats rather than dogs, judging from the relatively dainty teeth marks.

"It's like mosquitoes," McCarthy said. "They either like you or they don't."

The sun was low in the sky by the time they reached the designated compound. Everyone not assigned to security duty congregated on the roof to watch the bombardment.

The sky was ablaze, another stunning sunset in a landscape spectacularly oblivious to violence perpetrated for the sake of tradition or progress, in the name of this or that god. Empires came and went and the desert endured, unfazed. There was something comforting or menacing about its resilience. It would survive the apocalypse.

They could hear but not yet see Bradleys rolling into the neighborhood. Two Cobras crisscrossed the sky and disappeared. As usual, calm descended before the firestorm. The ubiquitous din of gun battles was conspicuously absent in the wake of the retreat. All the mosques in the vicinity had already been silenced. Sinclair noticed for the first time that his ears were ringing. Back home in Montana he loved the quiet. In Fallujah he had learned to dread it.

You could never see them coming, even in the desert. Fighting Falcons materialized instantaneously, precluding defensive measures, let alone evacuations, standard air raid precautions in days of yore. Blinding light eclipsed the sunset. The platoon was far enough away to avoid friendly fire but close enough to feel the secondary impact of laser-guided warheads. They waited for someone to crack the inevitable jokes.

"Just like the Fourth of July."

"Minus the keg."

The display of force was impressive, though nothing compared to Baghdad. There had been no-holds-barred there. Specter gunships. Close-support aircraft. Artillery. Everything except helicopters, which were too clumsy to keep pace with the bombardment. Spontaneous combustion. Smoke detectors from Libya to Pakistan must have been going off like crazy, alerting terrorists that there was a new gun in town. Good old Uncle Sam with a holster filled with everything but nukes. At first they had oohed and aahed in jest, like kids at a fireworks display. Pretty soon they weren't kidding around anymore. Even McCarthy stopped making Armageddon jokes.

Every time they thought the assault had peaked, explosions redoubled. Smoke billowed half a mile high above Baghdad. Tracers arced across the sky, lacing over bright bursts of color. Red. Orange. Blue mushroom clouds. The lighting effects beggared description. It would have been counterproductive to view the spectacle as anything other than a pyrotechnic marvel. They were soldiers, not Red Cross nurses. If hospitals and schools and playgrounds were destroyed, nobody could see them. If actual people were incinerated in beds, at desks, and on merry-go-rounds, nobody could hear them. Assuming the bursts of color had faces, it was best not to make eye contact.

In Fallujah, air strikes hit way too close to home. There was no getting around the fact that familiar landmarks, if not people, were being wasted, neighborhoods the platoon had patrolled on a daily basis. Proximity to targets was physical as well as emotional, just blocks away. Within earshot. The screams of insurgents burning to death haunted Sinclair. His phobia of suicide bombers was matched only by his fear of death by fire. He could never have been a firefighter like McCarthy, whose thick skin was like psychological body armor. Of course you wanted your enemy to suffer, given the alternative. It was either him or you. But there was a limit to how much Sinclair could take, at least in theory. In practice, he had already exceeded the limit. Sometimes he envied drone pilots. They complained about being too far removed from the action, claiming boredom was even worse than sensory overkill. If it wasn't one thing, it was another.

Heavy artillery had positioned itself in the middle of three intersections a block apart. Bradleys and Abrams tanks. They mortared the target sector, sending gusts of shrapnel-laden debris in every direction. Sinclair refrained from hoping they wouldn't haul out the white phosphorous. He was too good a soldier to second-guess strategic decisions. Special Forces would either flatten the block, the quick and dirty way, or mount a Shake and Bake offensive, flushing insurgents into ambushes. The virtue of the more complicated tactic was that buildings would be left intact, yielding potentially vital intelligence. The more information you had, the better your chances of eluding the enemy. It was messy, but it saved American lives.

Special Forces went with Plan B. Artillery squads started alternating between white phosphorous and high explosives. Rivers of fire shot through the air, through doors and windows, glazing everything in flames. Sinclair relinquished his front-row seat on the roof. Guys jostled to take his place. Downstairs, windows were packed with more men craning to see. After particularly violent concussions, his buddies clapped and slapped each other's helmets. Teacups rattled in the cupboards. Sinclair staked out a seat at the kitchen table, as far away as possible from all the excitement, and started cleaning his weapon.

"Nothing I like better than fried chicken," Trapp said. "The crispier the better."

"I love the smell of Willy Pete in the morning," Wolf said.

Wolf was a wealth of movie and television trivia. He and Trapp liked to stage contests to see if they could stump each other with obscure references. Everyone knew this one. It was a cliché in Iraq where WP was used almost as frequently as napalm in Vietnam. Infamous *Life* magazine photographs had forced the US military to stockpile its napalm arsenal. White phosphorous had the advantage of having not yet had its fifteen minutes of fame.

"*Apocalypse Now*," Trapp said. "Vintage Brando."

Johnson was on his satellite phone with CNN, reporting live. Sinclair wondered if the audience back home could hear the screams of people burning alive in the background. They probably dubbed them out. Television audiences had a tendency to misinterpret the significance of cries for mercy. Radio listeners were even less reliable.

Without the benefit of visual evidence, their imaginations ran wild. High-pitched screams didn't necessarily mean the target was a woman or a child. In distress even terrorists sometimes sounded pathetic and defenseless.

Johnson had resolved or repressed his ethical qualms. The only way to counterbalance Al Jazeera's bogus reportage was to provide real, albeit carefully curated, photographs. A CNN news anchor confirmed that a major insurgency stronghold was under siege, not a neighborhood of middle-class homes. True as far as it went. Had the screams been allowed to air, she would have described enemy combatants flushed from their lairs, not victims burning alive. Six of one, half a dozen of the other. CNN wasn't really withholding information, just strategically manipulating its interpretive lens, more an act of patriotism than anything else. Waging war with images was bound to result in ethical collateral damage.

Sinclair heard a chorus of cheers as bombs hit the cell's central weapons cache, leveling an entire city block. Still not as mind-blowing as Baghdad, but definitely worth the price of admission. Radetzky started breaking up the party, ordering everybody to bed down. The decision to use white phosphorous pretty much grounded the platoon for the night. WP had an insatiable appetite and would burn for hours. The heat was so intense, undetonated ammunition might decide to cook off, firing in random directions. The area would need to cool down before they could resume the ground offensive. Radetzky told them it would probably be awhile before they had the luxury of another night's rest. He didn't tell them why.

Outrage over staggering casualty figures was flooding the airwaves. If the American media didn't regain control of the narrative, Washington would be forced to initiate a cease-fire. It wouldn't be the first time public pressure hobbled the war effort. Bleeding-heart liberals were forever hijacking the moral high ground, as though liberating a country weren't high-fucking-minded enough for them. They blamed coalition forces for civilian casualties, oblivious to the fact that the insurgency was using them as human shields. Thankfully diplomatic wheels in Baghdad turned even more slowly than in Washington. Radetzky assumed Centcom would step up the pace of the attack to take full advantage of the time political posturing took to run its course. If they were lucky, Operation Vigilant Resolve would achieve its strategic objective before the Coalition Provisional Authority wimped out.

With the exception of hunkering down after the mosque attack, the platoon had been fighting almost nonstop for three days. In spite of having to literally slap himself awake during sniper duty, Sinclair had avoided popping Provigil pills in anticipation of precisely this scenario. A few hours' respite in the relative quiet of post-bombardment darkness was as close as you could get to ideal snoozing conditions. He stretched out next to Logan, who was sleeping the sleep of the righteous, as usual. Nobody conked out faster than Logan, goddamn him. The familiarity of his breathing patterns helped Sinclair pretend they were back at the base, nowhere near the bombed-out quarter. He was careful not to think of the white phosphorous, still burning in bright pools just beyond the safe zone. The screaming had subsided but a sensory hangover lingered, an echo that was as bad or worse than the real thing. More persistent. He tried to visualize serenity, fly-fishing knee-deep in a mountain stream, to calm himself. What a joke. He finally gave up, pretending he was too tired to sleep.

A group of insomniacs was clustered around McCarthy in the master bedroom. He was holding court, as usual, regaling them with bedtime stories. Combat fatigue kept them all awake. Something somewhere was still at the ready, fending off unremembered trauma lodged too deep to access alone. There was safety in numbers both on and off the battlefield. Wolf and Trapp had taken off their boots and joined McCarthy in bed. The box springs protested whenever anyone moved, three huge men sprawled with legs and arms spilling over the edge of the sagging mattress. Guys on the floor were using their rucks as pillows.

After every random act of violence, they rehashed what happened, or what might have happened, trying to salvage some semblance of meaning, if not the illusion of being in control. Lost buddies were commemorated. Scapegoats were mocked. In the unfolding narrative of the Thundering Third's adventures in Iraq, enemy combatants were little more than stick-figure foils accentuating the epic stature of heroic Americans. When there weren't battles to remember, they recounted exploits on patrols and raids. Narrowly escaping yet another roadside bomb explosion. The haunting look in the eyes of suicide bombers. Surprising feyadeen in shower stalls, on the crapper, one time even in bed. They let the woman escape, wrapped in sheets, before they gunned him down.

"The ultimate coitus interruptus," McCarthy always said.

He had told the story numerous times, invariably concluding with the same punch line. The entire squad had been involved in the sting operation, but they always let him do the honors. No one else could do justice to the delicious blend of the burlesque and the macabre that made the story an all-time favorite. They laughed as hard on the tenth telling as they had on the first. McCarthy was like a one-man warm-up band. Once he loosened everybody up, he made sure they all got a chance to unload, telling their versions of the day's exploits. Stories were like ballast. They kept the platoon afloat.

"What's up?" Sinclair said, taking a seat next to Percy on the floor.

"Funny you should ask," McCarthy said, making a lewd gesture. He pointed at Vasquez, who made a show of covering his crotch with his helmet. "Goldilocks here is in the middle of one about three bras."

"Next thing I knew, this freaking bra was three inches away," Vasquez said. "Eye-level. Black lace, no less."

"So much for the chastity of Muslim women," Percy said. As usual, the peanut gallery was in full force.

"Get real," Wolf said. "Underneath it all, they're as hot to trot as your high school girlfriend."

"Those burqas are a come-on, if you ask me," McCarthy said.

"Reverse psychology. Playing hard to get."

"Works for me."

"What's a bra doing hanging off a bedroom door, you may ask," Vasquez continued. He had unwittingly picked up the habit of asking rhetorical questions, a surefire way of heightening dramatic tension. McCarthy's inspiration was apparent even when he wasn't actually telling the tale.

"The suspense is killing me."

"It would have killed me too, if I hadn't had my wits about me."

"You got lucky. All your wits were really thinking about were tits, just like the rest of us."

"Unlike you, I can walk and chew gum at the same time."

"Or think of tits and ass at the same time, as the case may be."

"Anyway we get the picture. The old femme fatale trick."

Even if they hadn't actually encountered booby-trapped lingerie, they'd all heard tell of it. This particular lace number had been attached to a bundle of wires leading to plastic explosives concealed in a laundry hamper. Had Vasquez grabbed the doorknob, or even disturbed the dangling bra as he sidled into the room, they would have had to scrape him off the walls. No one knew whether femme fatale explosive devices were planted by the women themselves or by their husbands. One way or the other, the more intimate the bait the more deadly the trap. Searching tampon boxes for grenades was standard procedure. Iraq had given a whole new meaning to underwire bras.

"What you're telling us is that you got a boner and almost blew up the joint," McCarthy said.

"Lucky for you I snipped the trip wire before giving into temptation," Vasquez said.

"That's my definition of a hero. A guy who puts booby traps before boobs."

"I thought you said there were three bras," Sinclair said.

"You missed the first half of the story," Vasquez said. "There were two more in the bureau drawer. Needless to say, I had to search through all the underwear to make sure the lady of the house wasn't concealing any weapons."

"You can't be too careful."

"How long did it take?"

"Less than a minute," Vasquez said. "Like I said, black lace is my favorite."

"Nowhere near as sexy as red."

"Tell your own goddamn story."

"Does it have to be about jerking off?"

"Only if you finally manage to get it up."

Wolf had actually witnessed Vasquez's run-in with the bra, which may or may not have been life-threatening. But he refrained from editorializing. No one ever experienced the same incursion the same way. One member of the squad would remember being attacked by a dozen insurgents. Another would swear it was double the number. The only real consensus was that the enemy was armed to the teeth. This didn't mean reality was relative. There was one unwavering measure of what really happened in combat. You either survived or you didn't. Survivors were entitled to tell the version of the truth that enabled them to cope with the emotional burden of the memory. The closer the call, the more outrageous the story, as long as none of their buddies were killed. Death was the only thing that wasn't funny. Everything else was a laugh riot. There was no other way to neutralize the fear.

Sergeant Troy had planted the storytelling seed in boot camp. Ruthlessly denigrating recruits was the best way to transform milquetoasts into US Marines, but only if you gave them the psychological tools to survive the abuse. At night when the platoon collapsed in their bunks to lick the day's wounds, they were encouraged to vent their frustrations. Confess their fears. Brag or bitch or moan or whatever it took to put the day's indignities behind them. If they demurred, he suspended their Internet privileges. At first it was excruciating for introverts, possibly even worse for macho types who never confided in anyone, not even their girlfriends. Everyone got over their initial reluctance when they realized the toughest guys actually told the best stories. By the time they deployed to Iraq, they were spinning yarns like spiders.

Without military experience, recruits were forced to talk about themselves. What it was like growing up in Harlem or the Bible Belt. Unexpurgated versions of how they spent their summer vacations. Sergeant Troy wanted them to get down and dirty. In the heat of battle, they needed to know why they were risking their lives for one another. What made Logan worth evacuating under fire. Why Wolf was worth obeying instantaneously, always and without question. Some platoons relied on blind loyalty and obedience. Sergeant Troy believed that if you really understood how McCarthy ticked, you'd be more likely to take a bullet for him. Marines who fought as one won wars.

Everyone had to divulge a deep dark secret. Sergeant Troy had heard a lot of hair-raising stories over the years. He kept raising the bar. They were required to describe the proudest and most humiliating moments in their lives. Recruits tried to bluff their way out of telling the truth, hiding behind sensational stories. A case in point was Vasquez's infamous date with a transsexual, complete with graphic details about the inevitable unveiling in the backseat of his car.

"That dude was lucky he got out of there alive," Vasquez had said.

"Only in San Francisco."

"Soon to be showing at a theater near you," Wolf said. "New York is crawling with them."

Everyone was scandalized except Sergeant Troy. He could tell from Vasquez's body language that the incident had revolted and pissed him off, but not really wounded him.

"When I say shameful, I mean mortifying. So bad you'd rather die than tell anyone. Ever. Try again."

It took Vasquez four times to get it right. When he finally told the story about the scene he made at his father's funeral, high on crack, he was off the hook.

At first Trapp was the most adept storyteller. He had honed his skills hanging out with Vietnam vets, who were still telling the same stories that had kept them alive in the jungle. But even he had to be prodded. It took him a month to admit he'd gambled his wife's inheritance away. She still didn't know the extent of the damage done to their nest egg. A week later, McCarthy told almost the same story except that he had squandered his own inheritance, the money his uncle left him for college. They stayed up half the night discussing which was worse, betraying yourself or someone else.

Sergeant Troy insisted the devil was in the details. Nobody minded elaborating on their proudest memories. But when something really upset them, it seemed cruel to drag things out. Eventually they learned to trust the process. Guys started telling stories without really knowing why. Then they'd stumble over a secret kept even from themselves, embedded in a seemingly incidental fact or feeling. Things got pretty hairy at times. You wouldn't have wanted cops listening in. The platoon was unconditionally nonjudgmental, the ultimate safe space. Nothing brought men closer together than confession and absolution.

Sinclair was horrified by the idea of divulging anything personal. It was the most grueling part of boot camp. He was as emotional as the next guy, maybe more so. But he distrusted verbal expression. Words cheapened everything, especially feelings. He finally managed to tell a story about hating his father, something he had previously only admitted to Pete. Sergeant Troy was unimpressed.

"Big deal."

"Yessir."

"Are you proud or ashamed of the fact you can't stand your old man?"

"Ashamed, of course."

"Aren't you forgetting something?"

"Sir!"

"You're stalling, Sinclair. If I had a nickel for every jarhead who hates his father, we'd buy Iraq instead of having to invade it."

Sinclair was on the brink of making shit up, the way his Catholic friends back home invented sins to spice up their confessions. In desperation, he started talking about Pete. For all his bluster, Sergeant Troy was remarkably sensitive to emotional nuances, especially the body language of men who were disinclined to express themselves more directly. Whenever Sinclair mentioned his buddy Pete, he avoided eye contact. Now they were getting somewhere. He tried to cut to the chase, the part of the story where the police showed up. Sergeant Troy made him start at the beginning. The whole point was to try to remember every last detail, no matter how trivial. Everyone was lounging in the bunkhouse, ready for the long haul. Logan's sister had sent another care package from Des Moines. They ate chocolate chip cookies while they listened.

Grandpa had promised them a trip when they graduated from high school. Sinclair half expected Pete to pretend he couldn't get off work. By then he was hiring himself out as a buckaroo on neighboring ranches. The plan to attend college together had already been scrapped. But the fact that they hadn't been getting along for a few months didn't change the fact that they'd been dreaming of this trip for years, unbeknownst to everyone else. Grandpa kept throwing out ideas, one more extravagant than the next. They pretended to weigh their options, knowing full well where they were headed.

"I've always wanted to fly-fish No Tell-Um Creek," Pete said.

"Think big," Grandpa said.

"We could go to Denver for rodeo season," Sinclair said.

"Maybe even Fort Worth."

"Why not both?" Grandpa said.

"Too expensive."

"I'm paying. Remember?"

Planes, trains, and even Greyhound buses would have taken them farther faster, all the way to Mexico or the Pacific Ocean, which neither of them had ever seen. But they had their hearts set on riding as far west as possible on their horses, Buck and Paco. It was a quixotic journey, next to impossible with all the housing developments and shopping malls and freeways, let alone barbed wire every which way but up. But there were still plenty of ranches scattered between Frost Valley and Yellowstone Park, and contiguous deserts and mountains across the border in Idaho. Their history teacher claimed a century had passed since the closing of the frontier. They refused to believe it. If necessary they'd cross property lines by cover of night. Young and romantic in a quintessentially western way, they'd be damned if anyone was going to tell them what they could or could not do.

Even Grandpa thought they were spending the month camping in the Beartooth Mountains, just north of the ranch. No one would be the wiser if they just kept riding into the sunset. Sinclair's mother kept insisting they pack a mule with food and a tent. They resisted the idea, pretending they wanted to rough it. The real reason was mobility. The lighter they traveled, the faster they could make their getaway. Besides, mules were ornery and notoriously afraid of traffic.

"There might be a highway or two involved," Pete said, out of earshot.

"And a fair amount of fence jumping," Sinclair said.

"All we really need is bedrolls, fishing rods, and rifles."

"Maybe a few carrots."

"For rabbit stew?"

"For Buck and Paco."

Everyone made a fuss when they left. Even Pete's father made an appearance, hiding the previous night's dissipation behind reflective sunglasses. He stood apart, next to the old elm, watching them check their gear one last time. Sinclair's mother made them pose for pictures with the horses. Buck and Paco had never looked so handsome. Grandpa had given them both brand new Circle Y saddles equipped with rifle holsters. The leather was impossibly soft and supple, like butter, Candace said. She kept rubbing Buck's saddle, tracing its elegant lines from the swell to the cantle.

"Too bad Circle Y doesn't make purses," Candace said. She leaned over and breathed in the leather's fragrance. "Or perfume."

For some reason, Pete got a big kick out of her shenanigans. They kept yukking it up and all Sinclair wanted to do was get the hell out of there. He couldn't wait to leave everything behind them. His cloying sister. All the bad blood with their fathers. He blamed everyone but Pete for their adolescent growing pains. When they were boys, everything had been so simple. Perfect, really. Sometimes he wished they'd never grown up.

By the time they finally tore themselves away from their families, half the day was wasted. They rode past one after another of their boyhood haunts. The hollow log, great-great-grandfather Tyler's mythic hiding place a century ago. The ruins of a cliff fort reduced to rubble by a thousand winter frosts. Their favorite skinny-dipping pond. Every day after mending fences or branding colts, they used to swim off the day's grime. The ranch was on a high plain surrounded by the foothills of the Beartooths on the north and the Absarokas on the south. It never got all that hot at five thousand feet. But ranching was dusty work and the stinging cold water felt like a brisk slap, heightening the glorious sensation of being strong healthy boys preparing to be men.

Two creeks converged in the pond. When they were very young, they used to race frogs through the lily pads. They ran separate qualifying heats to select the sleekest swimmers. It was terribly exciting until they turned eight. Then they couldn't believe they'd ever been so juvenile. They started catching snakes instead. Pinching behind their heads to avoid bites, they stretched them out to see whose was longer. The winner got dibs on the best hunting blind that afternoon. They worked the ranch from six to three and swam and hunted the rest of the day. A more sublime boyhood was unimaginable.

When they reached the aspen grove, they stopped to water the horses. Sinclair hauled out the lunch his mother had packed, roast beef sandwiches, potato salad, and peanut butter cookies with crisscross fork patterns, their last civilized meal. They ate in the shadow of the moose rack mounted in the center of the grove. Pete pointed to two smooth round stones commemorating one of myriad rituals they had once performed with the incomparable moral gravity of little boys.

"Remember that?"

"I remember everything."

"So do I."

That first night out, camped by Willow Creek, they stayed up late, watching stars reel across the sky. The night was warm. Pete made a fire anyway. It had been a long time since they just lay quietly together, listening to a fire under the stars. Some sort of truce had been called, quelling a fight Sinclair wasn't aware they were having. He only knew it was an immense relief.

Dawn roused them, a minute or two earlier every morning as the solstice approached. Still half asleep, they rolled up their sleeping bags and climbed on their horses. Buck and Paco made good time, not that their riders were going anywhere in particular. They were devoted to the idea that the middle of nowhere still existed. It may have been an illusion all along, their most cherished boyhood fantasy. If they hadn't begun to doubt its existence, they would never have tested its limits by heading out to the territories. Pete knew this. Sinclair didn't. The wilderness seemed eternal, an endless tract of virgin land. He implicitly believed that by riding west they might turn back the clock, returning to a bygone age of innocence just out of sight over the next ridge.

Sinclair had packed plenty of maps, none of which they needed in Montana. It would take four full days to reach unfamiliar territory. They skirted the Walker Valley Ranch, so vast a day's hard ride left them still encamped on its western boundary. No use asking for trouble. The Walkers were relative newcomers to the area, Los Angeles speculators who bought up land when scores of dairymen went bust during the Great Depression. Real locals considered them outsiders. Homemade signs bearing timeworn slogans spontaneously appeared when the Walkers' huge herds drove down the price of beef.

Don't Californicate Montana
Buy Local. Boycott Big Beef

The Sinclairs disliked the Walkers for the simple reason that cattle and horse ranchers never saw eye to eye on anything. Breeding horses was a privilege. They were man's better half, his very soul embodied in flesh. Cows, on the other hand, were almost as bad as sheep. Cattle ranches were nothing but glorified fast-food joints.

"Hamburgers with a heartbeat," Pete used to say.

Grasslands gave way to foothills too steep for grazing. Still navigating by memory, they threaded through valleys and passes. They fished streams with gene pools unsullied by farmed stock, feasting on the sweet pink meat of rainbow trout. It was too early for berries. They followed bear tracks to patches of earth where sows taught their cubs to dig deep into the loam. There were plenty of roots, even a few tubers. They boiled them until they were soft enough to mash into what looked like potatoes and tasted like the earth smells after summer rains.

On the third day they ascended the final ridge of the Beartooths overlooking Wyoming. Sinclair hauled out the maps for the first time, consulting them not to locate but to avoid roads and towns. They would weave their way through blank spaces, taking refuge in uncharted territory. Yellowstone was a mixed blessing, chock-full of people but conveniently free of fences. Pete had a coil of barbed wire strapped to his saddle, covered with burlap to protect Buck's flanks. When they couldn't steer clear of fences, they'd cut and mend them. Yellowstone postponed this inevitability by some thirty miles.

The park was crawling with tourists, herds of them snapping pictures of buffalo wandering in and out of traffic jams. Even hiking trails were overcrowded. Sticking to designated bridle paths to blend in, Pete and Sinclair camouflaged their rifles, wrapping them in their bedrolls. They had entered the area illegally, on horseback rather than by car, and were subject to stiff fines, if not outright arrest. Fortunately forest rangers were too busy policing Old Faithful and Mammoth Hot Springs to notice outlaws traversing the park without a permit. Far too many people crowded far too close to geysers and paint pots, which never looked as good in person as they did on the website. The appeal of vomitous shades of mud-belching sulfide gas eluded city slickers, but they couldn't tear themselves away. Unconsciously they were still mesmerized by the promise of transcendence.

"Grandpa used to warn me about bubbling pots. He said they'd melt the skin right off your bones."

"Sounds familiar. Remember Uncle Joe?"

"It's hard to forget a guy with a stump."

"He claimed he lost his arm fishing his hat out of Dragon's Mouth Spring."

"Did you believe him?"

"He had proof, didn't he?"

Having so recently eaten the earth's subterranean fruits, they understood the subliminal attraction of fumaroles and steam vents. Deep down, even people with New Jersey license plates wanted to dive back into the earth that had birthed them. Little girls wandered down wooden walkways, gawking at transparent pools that erupted with violent regularity. Their fathers whisked them back to cars laden with souvenirs. Plastic facsimiles of geysers. Teddy bears. Postcards of everything they hadn't really seen.

Pete and Sinclair camped in the woods, without a fire to avoid detection. Bears kept waking them up, looking for midnight snacks in their packs. Nothing was really wild in Yellowstone, not even wolves and panthers, which were tagged and monitored by Fish and Game wardens. What had once been a natural wonder of the world was now a glorified zoo. When they finally slipped past the western gate of the park, elk started fleeing instead of staring back, chewing their cuds like cows. They hauled out their rifles again. Lush forests gradually gave way to arid plains. They kept riding.

Vivid geometrical expanses of green, mostly potato farms, sprouted out of the prevailing brown landscape. Harvest was still months away and virtually no one was in the fields. They rode along irrigation ditches, picking wild asparagus and hunting jackrabbits. Ranches started outnumbering farms. When sagebrush appeared they knew fences wouldn't be far behind. There still wasn't a soul in sight, but Buck and Paco started getting jumpy. The threat was imperceptible, purely intuitive. Horses knew what they were feeling before their riders did.

The mentality of farmers and ranchers was miles apart. Guys who tilled the land for a living were as territorial as the next gun-toting redneck. But they rarely took potshots at trespassers. Ranchers, on the other hand, gave the Second Amendment a bad name. You couldn't even hunt pheasant in cattle country without taking your life in your hands. Never mind the fact that the days of rustling herds were long gone. What had once been prudence had evolved into paranoia. Warning signs were posted on every other fence post. Enter at your own risk.

Pete and Sinclair started traveling by night. In high desert country, even waning moons provided ample illumination. Coyotes serenaded their progress. When dawn spread across the eastern horizon, they bedded down in ravines hidden from the heat of the sun and the watchful eyes of ranchers. Occasionally they heard pickups patrolling the range. One of them stopped to inspect a fence that had recently been snipped and mended by yours truly.

"Must be admiring your handiwork," Sinclair said.

"Maybe he'll offer me a job," Pete said.

The driver took one look at telltale tracks and another at the only ravine within spitting distance, and put two and two together. The pickup started barreling in their direction. It was an old Ford, jacked up enough to clear pretty much everything but boulders. They had already rolled up their bedding and secured their gear for what promised to be a rough ride. Buck and Paco took off quite literally at breakneck speed. One misplaced gopher hole and they'd be done for.

"*Vámonos!*"

The chase was on. The pickup kept gaining on them, throwing tumbleweeds every which way as it gathered speed. They reined their horses in the direction of a low rise, perceptible only to trained eyes. Galloping over the crest, they spotted a river in the distance. With any luck, they'd reach its banks before the truck overtook them. It would be a tight race. Spurring hard once, they relinquished control of the reins and let the horses fly.

Pete let out a whoop even before the rifle cracked. They could tell from the angle of the sound that it was just a warning shot. Buck and Paco couldn't tell the difference between blanks and bullets, let alone their trajectories. They bolted forward even faster, and both boys whooped. Another shot rang out, and then a pair in rapid succession. One of them ricocheted not ten feet from their thundering hooves. The rancher was still gaining ground, but the sheer joy of velocity made them feel invulnerable. The land was bigger than he was, bigger than the fences that tried to tame it. The trappings of civilization were just that. Traps.

When they reached the river, Buck and Paco tried to veer away, their huge heads mutinous with terror. Pete and Sinclair reined them tight and straight into the current. The riverbed dropped off precipitously, forcing them to swim. They calmed down immediately. Even in raging waters, horses entered a kind of meditative trance the minute their hooves lost contact with the ground. Survival instincts trumped fear.

The rancher raced to the brink of the river and jumped out of the truck, brandishing his rifle. Once he was stationary and could actually aim, he didn't even raise his weapon. A law-abiding citizen, he only felt justified killing trespassers. He didn't own the river, water rights notwithstanding. The Snake and all of its tributaries were the exclusive property of the state of Idaho. Curses, foiled again. He was shouting something, but the rushing water swallowed up the sound.

Sinclair and Pete strained to hear from the opposite bank of the river.

"Probably a dinner invitation."

"Too bad we didn't pack dress clothes."

The rancher drew his finger across his throat.

"Sweet of him. Offering to slaughter a heifer, just for us."

"A big juicy steak sounds pretty damn good, right about now."

"Maybe next time."

They waved and wheeled the horses around to continue the journey west. With each passing mile, the landscape grew drier and the population grew denser. The threat of fences was superseded by even more dangerous obstacles. Highways. There was no avoiding them. Their only hope was to sneak across after dark when traffic died down. On a good night they managed to cross three or four highways before nine-to-fivers hit the road at dawn. They dismounted to spare the horses' hooves on the hard pavement.

The going was slow. Thanks to unrestricted urban sprawl, a hallmark of freedom in these here parts, once isolated desert roads were jammed with honking cars and SUVs. Living the dream, dontcha know. Commuter highways gave them plenty of practice before reaching the interstate running north to south through the Snake River Plain. They had to cross I-15 to get to the Sawtooths, a wilderness area that would protect them for a good thirty miles. It was the only road with a median, the only one crawling with state troopers. When they finally spotted the freeway in the distance, they stopped for a while to gauge the traffic flow and stake out the fuzz.

Troopers were notorious night owls. They killed their lights and sat in the dark, licking their chops. In Montana you could speed your way from one end of the state to the other during the day. The minute the sun set, you'd be pulled over and frisked. Idaho appeared to be even more of a police state. Instead of one trooper per twenty miles of highway, there were three with overlapping jurisdictions. Two were preoccupied with making money for the state, catching speeding drivers like suckers in a pond. Routine stuff. The third was far more judicious, ranging up and down the freeway looking for trouble. He obviously had bigger fish to fry.

"He's a wily one," Pete said.

"Takes one to know one," Sinclair said.

They monitored the rover's movements for several hours without discovering a pattern. All they knew for sure was that he passed by with alarming frequency. There must have been turnarounds every mile or two. Either that or he just plowed across the median at will. The only viable strategy was to cross the minute he whizzed by and hope for the best. They crept as close as possible to the freeway, leading Buck and Paco by the reins. Truckers were out in full force, especially at night. The horses danced every time a big rig rolled by. Then they saw him coming.

They knew it was the trooper because he drove way over the speed limit. Cars scooted into the right lane to make way for him. When his taillights rounded the bend, they made their move. It was clear sailing on their side of the median. They traversed the northerly lanes, calming the horses with rough endearments. Almost immediately, Pete managed to sprint the rest of the way with Buck in tow. But Paco balked twice before Sinclair could coax him across the southerly lanes. They jumped into the saddle the minute both of them cleared the pavement, spurring their horses for the second time during the journey west.

A wise-guy trucker blew his big-throated horn, spooking the horses again. Hunkering down in the saddle, they managed to channel panic into meteoric forward motion. Not a moment too soon. They heard the siren first, and then the desert sky started flashing. Tires skidded to a stop. A surprisingly high voice barely caught up with them.

"Halt, or I'll shoot!"

Almost instantaneously a gun fired, this time a pistol. All of Idaho was trigger-happy. They assumed it was just another warning shot. They were committing a crime, no doubt about that. But state troopers were less likely to shoot them than crazy old ranchers. Badge or no badge, killing a young man for daring to ride a horse would make nasty headlines in the local newspaper. He'd post an all-points bulletin, for what it was worth, a warrant for the arrest of two latter-day cowboys on the run. Lucky for them, the days of mounted posses were long gone. By dawn they'd disappear into the mountains without a trace.

"We're home free!"

For several strides they rode side by side, keeping pace. Sinclair looked over at Pete, hoping to catch his eye. He was startled by the exuberant expression on his face. Pete was obviously in his element. Sinclair, on the other hand, was conflicted. There was a part of him that revered authority as much as Pete disdained it. Following orders was an expression of his true character. At the time, all that registered was that a man in uniform was demanding he stop and surrender himself to custody. It was the right thing to do.

Pete's elation stemmed from unencumbered liberty, not license. He knew damned good and well that what they were doing was technically illegal. Big whoop. Surely even Sinclair knew that breaking stupid laws was far less ignoble than obeying them. One way or the other, he must have underestimated the significance of the defining moment of the trip. Pete would have gone to hell in a handbag as long as Sinclair went with him. Loyalty was the one true measure of friendship. If abstract principles got in the way, they were bogus and inconsequential.

Sinclair let his horse's pace slacken, taking refuge in passivity. That way he could blame Pete for what happened. A true friend would never expect him to compromise his principles. Pete swiveled in the saddle the second Sinclair left his side. They were in this thing together. The two boys beckoned one another with mirror gestures, one urging his buddy to hurry up, the other to give up. Sinclair would never forget the look on Pete's face. He must have worn the same expression when he slid the shotgun into his mouth three months later. Defeat. Defeated trust, defeated dreams, generations of defeat too relentless to be housed in a single wounded heart.

That was pretty much the end of the story in more ways than one. Grandpa's horse trailer pulled into the police parking lot late the following afternoon. He paid the fine and promised not to breathe a word to Sinclair's father. Pete barely talked the whole long drive back home. The fact that they were driving east instead of riding west said everything. Talk about a fall from grace. If Sinclair had acknowledged what he had done wrong, Pete might have forgiven him. It wasn't until he told the story to his buddies at boot camp that he finally found the courage to take responsibility for his betrayal.

"That's some story," Sergeant Troy said. He walked across the bunkhouse, weaving between beds to get to Sinclair's.

"Yessir."

"Where's Pete now?"

"He's dead."

"How long ago?"

"A few months after our trip."

Sergeant Troy put his hand on Sinclair's shoulder. He had never touched any of them before. Most of the men were embarrassed by the gesture. Novices in blood brotherhood, they mistook the power of empathy for mere sentimentality.

"Let it go, son."

"Yessir."

"You'll make a fine marine. But you've got to learn to let things go."

He started to leave, and everyone jumped to their feet to salute.

"Sir!"

"At ease."

Nobody knew what to say after Sergeant Troy left, so they said nothing. The entire bunkhouse simulated sleep, leaving Sinclair in the lurch. He was obviously on the verge of a meltdown, something they equated with weakness rather than catharsis. They had yet to witness Trapp weeping uncontrollably, cradling a dead comrade in his arms. Logan hadn't kicked the dead bomber's face to a bloody pulp, calling on God to damn his soul to hell. Nobody had shit his pants in abject terror, not yet anyway. They were still invested in the superficial trappings of machismo that seasoned marines, unencumbered by inhibitions, learned to consider trivial.

Two years later in Fallujah, they had enough combat experience to process raw emotion without the help of Sergeant Troy. They exorcised guilt and anger by scapegoating the enemy and exonerating themselves, one tale at a time. Nobody could top Vasquez's epic encounter with the three bras, but that didn't stop them from trying. Wolf told a story about the mosque attack. Percy entertained them with impersonations of Colonel Denning and Captain Phipps. Everybody was drowsy by the time they'd talked themselves out. Sinclair was already asleep. What was terrifying once upon a time had been successfully tamed into bedtime stories. The simple fact that they had lived to tell the tale made them all feel safe.

Radetzky roused them at 0500 hours. Tactical Operations had finally given the all clear in the wake of the bombardment. He split the platoon in two. Half were assigned to reconnaissance while the others resumed search-and-destroy missions. Sinclair finally broke down and popped a Provigil. Three hours of shut-eye had left him more groggy than none at all, and he was afraid of losing his edge when he needed it most. Traversing bombed-out terrain was especially dangerous in cities. Damaged ordnance was often buried in the rubble. What looked like a wasteland could actually be a minefield.

Puddles of white phosphorous still burned in streets and courtyards. They tucked their pants into their boots. If clothing caught fire, almost nothing could smother the flames. Certainly not water. Phosphorous ate traditional fire retardants for breakfast, let alone pant legs. They moved carefully but quickly, Wolf in the lead. Many of the compounds were still standing, burned-out shells of their former selves. The smell of burning flesh lingered in the air.

"Remember Othman?" Trapp asked.

"Yeah, why?"

"That was his house."

Sinclair couldn't believe he hadn't recognized the place. He had earned a reputation for instinctively knowing where they were and where they needed to go. Back home, hunting had honed his sense of direction, something his buddies had learned to trust. During Operation Iraqi Freedom, he helped the platoon navigate hundreds of miles across the desert without once losing his bearings. Even Radetzky routinely consulted with him to confirm coordinates, especially when trying to avoid friendly fire. Either Trapp was wrong or something had seriously disoriented him. Fallujah was really kicking his ass.

Sinclair looked north and south along the main street fronting the house. There was still too much smoke from phosphorous fires to see more than a block or two in either direction. In the City of Mosques, they verified locations by identifying nearby minarets. If the ones in the vicinity were still standing, they were obscured in the haze. Sinclair followed Trapp, straddling a fallen column to get to the porch. There was Othman's bicycle, covered with a thick layer of ash. It had fallen over but was otherwise unscathed. Bombs were funny that way. Here and there, random things were spared.

"Let's just hope he got out in time."

Neither of them said what they both knew. Othman never would have evacuated without his beloved bike.

"Good old Othman."

It was hard to believe that just over a week ago Sinclair and Trapp had been walking the beat with Othman, a young Sunni fresh out of security training. In an effort to dispel the appearance of martial law, marines partnered with equal numbers of local police. Coalition forces patrolled the same neighborhoods every day to foster community support. They even got to know people by name, as long as tribal leaders hadn't poisoned the well. In theory, peacekeeping initiatives were more likely to win the war than combat missions. Too bad the Eighty-Second Airborne Division hadn't spearheaded more joint initiatives. The Marine Corps would have inherited a less antagonistic city.

Providing security was just the beginning. Using interpreters, platoons asked Fallujans themselves what they needed most, as if it weren't obvious. They needed everything. Clean water, electricity, a pot to piss in. Engineers were only contracted to handle bigger jobs, things like digging new sewage systems and refurbishing power plants. Leathernecks tackled everything else, working with locals to rebuild infrastructure.

At first they attracted a great deal of attention ranging from guarded curiosity to men flashing the soles of their sandals, the ultimate insult. A native Fallujan, Othman was particularly sensitive to the prevailing mood. He often lagged behind, almost hiding, especially when they met with local sheikhs. Needless to say, McCarthy was skeptical of the advisability of meet-and-greet detail. Sinclair remained optimistic. The Coalition Provisional Authority was designed to help Iraqis get back on their feet, phase two of their liberation from the jaws of tyranny. He refused to believe that winning the hearts and minds of the people was just a slogan.

Sinclair had obviously misread all the signs. Women weren't the only ones hiding behind veils in Iraq. The blank expressions on elders' faces conveyed carefully controlled hostility, not tacit acceptance. Scores of unemployed men congregated on street corners. The fact that they didn't betray resentment didn't mean it wasn't seething beneath the surface. Patrolling with Othman must have lulled Sinclair into thinking they were comrades-in-arms, especially after he asked the squad to walk past his house. They thought he wanted to show off his new Iraqi police uniform to his wife. He waved to an upstairs window. Sinclair and Trapp looked up just in time to see her duck out of sight.

"Can we meet her?"

"That is impossible. She is not veiled."

Sinclair decided not to push the point. Why she couldn't just throw on a burqa was beyond him, but he was trying to be sensitive to cultural differences. Joint patrols notwithstanding, Othman had no intention of letting his wife be seen fraternizing with American soldiers. Dethroned Ba'athists frowned on young men joining the police force, no matter how much they needed the salary. Othman had orchestrated the entire excursion as a show of force to warn underground authorities to back off. It wasn't the first time Americans played the part of unwitting pawns in sectarian turf wars. They would have to learn to discern the various factions in order to defeat them.

Othman's circumspection seemed impregnable. He willingly talked about the weather and very little else. Occasionally they caught him wagging his head and mumbling, as though he couldn't contain himself. Their interpreter, Sajad, maintained a divided loyalty that thwarted efforts to decipher these asides. Terps routinely translated even the most outrageous civilian diatribes but soft-pedaled communication with the police. Finally after a particularly volatile interrogation in an elder's household, Sajad relented. Presumably Othman had given him the go-ahead.

"With all due respect," Sajad said.

"Don't mince words," Trapp said.

"I'm not. Othman himself said 'with all due respect,' not me."

"Figures. Get on with it."

"It is vaguely possible that coalition forces shouldn't humiliate Iraqi husbands in front of their wives."

"What are you talking about?"

"In particular, frisking Iraqis in prone positions, faces smashed in the dirt, is probably not a good idea."

"It is if you don't want them to pull a knife on you," Sinclair said.

"Yes and no."

"Who said that? You or Othman?"

"Me. He said their dignity might require retaliation."

The evasiveness of the translation seemed true to the original. But there was no way to verify its accuracy. When Trapp tried to clarify what Othman meant by retaliation, he clammed up completely. Several days later, for reasons Sinclair didn't understand until it was too late, Othman finally spoke his mind. This time around, retaliation took the form of an Iraqi boy throwing a stone at the patrol, an increasingly common occurrence the week before the Blackwater lynchings.

"There is no God but Allah!" he shouted in retreat. "America is the enemy of God."

The stone pinged off McCarthy's helmet. Kids shrieked with delight in the distance, pretending it was just another juvenile prank. McCarthy swore under his breath but kept his cool. They were in meet-and-greet mode.

"This never happened in Baghdad," Sinclair remarked, not for the first time.

"Baghdad is a Shiite town," Othman said. "We're Sunnis."

"And we're Americans. We don't take sectarian sides."

"You're in Iraq now." Sajad measured Othman's words very carefully. "Everything has a sectarian side."

"Fair enough. But why do those boys assume we side with Shiites?"

"Last I heard Saddam Hussein was a Sunni."

"Saddam Hussein was a tyrant."

"And a Sunni."

"You can't tell me you wish he was still in power."

Othman stopped walking and turned to look Sinclair square in the eyes, something he hadn't done since they were first introduced. When he lowered his voice, Sajad followed suit.

"Respected Sunni clerics warn that you will hand the city over to Shiites," Othman said. "What are the people of Fallujah to believe, given the example of Baghdad?"

"We're patrolling with you. Sunnis, not Shiites."

"They are afraid politics will corrupt our faith in the true Muslim religion."

Sinclair wanted to ask whether politics and religion could ever be disentangled, but he was afraid of offending Othman. Patriotism was very complicated in Iraq. He tried to think of a less confrontational way to pose the question.

"Can't they believe in freedom and Allah at the same time?"

"That remains to be seen."

"Why? Everyone wants to be free."

Othman remained silent, and Sinclair assumed the conversation was over.

"Your definition of freedom is foreign to the people of Fallujah," Othman finally said. "It looks a lot like occupation to them."

"What will it take to change their minds?"

"Do you really want to know?"

"Of course."

"You must leave Fallujah."

"All hell will break loose."

"It will break loose anyway."

The following morning Othman failed to show up for patrol duty. His candor had been a parting gesture. Ba'athist bigwigs hadn't been intimidated in the least by their show of force. Othman had already received death threats warning him to stop collaborating with infidel invaders. This time they targeted his family. Another Sunni officer, a bachelor, was assigned to take his place. In the heart of Anbar Province, loyalties hadn't toppled along with the regime. Tacitly accepting the inevitable presence of American soldiers was one thing. Collaborating with them was another. Sinclair could only hope that Othman's wife had evacuated without him.

White phosphorous had incinerated a swath four blocks wide and seven blocks long. It took Wolf's squad two hours to pick their way through the charred rubble. Radetzky's half of the platoon got hung up disabling a vehicle-borne IED. TOC couldn't spare any combat engineers, and the threat was too grave to leave parked on the street. Yet another Iraqi Intervention Force unit had gone AWOL, and there was still no one watching their backs. By the time the platoon reached the next phase line, the rest of the company had already been briefed for the last leg of the offensive.

At 1700 hours, Operation Vigilant Resolve went into overdrive. The Thundering Third had never been asked to sustain such a furious pace, not even speeding across the desert to Baghdad. It felt like an omnipotent boot was pressing the accelerator to the floor, completely oblivious to twists and turns in the road ahead. Lucky for them, they encountered very few obstacles. Contiguous platoons raced to keep up with each other, clearing house after house with the relative ease of the first few days of the campaign. Lack of resistance seemed ominous given the fact that they had penetrated so far into East Manhattan.

"The calm before the storm," Trapp said. They figured he ought to know, having weathered many a hurricane season on the Gulf Coast.

Combat time set in. One minute it was midnight, the next noon. The only difference between night and day was the presence or absence of night-vision goggles. The men were on autopilot, fighting all the more effectively when they were too tired to think. Up to a point. The armed forces had yet to invent a drug that could replace sleep altogether. On day five of the offensive, Radetzky initiated catnaps on a rotating basis. Squads worked ten-hour shifts and then crashed for an hour or two in makeshift bunkers. Acting as chief medic in the absence of Doc Olsen, who was god knows where, Trapp was concerned that Provigil was taking a toll on the men's nervous systems.

"We can't go on like this forever," Trapp finally said.

"You won't have to," Radetzky said. "Centcom is bringing in another battalion. They think we can close the deal in another couple of days."

"What's the rush?"

"Plunge before they pull the plug," Radetzky said, and left it at that. An aerial photograph of the city monopolized his attention. Lines of thumbtacks were at the ready, poised to attack.

"That's not our man Radetzky talking," McCarthy said, out of earshot. "Sounds more like a slogan than an op plan."

"He's quoting somebody," Sinclair agreed.

"Somebody high and mighty and clueless."

They disliked fighting in the dark without a clear sense of how their mission fit into the overall war effort. Whenever possible, Radetzky kept them in the loop. Very few commanders briefed their platoons with such attention to strategic detail. But he was too good an officer to jeopardize his men's morale for the sake of transparency. Sometimes too much information was a burden. He almost wished he weren't privy to the politics of the invasion, a conflict concocted in Washington and hotly contested in capitals around the world. There were definitely too many cooks in the kitchen, a recipe for disaster.

Sunnis in the Iraqi General Council were threatening to resign because US Marines were trouncing their cronies in Fallujah. Doves in London were squawking about civilian casualties. Paris issued a statement denouncing excessive use of force in Anbar Province. As usual, hawks in Washington were impatient with the political posturing of their allies, even though their own approval ratings were slipping precipitously. Press coverage had swung to the left, and Operation Vigilant Resolve was being portrayed as a slaughter of the innocents rather than righteous retribution for the Brooklyn Bridge atrocities. If the political climate didn't improve, Centcom might be forced to issue a ceasefire, even though conditions on the ground promised to bring the city to its knees within a matter of days.

Colonel Denning had originally questioned the advisability of the offensive. Now that his troops were in the thick of it, he wanted to finish what they had been compelled to start. Whatever goodwill had been spawned by meet-and-greet detail had been snuffed by recent incursions. A cease-fire might look good on paper, but it would strand soldiers in the middle of a hostile city. They were fighting on two fronts, one in Fallujah, the other at the Pentagon, where military strategists were trying to wrench the reins back from the White House. Marines were caught in the crosshairs of almost unprecedented levels of government dysfunction, all the more reason to strike while the iron was hot. Pulling punches now would be suicidal.

The good news was that the funnel was working. Kilo Company was intercepting insurgents fleeing from the Jolan offensive. The bad news was that the insurgents in question were family men. Radetzky was furious. His bid for promotion had been jeopardized more than once by civilian casualties. He might have been a captain by now if women and children had stayed out of his way. His commanding officers thought he was too humane for his own good, a misunderstanding of his primary motivation. He was actually protecting his platoon from the threat of so-called innocent bystanders. Turning a blind eye to indiscriminate killing always backfired, leaving deep emotional scars in the wake of the slaughter. He owed it to his men to bring them home in one piece, psychologically as well as physically.

Radetzky reported the civilian exodus to Colonel Denning. With three battalions advancing in concert, there were too many moving pieces to let platoon commanders make vital strategic decisions. From here on out, battalion headquarters would be calling the shots. If even one squad lagged behind, a dangerous breach in the line of scrimmage would leave the whole company vulnerable to attack. Funnels could work both ways, allowing civilians to trickle out and insurgents to rush back in. That's where intelligence came into the picture. Identifying the source of the leak might actually help speed things up in the long run. Unfortunately, given the accelerated pace of the offensive, there was no guarantee there would be a long run. The colonel adjusted his strategy accordingly.

"Find out where the hell they're coming from," Colonel Denning ordered.

"Then what?" Radetzky asked.

"Plug the hole."

"What about the women and children?"

"What about them?"

"What the fuck am I supposed to do with them?"

"They're on their own, Radetzky. We're a military outfit, not a babysitting service."

There were orders Radetzky couldn't issue with a clear conscience. But he could obey them just as his men obeyed them, without question. Working around such ethical dilemmas was part of being a good officer. He left his radio frequency open, allowing the entire platoon to hear the revised rules of engagement, straight from the horse's mouth. Colonel Denning's command was incontrovertible. They would engage with civilians to gather intelligence. Otherwise they would ignore them.

Easier said than done. Squads stacked through front doors and families rushed out the back. Sinclair watched them dashing across courtyards and snaking down alleyways. Snipers had the advantage of seeing them out in the open. They could shoot around them, conditions permitting. He pitied gunners who had to guess who was on the other side of a closed door. They found women locked in bathrooms and children cowering in bedroom armoires. Mistakes were made.

Sorting out civilians and combatants had been much more straightforward the first few days of the operation. The groups were smaller, usually just a mother and her children. Occasionally a father showed up. Determining whether he was armed with malicious intent could get tricky. Using families as camouflage to move from one position to another was standard practice. Desperate men deployed more desperate measures. In Ramadi Sinclair's platoon had confronted an insurgent grasping his daughter in one arm, a pistol in the other. Sinclair managed to pick him off without harming the girl. Overcome with grief, she threw herself on her father's body, oblivious to the fact that he had just used her as a human shield.

"Blood is thicker than water," Wolf had said, prying the girl loose so they could search the corpse.

"Tell her father that," Sinclair said.

He grabbed one of her wrists but she twisted free. Logan rushed over. It took three of them to restrain her.

"The prick."

Untold numbers of families risked their lives to remain in the combat zones they called home. Born and bred with the taste of war on their lips, they had grown accustomed to its bitterness. Perhaps filial devotion and patriotism were more closely aligned in the Middle East than in the West.

At every turn, cultural differences seemed to favor the cause of the insurgency. Winning wars against armies was one thing. Fighting the combined forces of religion, regimes, and kinship ties was far more daunting. Americans had superior military might on their side. The question was whether weapons alone could prevail over so many convictions so deeply rooted in the marrow of the land.

A burqa appeared in the window of a posh three-story residence. A minute later a woman emerged from the back door, five kids and a teenage boy in tow. Her clothing was far more modest than the house. Sinclair assumed she was either a servant or just passing through the neighborhood in search of increasingly elusive asylum. The children's heads were bowed, as though their safety depended on keeping their gazes glued to the ground. Only the teenager's eyes wandered, almost imperceptibly. He was dressed in jeans and a T-shirt, a sign of either Western influence or a disguise masking his militancy. The only certainty was that he walked suspiciously close to the woman. The others were young enough to want to cling to her. But older boys usually kept their distance, asserting a modicum of independence even in kill zones. Sinclair zoomed in, looking for concealed weapons.

"Heads-up," Sinclair reported into his headset.

"Location?"

"Crossing the courtyard."

"That woman and her kids?" Radetzky demanded.

"Could be a decoy."

"Got that, Wolf?"

"Roger that."

Wolf's squad was clearing a house just east of the civilian incursion. Gunners immediately manned the windows facing the courtyard. Sinclair could see that their angles were blocked by an old olive tree. Furtive patches of shade dodged Fallujah's relentless sun. Radetzky's team exited the neighboring compound, covering him as he shouted in Arabic.

"Stop right there. Put your hands up."

The woman raised her arms in the air. Everything about her seemed to signal innocence. The teenage boy stood behind her, just beyond the perimeter of shade. Only Sinclair had a decent view of him. Something glinted. It might have been a belt buckle. No one in the squad noticed. They were wary but not alarmed, relying too heavily on Sinclair's cover.

"That goes for your kids, too," Radetzky said. "Tell them to raise their hands over their heads."

The teenager took a small step to his left, compromising Sinclair's sight line. Fortunately he was considerably taller than the woman, whose voluminous burqa all but obscured his torso. Something glinted again, and the barrel of a rifle poked out. The only possible target was the boy's head. Sinclair squeezed the trigger, and the woman fell to the ground.

"What the fuck—"

A single shot had been fired, a bull's-eye. The head exploded, spraying the woman and her children with gore. Sinclair told himself she couldn't possibly have been wounded. He zeroed in on her face. Her eyes were closed. He scoped her chest, which rose and fell with each labored breath. She must have fainted.

"Hold your ground," Radetzky ordered.

No one made a move to succor the woman. She lay dazed until the cries of the other children roused her. Radetzky's squad kept their automatics at the ready as she tried to comfort them. Women were often used as bait in ambushes, even when they weren't complicit. Sinclair surveyed the entire neighborhood. Another platoon was engaged in a firefight several blocks west. There were no threats in the immediate vicinity.

"All clear," Sinclair confirmed.

The woman rose and led her brood away from the decapitated corpse. The youngest was still crying. The rest had resumed their guarded expressions, eyes trained on their feet. The self-possession of children in Iraq amazed Sinclair. Even toddlers comported themselves with preternatural calm. They made him wonder whether immaturity was more a performance than a state of mind, something kids staged to attract attention. Not that he begrudged them their little indulgences. Childhood wasn't just a luxury. It was a basic human right, another casualty of war.

The woman was picking bits of flesh out of their hair. She wiped their faces with tissues extracted one-by-one from a miniature Kleenex dispenser. There was something surreal about the sight of an American brand name amidst the carnage, a product specifically marketed to carry in purses, just in case. Judging from her impassive expression, she might have been blowing their noses. She was meticulous. Each bloody Kleenex disappeared into a pocket concealed in her robe, a deep-seated habit to avoid littering. If she had been complicit with the dead boy, she was hard-boiled. She would have made a perfect spy.

"Trapp," Radetzky barked.

"Sir."

"Take them back to the cleared compound."

"Yessir."

Radetzky's squad was long overdue for a catnap. In the meantime, Captain Phipps granted permission to interrogate the woman. Radetzky ordered Sinclair to cover the area until Wolf could spare a couple of gunners to pull guard duty. Wolf took his sweet time. They had encountered resistance in an adjacent alleyway. It was almost predictable. The minute civilians showed up, the fighting escalated. Sinclair hated to think that innocent bystanders were being used as decoys. But it was the lesser of two evils. The only other explanation was that there was no such thing as innocent bystanders in Fallujah.

A half hour crawled by before relief showed up. Sinclair kept scoping possible targets, trying to keep busy to stay awake. The last thing he wanted to do before a coveted catnap was take another Provigil. He watched a pack of dogs slink down the alleyway. One of them raised its snout and caught the scent of his last kill. He stopped watching when they started nosing around the headless corpse. Finally he lost the battle and popped a pill. There'd be hell to pay if he couldn't sleep when he joined the squad in the compound below.

When he finally descended from his perch, Sinclair made the mistake of walking past Radetzky's command center. He could have easily avoided it. Radetzky never failed to colonize the kitchen. Other lieutenants preferred the study, if there was one, or the living room. The kitchen must have been the command center of Radetzky's home growing up. Johnson was leaning against the refrigerator, filing a report with Fox News. Radetzky was on the radio with Colonel Denning, confirming grid coordinates. The woman was sitting with her hands folded on a checkered tablecloth.

Sinclair was surprised she was still there. Radetzky disliked civilian interrogations. He usually got them out of the way as quickly as possible so he could get back to the business of waging war. They must have let her wash up first. Her robe was covered with wet circles where she'd scrubbed out the blood. Otherwise there was no evidence of the shooting. A kettle steamed on the stove. A full cup of tea sat, untouched, in front of her on the table.

She pretended not to notice Sinclair or anyone else. She looked at her hands the way her children had looked at their feet, as though she might escape notice if she kept to herself. Sinclair wondered if she knew that he was the one who killed the teenager. Her son. Whoever the hell it was. Her composure certainly didn't rule out the possibility. An untrained eye might have mistaken it for detachment. Sinclair knew better. He had witnessed countless Iraqi civilians, mostly women, with that same distant expression. Burqas hid very little once you learned their body language. They tended to focus rather than mask emotions.

Sinclair grabbed an MRE before going upstairs to crash. He stood, gazing out the window, while he ate. He could feel the woman staring at his back even though he knew she was still watching her hands. Iraqi women had learned to compensate for Sharia law against making eye contact with men. They could stare you down without even looking at you. She reminded him of the mother of the shepherd boy they had gunned down near Mosul. They had the same mute ferocity.

His squad had been ordered to seize an airstrip. They were told in no uncertain terms that the area was crawling with hostile forces. It was high noon, so hot the desert horizon shimmered the way it does in old movies. Even the requisite camels were there, silhouetted against the glare. Then somebody fired the first shot. Camels flew one way, enemy combatants with rifles the other. The squad let loose, mowing down everything in sight. Only they weren't enemy combatants with guns. They were shepherds with staffs, teenagers and their little brothers. And they were all dead except one. His mother was by his side almost before the storm of bullets subsided.

"Shit!"

"Is she armed?"

"Where's the medic?"

They had just shot and almost killed her son, who had provoked them with nothing more than a herding stick. She turned to them, supporting the boy in her arms, without a trace of malice. All that mattered was saving his life, and only the soldiers responsible for his wounds could dress them. She didn't humble herself. Her speechless supplication bristled with the power of mothers protecting their young. Rules of engagement notwithstanding, they suspended combat operations to treat the boy. She never thanked them, never even really saw them. The desert was filled with nameless, faceless threats. They were all the same to her.

It was an unfortunate incident, the most ill-advised attack during their first tour of duty. But they knew better than to second-guess their impulse to defend themselves. If nations agreed to let gladiators decide the outcome of political conflicts, collateral damage could be avoided. Until then soldiers who served honorably were blameless, even heroic. Commanding officers were adamant on this point. Teaching men to kill without remorse was almost as important as teaching them to kill in the first place.

"As long as you follow orders, you'll never be guilty of war crimes."

Whenever shit hit the fan, Sergeant Troy's voice came to the rescue, providing the ethical armor necessary to survive in Iraq. Too bad he never told them how to defend themselves against women. Not that they posed a direct threat. But if there were chinks in Sinclair's armor, he knew damned good and well how they got there. Something about the woman in the kitchen got under his skin even more than the mother on that godforsaken airstrip. It might have been nothing more than proximity, the fact that he could reach out and touch her. House-to-house combat was claustrophobic enough without this shit.

Sinclair finished bolting down his food. He threw the empty containers in the garbage and prepared to leave the kitchen. But something about the woman held him captive. Whether or not she was the dead boy's mother didn't alter the fact that he'd been carrying a German Mauser. The more important question was whether she knew he was armed. Johnson was apparently interested enough to forgo sleep to find out. He had finished filing his report and was sitting with his back against the refrigerator, waiting for the interrogation to begin. Sinclair sat down next to him. Johnson's curiosity, which was purely professional, made Sinclair's seem less inappropriately personal.

"Think she was in on it?" Sinclair asked.

"I doubt it," Johnson said.

"They're all in on it as far as I'm concerned." Sinclair wasn't entirely sure what he meant, but somehow it made him feel better. "Otherwise why would they be here?"

Sajad was taking down the woman's vital statistics. Then Radetzky started conducting the actual interrogation. His knowledge of Arabic was good enough to carry on rudimentary conversations. He must have thought the woman could provide more nuanced intelligence, things he couldn't comprehend without the help of an interpreter. The fact that her children were in custody provided the kind of leverage Radetzky needed to tighten the screws, if necessary. He spoke in a disarmingly gentle voice, one Sinclair had never heard him use before. Her responses, though barely audible, were remarkably forthright.

"I'm Lieutenant Radetzky. Please tell me your name."

"Afaf Pachachi."

"Why are you still here?"

"They told me you wanted to talk to me."

"I mean here in Fallujah."

"I live here."

"Where exactly?"

"In the Jolan District. Our house was bombed."

"What are you doing in this neighborhood?" Radetzky leaned forward. He was obviously modifying his body language in response to the tone and tenor of Afaf Pachachi's answers. Successful interrogations were a kind of dance, a movement back and forth between civility and coercion, especially when women were involved. If Sinclair had been in charge, there would have been far less give and take. He would have relied more on intimidation than trust, overcompensating in self-defense. Radetzky's sangfroid was instructive.

"We've been taking shelter wherever we can."

"You were told to evacuate."

"I couldn't."

"Why?"

"My husband—"

"What about your husband?"

"He's my husband. I belong by his side."

Sinclair could have predicted her answers, almost word for word. He had heard dozens of women profess what amounted to marriage vows, loyalty till death do us part. The real issue was whether this was an exclusively matrimonial allegiance. Too often, sacred laws shielding women from public life didn't prevent their participation in guerrilla warfare. Sinclair scooted across the floor to get a clear view of Afaf Pachachi's face. He studied her eyes for signs of subterfuge. No doubt Radetzky was doing the same.

"Where is your husband?"

"I don't know."

"When did you last see him?"

"Yesterday."

"Where?"

"In the mosque."

"Is he armed?"

"I don't know."

She raised her right hand to adjust her veil, which didn't need adjusting. Sinclair assumed the gesture was a decoy, a way of camouflaging emotion or deceit. She probably hadn't lied yet. It was much more likely that she was afraid her husband had been killed. Every able-bodied man in the entire country carried a weapon. If he wasn't armed, he was dead.

"You have five children?"

"Four. The younger ones are mine."

"What about the older boy? The one who was shot."

"My neighbor's child." Her eyes betrayed her feelings again. This time she didn't brush them away with her hand.

"He was armed."

"Yes."

"You were harboring an armed insurgent."

"A neighbor. He must have picked up the gun in that house."

"Which house?"

"The one with all the bodies. You must have seen them."

"Of course I saw them," Radetzky barked. The real interrogation began. "I have sent your children back to base camp. They're safe, but I want you to cooperate with me."

"Of course." A note of urgency crept into her voice.

"What was your husband doing in that mosque?"

"What they were all doing."

"Stop playing games. What were they doing?"

"They were doing what you're doing. Fighting. Making war."

"And you? What are you doing here?"

"I am trying to save my family. I can't stop my husband fighting any more than I can stop you," she said, finally breaking down. She bent over in her chair to conceal an unwonted display of emotion, which she considered indecent.

"Escorting armed teenagers is a far cry from saving your family."

"He promised he wouldn't get involved."

"This is war, goddamnit!" Radetzky shouted, slamming his fist down on the table. "You can't just politely refuse to get involved."

"I am trapped," she said, fighting to recover her composure. "You think I would deliberately risk the lives of my children?"

"You should have left the city. To protect your children."

"Perhaps you are right," she said. Her acquiescence was barbed with defiance. "But I would rather die than abandon my husband."

"That's enough," Radetzky said to Sajad. "Get her out of here."

Radetzky was obviously disgusted with her blind loyalty. For him the interrogation was a complete waste of time. For Sinclair it was a catastrophe. This woman's willingness to die for love hit way too close to home. He traveled halfway around the world, trying to elude this kind of passionate intensity, but it hunted him down. Everyone thought he enlisted because of the terrorist attacks on 9/11. They underestimated the impact of Pete's suicide, the ultimate betrayal. Even now a part of him refused to believe what his fucking sister tried to tell him all along. The crime wasn't so much that Pete fell in love with Candace but that he was unfaithful to a masculine ideal that transcended love itself.

The fact that he killed himself in the aspen grove seemed inexplicable. They had performed secret rituals there, cleansing their weapons in the blood of totem animals. If Pete felt compelled to throw it all away for a girl, let alone Candace Sinclair, he should have done it somewhere else. Anywhere but there, on hallowed ground. Fighting side-by-side with his buddies in Iraq, Sinclair recovered a modicum of what he had lost. But it was a tenuous recovery, as susceptible to encroachment as the forest itself, which had once seemed inviolable. Surely men were entitled to be men, unmolested, if only in combat zones. Maintaining military ethics was tough enough without being ambushed by women at every turn, their children's toys and dolls strewn like booby traps across nursery floors.

Sajad was debriefing Afaf Pachachi, verifying details before submitting a report to TOC. She kept her eyes trained on the kitchen table, waiting to be escorted back to her children. Sinclair was still sitting cross-legged on the floor next to Johnson, who was fiddling with his equipment. Johnson finally found what he was looking for, a special lens he almost never had occasion to use, given the blistering pace of urban operations. The woman hid her face in her hands, a vain attempt to elude the eye of the camera. The more she concealed herself, the better the photograph. *Vanity Fair* in particular loved this kind of thing, candid shots of beleaguered modesty. He kept shooting until Sajad escorted her out of the room. Once the show was finally over, Sinclair and Johnson made their way upstairs for some shut-eye.

"Think she was telling the truth?" Johnson asked.

"About what?"

"The kid. Not being involved."

"Does it really matter?"

"You're damn right it matters. Fighting a handful of insurgents is one thing. Taking on an entire country is another."

"The whole country's involved one way or the other. Even if they just get in the way."

Sinclair collapsed onto a blanket between Logan and Trapp. The space was so cramped he could feel their bodies against his. The contact comforted him. The squad had crashed in a young girl's bedroom, par for the course at this point. Sinclair felt like he was being stalked. Pictures of horses painted on black velvet lined the walls, just like the ones in Candace's room back home. Once she got all frilly in high school, she took down every last one of them. The romance between girls and horses must have been universal, if not the velvet paint sets, which were probably imported from the States. On second thought, Sinclair had no way of gauging whether the room reflected the Western influence excoriated by local imams. Scarves and veils were draped everywhere, looking more ornamental than decorous. A silver comb and brush graced the top of a hand-carved teak dresser, which might have passed for a vanity, had there been a mirror. Brightly colored vases adorned the windowsills, their glass translucent in the sunlight.

Sinclair must have dozed off because the attack caught his reflexes by surprise. He jumped to his feet before Logan could pull him back down. Streams of bullets were shredding the walls and ceiling. Shards of broken glass were everywhere. They grabbed their automatics and crawled over to the closest window, where McCarthy was already cranking out rounds. Trapp and Vasquez were stationed at the only other window, facing east.

"I've got this one covered," McCarthy hollered. "See if Wolf knows what the hell is going on."

Wolf was in the hallway, trying to reach Radetzky on his headset. Given the danger of keeping all their eggs in one basket, they were almost never in the same place at the same time. Radetzky's men had moved out the minute he finished the interrogation. They were in striking distance, strategically positioned two blocks away. Almost inevitably, the minute a squad took a catnap, all hell broke loose. Murphy's Law.

"We need some backup!" Wolf shouted into his headset. The deafening blare of cross fire made it all but impossible to hear.

"What are you up against?" Radetzky barked back.

"We're outnumbered. The roof's raining grenades."

"Hang tough. We've got your back."

Radetzky's squad was perfectly positioned to defend the area from any direction but east. They had cleared the tallest residence on the block, a real beauty with whimsical architectural accents. The parapet was crenellated like a medieval castle, tailor-made cover for gunners. A lot of good it did them. Insurgents were attacking Wolf from their only blind spot, and there was no way to relocate without being bombarded by RPGs. Radetzky radioed Captain Phipps, requesting artillery support. Their only hope was to call in tanks or Strykers, preferably both, provided they weren't already backing up other platoons. They were in luck. A fleet of tanks was nearby, ready to rumble.

"Where the hell are you?" Wolf said.

"We're hamstrung," Radetzky said. "TOC is sending a couple of big boys your way."

"Better make it snappy."

"Ten minutes max."

Sinclair could hear McCarthy and Percy cursing into their headsets. Individual words were difficult to decipher in the din, but the gist was clear. Ten minutes was a hell of a long time, under the circumstances. Logan, Trapp, and the rest of the gunners had staked out virtually every window in the compound. They took turns ducking in and out of firing range, timing their rounds to maintain a steady output. Their efforts were purely cosmetic. Without anyone on the roof to pick off insurgent grenade launchers, the chances of actually connecting with targets were practically nil. Their posture was strictly defensive. The best they could do was pin down the enemy, forcing them to maintain their present positions. Any alteration in the delicate balance between offense and defense, and they'd be done for.

Grenades kept bouncing off window frames before exploding on contact in the courtyard below. RPGs were notoriously difficult to lace through windows, thank god. They hadn't been so fortunate on their first tour in Baghdad. During an almost identical standoff, a grenade had ricocheted into their stronghold. Instinctively, Private First Class Smythe dove across the room, landing right on the money. They had to wipe bits of his body off their night-vision goggles. Everyone learned something that day. A medium-sized man could completely absorb the impact of a loose frag. Smythy was an ace baseball player, known for executing crazy-ass steals without getting picked off. His example had set the bar very high. Since then they were all prepared to cover the bag in the event a grenade took a bad bounce. Teamwork.

An explosion shook the entire building. At first Sinclair thought they were taking mortar fire. Then he realized it was collateral impact from their own SMAW. Percy was pummeling the enemy from a window on the ground floor. Sinclair ran downstairs to see if he needed cover. The entire world seemed to shake in its boots when the SMAW made contact. But when the dust cleared, the adjacent compound was still standing. His objective, born out of desperation, was to hammer away until it collapsed, burying the enemy in rubble. But his angle was compromised by cross fire. Sinclair stationed himself next to Percy, spraying a stream of tracers back and forth across the courtyard. Enemy gunners retreated enough to allow Percy to score a direct hit, ripping a sizable hole in the foundation. But the compound was built like a goddamned fortress. Better luck next time.

Sinclair strained to hear the distinctive grind of tank tractions amidst the melee of explosions. He had a sixth sense that could detect aberrant sounds beneath the white noise of battle. Something must have been holding up the tanks, which usually rolled in within minutes of an SOS. At the very least, TOC should have updated them on their progress. When Radetzky lost his temper and started cussing out Captain Phipps, everyone thought it was McCarthy launching into one of his tirades. They had never heard Radetzky swear like that before, let alone question an order. No one, with the possible exception of Sinclair, was more respectful of the chain of command.

"You've got to be fucking kidding me."

"I wish I were," Captain Phipps said. "They've declared a cease-fire."

"Who's they?" Radetzky demanded.

"I wish I knew."

Someone somewhere had ordered a unilateral cease-fire. Planes were grounded. Tanks were parked on Highway 10. Reinforcements were twiddling their thumbs in the desert less than a mile away. Operation Vigilant Resolve was frozen in its tracks. Sinclair was too patriotic to point the finger at Washington. He blamed Baghdad instead, not without reason. Sunnis in parliament didn't appreciate the fact that American marines had invaded Fallujah. They threatened to boycott the provisional government if the offensive continued. Sinclair's buddies, who had less faith in the wisdom of their commander in chief, assumed the White House had ordered the cease-fire. An election was on the horizon, and the president was behind in the polls.

Sinclair refused to believe that public opinion could sway military policy. This was new-millennial warfare, not a sixties sit-in. He was right about one thing. The days when Washington heeded the voice of the American people were long gone. But he underestimated the power of the press. Civilian casualties were nothing new, but the liberal media were blowing everything out of proportion. The cease-fire was a publicity stunt, not a military strategy. What may have looked good on paper wreaked havoc for boots on the ground.

"Throw us a bone," Radetzky shouted. "One lousy tank—"

"One lousy tank could get us both court-martialed," Captain Phipps said.

"Not if the order preceded the cease-fire."

"My hands are tied, Radetzky. But yours aren't."

Even unilateral cease-fires made provision for self-preservation. The platoon was authorized to defend their positions, if need be, as long as they refrained from mounting attacks. Forget the fact that even the greenest boot-camp rookie knew that offense was the best defense. Fortunately no one was around to monitor whether they were actually initiating or just repelling attacks. Their lives were on the line, and they were in no mood for fine distinctions.

"Guess that means it's up to me," Percy shouted, shouldering his SMAW. Sinclair took stock of their trajectory options. The most effective angle left them marginally exposed, a calculated gamble. On sniper duty, the odds were more predictable. Sheer velocity exposed gunners to multiple, more immediate threats. Sinclair's M249 fired five times as many rounds as enemy AK-47s, which meant he could probably double the risk without losing his advantage. He inched farther into the window, channeling Sergeant Troy's training again. His voice still echoed in Sinclair's ear, a brusque guardian angel forever shouting strategic directives.

"It's a game of inches, men!"

Invariably one of the recruits made a joke about size queens.

"That's right, jack-off," Sergeant Troy said. "Stick it out too far, and you'll get the whole damn thing blown off."

Sinclair edged sideways until his tracers cut off an enemy gunner's angle. The stream of bullets threatening Percy's position stopped long enough for the SMAW to waste an entire room in the enemy compound. The fact that Sinclair felt perfectly in control of the situation meant he was being too cautious. He edged out a little more and caught sight of someone crouching next to a garden wall. The man in question wasn't toting a rucksack or wearing a kaffiyeh in the manner of insurgents. He appeared unarmed, though his jacket might have concealed a weapon. A volley of rounds burst from a window, just missing Sinclair's head. Shifting his position a full inch had put him at risk of being picked off. He tried half an inch. The window remained silent. He had discovered his optimum angle.

Sinclair's main objective was backing up Percy's SMAW. Without artillery support, it was their only ticket out of there. Necessity had honed his peripheral vision, allowing him to keep an eye on the garden, just in case. He saw a lizard flicking its tongue on the wall, but the man had disappeared. Burning bushes were scattered helter-skelter, their charred roots exposed. A limp tomato plant dangled from electrical wires overhead. Still no sign of the lone man. Clouds of dust and debris continued to settle in the wake of Percy's bull's-eye. The sun broke through, dappling the ruined garden. Suddenly the man jumped back into view. He looked heavenward. Blinding light illuminated his face.

He started sprinting in slow motion toward Sinclair's stronghold. He wasn't bulky after all, and he hadn't been wearing a jacket. Dozens of pounds of explosives were strapped to his torso. Everything else moved at the speed of lethal lightning—bullets ricocheting everywhere, pocking walls and coughing concrete clouds into smoky rooms shuddering from the impact of grenades pelting the roof like hail in a maelstrom—but this one man emerged unhurried and unscathed as though walking on water, the vortex swirling beneath him, above him, around him, but nowhere near him. Sinclair was pinned against the window frame, unable to retaliate without exposing himself to cross fire. The rest of the squad must have been equally besieged, allowing the man to keep floating toward him, so close now the beatific expression on his face came into focus, a serene ecstasy radiating from eyes that seemed to actually see Sinclair shrinking in terror more from the act of suicide than the fact of the bombs on his body. The expression was unfathomable. He had expected mania, not tranquility, fanatical compulsion rather than self-possession.

The specter that had haunted Sinclair since Pete's suicide confronted him not with nihilistic despair but with the pure clarity of conviction he himself so fervently desired. If anything, excess of faith motivated this headlong dive into death. Sinclair locked eyes with the bomber. It was more like looking into a mirror than into a void. The same expression of pure conviction must have shone in the jihadists' eyes as they slammed into the Twin Towers. Horror eclipsed Sinclair's fleeting identification with the enemy. He needed to believe that there was a difference between their ethic and his. Between their God and his. The sound of his buddies fighting for their lives roused him. They were soldiers, not martyrs. They had come face to face not with fellow Crusaders but with the nemesis of everything America stood for. Fanatics, not freedom fighters. Enemies of life and liberty.

Sinclair dodged into the window, leaving himself fully exposed to take his best shot. Firing multiple rounds into the torso of the bomber would have raised the odds in his favor. But he couldn't risk detonating the explosives strapped to the man's body. He aimed squarely at his mouth, precisely where Pete aimed the barrel of his shotgun to ensure the most lethal discharge. But it was too late. A split second before he pulled the trigger, the man managed to slip around the corner of the compound. Everything depended on anticipating his next move. Sinclair turned and raised his rifle just in time to blow the man's head off as he ran through the door.

"Fucking A," Percy yelled across the room. "I never even saw him coming."

Percy admired Sinclair's handiwork without breaking stride. The SMAW was reloaded and ready to fire within seconds of the attack. Sinclair was back at the window, covering him. They couldn't afford to suspend their assault. But leaving a body strapped with explosives on the threshold posed almost as great a threat as the enemy gunners next door. A stray bullet could hit his trigger switch, sending them all sky high to meet their respective makers. Sinclair shouted over and over into his headset, trying to reach Wolf. He feared the worst until a deadpan voice finally crackled back at him. When things really heated up, Wolf's sangfroid helped cool the squad down.

"Wolf's busy. Can I take a message?"

"Cut the crap. We've got a dead bomber down here, ready to blow."

"I'm on my way."

Wolf and McCarthy sidled down the stairs. They crabwalked across the room and flattened themselves against either side of the door. Wolf signaled McCarthy to stay put. He squatted and grabbed a splayed leg, testing the corpse's weight. Too heavy to heave. Wolf caught Percy's eye and pointed at the roof of the enemy compound. Percy nodded. He repositioned his weapon, angling it higher than usual. There was no way to actually pick off the RPG launchers on the roof. But targeting the parapet would temporarily stop them from dropping grenades as the team ventured into the garden.

Wolf gave the signal and Sinclair let loose with his automatic. Percy used the cover to lean out farther than usual, delivering a clean shot to the roof. The blast blotted out the sun. McCarthy and Wolf threw a couple of grenades into the garden. The space between the two compounds was choked with smoke, obscuring their movements. They grabbed the bomber's legs and dragged him back across the garden, all the way to the wall, then sprinted back and dove through the door. Everybody hit the deck, waiting for an enemy RPG to detonate the bomber's body. Shrapnel flew through the windows, scarring the walls. A chunk of metal seared into Percy's thigh. They all stared at it, not sure what to do, until Trapp appeared out of nowhere. He never failed to show up when someone was wounded. He clenched the pair of pliers he always carried in his medic bag.

"Hold him down!" Trapp shouted.

McCarthy and Wolf held his arms and braced themselves. Percy tried not to scream as Trapp pulled the smoldering metal from his leg. Luckily his charred flesh stanched the bleeding. Trapp started dressing the wound, but Percy waved him off. He was already shouldering his SMAW, oblivious to his injury. With death so close at hand, being wounded was a luxury. Pain was weakness leaving the body.

McCarthy and Trapp prepared to return upstairs, where Logan was trying to simulate the firepower of an entire squad. Their only hope was to fend off the attack long enough for Percy's SMAW to prevail. His persistence was paying off. One corner of the enemy compound was completely blown away. Water gushed from a floor suspended over what was left of the foundation. The building was on the verge of collapsing, crushing everyone inside. The enemy was apparently prepared to go down with their ship. They were either courageous or stupid. The distinction between the two often melted in the heat of battle.

"Stay put!" Wolf ordered.

"Logan needs backup," Trapp hollered.

"Logan needs to get his ass down here," Wolf said into his headset. "On the double."

"Yessir," Logan confirmed.

The logic of Wolf's strategy escaped them. There wasn't even enough room for all their weapons at the living room windows. Only Percy, who was also trained in demolition, understood that the architectural integrity of the neighboring compound had finally been sufficiently compromised to collapse. Wolf wanted them all together, poised and ready to evacuate. Radetzky's squad was just two blocks west, occupying a far more defensible building. If Wolf could get his men there in one piece, they'd have a better shot at surviving the cease-fire. Given Fallujah's chronic volatility, he found it hard to believe Operation Vigilant Resolve would be permanently suspended, political posturing notwithstanding. Surely the Pentagon wouldn't roll over and let them all get fucked by executive privilege. Somebody somewhere needed to make up his mind. They were either at war, or they weren't.

Logan came clambering down the stairs, his automatic strapped to his back. Sinclair and Wolf continued to provide cover for Percy. Trapp, McCarthy, and Logan queued up at the door, ready to roll. Timing was crucial. If they evacuated too soon, they'd be sitting ducks. Insurgents were still battering their building with machine guns and grenades. Waiting too long could prove equally deadly. The instant the enemy compound gave way, they'd have to be in transit to elude falling debris. Wolf raised his arm. Percy's SMAW hit home. Wolf's arm dropped and they all rushed out the door.

Sinclair followed Trapp. At first he thought they had jumped the gun. The air wasn't yet choked with death and destruction. But Wolf had timed everything perfectly. Glancing over his shoulder, Sinclair caught his last glimpse of the compound, wavering like a mirage in an impossibly blue sky. Suspended in time and space, it seemed to hold its breath not so much in terror as in disbelief. In war zones, buildings exploded. They burned to the ground. They didn't disintegrate into shimmering dust, falling almost delicately the way confetti descends from the heavens in ticker-tape parades. Déjà vu. Sinclair had an uncanny feeling that he had already witnessed just such a building collapse on just such a sublime morning. There had never been a more beautiful day. Both buildings hovered on the brink of improbability before plummeting into the inferno. Twin Towers.

Sinclair watched 9/11 on TV from what had once been the safety of his fraternity's living room. A stray plane hit the north tower. A terrible accident. The second plane slammed into the south tower. The apparent accident was actually premeditated mass murder. Living rooms would never be safe again, let alone skyscrapers. Americans couldn't tear themselves away from the spectacle, broadcast on screens from coast to coast. Even New Yorkers tuned in, if they were lucky, to verify what they couldn't believe they were seeing with their own eyes. The same footage aired over and over, one tower and then the other literally melting into thin air, without warning, just smoke leaking from a few iso-lated floors more like a campfire than a conflagration. The sky above remained preternaturally blue until the buildings dropped like bombs on Ground Zero, exploding through streets too narrow to contain the sheer volume of wreckage. Darting through the debris with his squad, Sinclair bore witness not to the destruction of a Fallujan family's home but to the carnage of 9/11. The sight of the one conjured up the other, steeling his purpose.

"It's payback time!"

They scrambled over rubble, expecting to take fire from the west. Lookouts had spotted enemy gunners in at least one of the two compounds en route to Radetzky's strong-hold. Both would have to be cleared in transit. Dust clouds still compromised visibility, but the enemy knew their des-tination as well as they did. The Iraqi resistance had come a long way over the past year. Ragtag bands of disgruntled

Ba'athists and foreign fanatics coordinated their efforts, united against the United States. A steady barrage of bullets guarded access to the next target compound. What looked like the squad's only strategic option had been cut off.

"Fatal funnel!"

"Shit!"

"Shadow me—"

The squad followed Wolf's lead, diving over a low wall to avoid the ambush. They all tried to roll back onto their feet, as he did, in one fluid motion. McCarthy was the least athletic. He crashed and burned and swore a blue streak before regaining his equilibrium. Percy was encumbered by his SMAW. Sinclair paused to help hoist him over and then ducked instinctively before diving over himself. Their cover was dissipating rapidly as the dust settled. Zigzagging in single file to reduce the threat of exposure, they ran for their lives. Their destination, the lip of a balcony, provided a modicum of cover. Plastered against the north wall of the compound, gasping for air, the squad prepared to outfox the next death threat.

They resumed stack formation, Wolf bringing up the rear. McCarthy, who was a connoisseur of doors, always led the way. Some were flimsy and could be opened with a swift kick. Others, especially in upscale neighborhoods, had to be blown open. On routine patrols they had the luxury of stowing chain saws in their Bradleys. In full combat mode, they carried the tools of the trade on their backs. McCarthy was prepared to jerry-rig a fuse, but he had the wherewithal to try the knob first. The door was unlocked. Somebody wanted them to waltz right in.

"Frag the fuckers," Wolf ordered.

McCarthy and Trapp grabbed grenades and lobbed them through the door, dodging the initial burst of shrapnel before storming inside. The room was ablaze far in excess of the combustive power of the grenades. The squad managed to skirt the flames, advancing to a far wall with a clear view of an open door leading to the kitchen. Sinclair put out Logan's sleeve, which had caught fire. Smack in the middle of the living room, a gas canister still burned uncontrollably. A housewarming gift.

"Storm the kitchen!"

Wolf's genius was his preemptive imagination. He was always five steps ahead of the enemy as well as his men. The hotter the spot, the more outrageous his orders, which were obeyed without hesitation. Anyone in their right mind would have waited until the canister fire died down, a dangerously predictable stratagem. As far as Wolf was concerned, sanity was overrated. Whoever left the flambé in the middle of the living room was cooking up something even worse in the kitchen. The squad needed to beat them to the draw, effectively ambushing the ambush. Wolf signaled Sinclair and Logan to watch their backs as they disappeared into the smoke.

Left alone in the living room, Sinclair and Logan scrambled over to the only door in sight, staying low to minimize smoke inhalation. Logan covered the stairwell while Sinclair kicked in the door. The adjoining room was empty. With the exception of the kitchen, the main floor was clear. They proceeded up the stairs, cautiously at first. Then they switched tactics and rushed the rest of the way, firing rounds into an empty hallway flanked by four rooms. They pantomimed a plan and nodded in agreement. Logan would take the two rooms on the left, Sinclair the two on the right. The sooner they cleared the upstairs the sooner they could rejoin the shoot-out below. Judging from the volume of cross fire, Wolf's team was outnumbered.

They moved down the hallway, perfectly in sync. They loved fighting side by side but seldom got the chance. Sinclair usually worked alone, watching his buddies duke it out from his rooftop perches. His role was important, too. Everybody contributed. But he relished the opportunity to really get his hands dirty, especially with Logan. Guys like McCarthy whipped themselves into a frenzy. The more pumped up they got, the better they fought. Sinclair and

Logan shared a more meditative approach to combat, favoring stealth over bluster. When things really clicked, they reached an almost trancelike state. Their way wasn't necessarily exemplary. It just felt more noble to Sinclair and more holy to Logan.

Wolf purposely paired them up, hoping they'd feed off each other's fervor or whatever the hell it was. He could see it in their eyes. Logan in particular looked like an angel of death, a latter-day Abraham sacrificing Isaac on the altar of righteousness. Sinclair's expression was more ecstatic than religious. Killing was primitive and ritualistic, an exalted form of hunting. Truth be told, his stories about bathing faces in the blood of slaughtered animals creeped out Wolf. But every soldier had his way of getting into the zone. As long as Allah wasn't involved, Wolf suspended judgment. The important thing was to get there.

Rifle fire rang out. An enemy gunner had been biding his time in one of the rooms at the end of the hallway, yet another ambush. Logan ducked into an open door on the left and started returning fire. His automatic overpowered the rifle, giving Sinclair the momentary cover he needed to smash through the first door on the right. He whirled in a circle, shooting from the hip to defend against anyone standing or crouching or hiding in what looked like a master bedroom. He didn't hear the shot over the racket of his own gun, but he felt a tremendous blow against his chest. It must have been a pistol. A bigger weapon in such close proximity would have penetrated his body armor. Either he was lucky or the enemy was ill-equipped. It was too soon to tell.

He kept spinning and firing, realizing too late that his automatic was too unwieldy for such intimate combat. Somebody tackled him from behind. He shoved his gun backward against the ribs of his assailant. Almost simultaneously, he felt the butt of the pistol smash his skull. Sinclair reeled but managed to take advantage of the blow. For that split second, he knew just where to find the pistol.

He grabbed the man's wrist and slammed it against the wall, sending the pistol skittering across the floor. The man pulled a knife and lunged at Sinclair, who had already unsheathed his. It was just the two of them, unencumbered by firearms.

The knife was a gift from Pete's dad, Eugene. Everyone else back home had given him a hard time about enlisting in the Marine Corps. Eugene gave him a going-away present, complete with a tutorial on how to use it. Sinclair knew exactly what Pete would have said, had he still been alive. Nothing like being taught how to knife fight by a drunken Indian, yet another example of his father's embarrassingly stereotypical behavior. Sinclair begged to differ. Pete's dad was the only one brave enough to let bygones be bygones, acting more like a father than his own goddamned father. Eugene's gift had saved his life more than once in Iraq.

Eugene taught him everything he needed to know one August afternoon. Sinclair was due at boot camp in a week, and time was short. His instruction was completely unorthodox. Everybody else in the world thought the trick was to keep your opponent off balance. Eugene said everybody else in the world was wrong. Knife fights weren't like fencing where you got points for looking pretty. All you had to do was stick the guy and stick him good. You could be falling over backward and still slice and dice the best of them. They'd be all smug, balanced on the balls of their feet, with their guts hanging out. Touché.

They fought for hours on end, secluded in an abandoned barn. Beds of hay cushioned their falls. Sinclair had carried a knife since he was old enough to clean fish. Now the blade needed to become part of his body, a new and more deadly appendage to fend off Eugene. At first, too much was happening too quickly. Eugene's limbs seemed to fly in every direction at once in random patterns. His blade glinted with the predictable unpredictability of a firefly. The minute you saw it in one place, it was in another, untraceable.

"Ignore everything but the knife. Keep it simple."

The less Sinclair tried to follow Eugene's every move, the more he was able to anticipate the next thrust of his knife. Everything started slowing down. He managed to insert himself into the action, finding fleeting slivers of unguarded air. Once he mastered a few offensive moves, they started working on psychological defense. Knives were more temperamental than firearms. Whether an Iraqi or an American fired a gun, the bullet maintained a strictly mechanical trajectory. Knives had personalities, nationalities, even socioeconomic backgrounds. Eugene started role-playing, fighting like lumberjacks and punks, soldiers and terrorists.

"How do you know how terrorists fight?"

"My ancestors were terrorists, remember?"

"Don't be ridiculous. Your ancestors were Americans."

"Tell that to General Custer."

"He fought the Cheyenne. Not the Sioux."

"They all looked the same to him."

Sinclair's clothes were slashed to pieces. He suffered a number of superficial cuts, friendly reminders of what not to do in knife fights. They kept sparring until he drew blood. His accuracy still left something to be desired. The wound he inflicted was a bit too friendly, more a gash than a knick. Blood soaked through Eugene's shirt. He shrugged it off.

"I've seen worse in the barber's chair. Next time follow through."

"Sure you're okay?"

"Nothing a little medicine won't cure. Let's go get doctored up."

They got liquored up instead. Eugene usually drank at home in his trailer. That night they splurged at the local bar. Eugene kept toasting Sinclair's illustrious future as an oil tycoon. That was the point of the Iraq War, wasn't it? To build a pipeline straight from Baghdad to your Chevy? He was mostly kidding. He'd have enlisted himself if he weren't such an old fart. Too bad his son hadn't lived long enough to fight the good fight, by which he meant any fight at all.

Sinclair took offense, of course. He insisted America was fighting for freedom, not just free enterprise. They kept circling back to this distinction as Sinclair got drunker and Eugene got more philosophical. Night fell in the bar. The regulars had long since taken the edge off and were pacing themselves. Johnny Cash dominated the jukebox, serenading their otherwise quiet kinship of beer and an occasional shot. Eugene and Sinclair were still drinking full throttle, trying to outpace their demons.

"I'm not fighting just for the sake of fighting, you know."

"God is on your side?"

"You're damn right he is."

"Lucky you. I wish Pete had your luck."

"He wouldn't have fought anyway."

"He'd have fought."

"Pete hated the military."

"He hated the government. Who doesn't?"

"I don't."

"Doesn't matter one way or the other. Pete couldn't pass up a good fight any better than you can."

"Last I heard, he trashed the army every chance he got."

"He was just trying to impress that girl."

"What girl?"

"Your sister. Who else, dick-brain?"

Eugene's hostility toward Candace caught Sinclair off guard. They were in dangerous territory, armed with nothing but tequila, equal parts truth serum and amnesic. Sinclair could count on one hand the times they'd seen each other since Pete's suicide. The gift of the knife came out of nowhere. It seemed conciliatory, even though he had no idea what, if anything, had estranged them. For the first time, he realized Eugene might be privy to things even he didn't know about Pete.

"I've asked myself a million times why he did it."

"You should have asked me."

"I'm asking."

"He was dishonored."

"By my sister?"

"By your father. Your sister just went along for the ride."

"What's that supposed to mean?"

"Like you don't know. Your father told Pete to keep his stinking Indian hands off his daughter. Candace didn't say a word in his defense. Not a goddamn word."

"You're making shit up."

"He's dead, isn't he?"

"Who ever heard of killing yourself for that?"

"It's a Sioux thing."

"For disgrace in battle. Not love."

"Honorable suicide, Billy. Something you palefaces wouldn't understand."

"Since when was Pete such a devout Indian?"

"Since they rubbed his nose in it. It was all he had left."

Either the tequila or the truth caught up with Sinclair. He was too sick to go home, so they both slept it off in Eugene's trailer. They each remembered about half of what was said that night. There were no hard feelings. Everybody had been blaming everybody else for Pete's suicide since Grandpa found him dead in the aspen grove. Surely they were the least responsible, they who had loved him most. They said good-bye abruptly that morning, trying to cover the intensity of what they were feeling. Eugene told Sinclair to keep his eyes open. He hadn't taught him how to fight just so he could get himself killed in Iraq. Sinclair said he'd do his best not to. It was his only real send-off. His own father didn't even drive him to the airport.

He kept practicing his moves at boot camp. Sergeant Troy was initially skeptical of his technique. Sinclair looked out of control, off balance. But nobody could get anywhere near him with a knife. Master of the long shot, he seldom got the chance to fight the way Eugene had taught him to fight, mano a mano. He had used his Ka-Bar to finish off a few dudes in Baghdad and Ramadi. But he definitely never met his match until Fallujah, the only town down and dirty enough to serve up a knife fight worthy of his training. The insurgent in the master bedroom probably thought he was leveling the playing field, stripping an infidel of his superior firepower. He was actually handing Sinclair his weapon of choice.

Eugene was right about how terrorists fight. The man's movements were veiled and devious. There was something fluid about him, almost incorporeal. His body seemed to vanish whenever Sinclair's blade approached. It was like fighting a mirage. The man was much older than Sinclair, much bigger and stronger and more experienced. He had the seasoned confidence of a holy mercenary, a mujahid trained in Pakistan or Afghanistan with nothing to lose and everything to gain in the hereafter. Sinclair could only win the fight if he stayed alive. This man would win either way. The odds were in his favor, yet another suicidal warrior embracing death as the ultimate victory, making it almost impossible to prevail over him.

The specter of suicide pricked Sinclair's concentration, opening a slit that widened into a gash as the man knifed his thigh. Resisting the impulse to look at the wound, he assured himself it was just a scratch. He felt a spreading warmth before slamming shut the part of his brain that registered pain. Though too late to deflect the attack, he managed to slash the wrist of the man's retreating arm. In the inevitable tit for tat of knife fighting, Sinclair had chalked one up. Unless his adversary was ambidextrous, he had lost his advantage.

This first physical contact changed everything. Neither man was bleeding profusely, but one's boot was full of blood and the other's hand was slick with it. The terrorist had known exactly where to find the main artery in Sinclair's thigh. He must have missed it by a fraction of whatever metric they used to measure fatality in his native country. Casualties in battle often resulted not from initial injuries but from the slow and steady bleeding out of wounds.

Both men started fighting more aggressively, racing against a clock with blood dripping from its hands. What had been hidden was unveiled.

The man attacked with what might have been a dozen knives. Sinclair tried to slow himself down, even as his opponent sped up. One mortal blow was worth multitudinous flesh wounds. The man's collarbone was like a plate of natural body armor. But there was one sweet spot. Like a surgeon, Sinclair probed with steely precision. His knife slid in all the way to the handle. They both heard, or perhaps felt, the spurting sound, a punctured artery in the neck. What had been dripping began gushing. The man fell forward, shuddering in Sinclair's arms. He held him tightly to make sure he wasn't playing possum, gathering strength for one last stab at victory. He wasn't.

The sound of battles being waged in other parts of the compound came flooding back into Sinclair's consciousness. Cross fire still raged downstairs. Logan and the lone rifleman exchanged periodic shots in the hall, ducking in and out of doorways. Sinclair sheathed his knife and wiped the blood off his hands. He picked up his automatic and tiptoed across the room in his steel-toed boots, ignoring his thigh wound as assiduously as the spectacle of the dead terrorist sprawled on the floor, eyes wide open. Wolf and the rest of the squad needed reinforcement. Time to wrap up this sideshow and get back to the main attraction.

Sinclair stood in the doorway where Logan could see him and the rifleman down the hall could not. He held his finger to his lips and Logan winked. A plan was born almost telepathically. Logan kept wrapping himself around the doorjamb, trying to take clean shots without exposing too much of his body. His automatic overpowered the rifle, but the ballistics were all wrong. Shooting from rooms on the same side of the hallway made it next to impossible to score. Sinclair had a much better angle. Once he mastered the logistics of their stalemate, he'd be ready to execute a standard bait and hook.

Logan was the bait. The strategy worked best when the quarry was either gullible or cocky. The rifleman appeared to be both. Every time Logan stuck so much as a big toe into the hallway, out popped the rifleman. He apparently assumed his pal the professional mujahid was making short work of Sinclair. A novice, no doubt about it. The only safe assumption was that enemies lurked around every corner. Sinclair positioned himself. Logan unloaded a decoy round. The rifleman appeared, right on schedule, and fell forward into the hallway. He died instantaneously, but his body kept jerking as Sinclair continued firing into it, emptying his magazine. It may have been overkill. He needed to reload anyway.

Logan followed suit. They both ducked back into the safety of their rooms and slammed in new rounds. They might not need full magazines to finish clearing the bedrooms. But judging from the continuous fire in the kitchen, they'd need an arsenal to get out of the compound alive. Bring it on. The US Army taught its soldiers never to fear combat. Marines were trained to embrace it. Better yet, crave it. When they weren't actually fighting, they reminisced about fighting or looked forward to the next fight. Half of Sinclair's platoon had volunteered for redeployment at the end of their active-duty service commitments. They couldn't bear the thought of their buddies fighting without them. It wreaked havoc on marriages. It won wars.

They stormed the hallway, side by side, so massive in full combat gear that domestic spaces could scarcely accommodate the enormity of their attack. Logan straddled the dead insurgent, pivoting to fire into the open room to the left. Sinclair kicked in the door to the right. Multiple rounds harmlessly ripped into the walls and mattress of what looked like a boy's bedroom. Clothes were strewn on the floor, waiting for his mother to tell him to pick them up. The upstairs fell silent. Logan had already stopped shooting.

"All clear!" Sinclair hollered.

Logan didn't respond. Sinclair squared off, preparing to rush headlong into the next room.

"Logan?"

"Clear," he finally said. He voice sounded huskier than usual.

"Everything okay?"

Logan appeared in the doorway, visibly shaken. He caught sight of Sinclair and his face hardened. What looked like a woman's arm was draped across the floor of the room. Logan stepped into the hallway, closing the bedroom door behind him.

"All clear," Logan repeated. "Let's get back downstairs."

"What happened in there?"

"Drop it."

"Was that a woman?"

The minute Sinclair asked the question he regretted it. No matter what happened in that room, it wasn't worth jeopardizing his bond with Logan. The long mission was taking its toll, and they were making mistakes. Correction. Sinclair had made a mistake. Logan was just doing his duty. If Sergeant Troy had told them once he had told them a million times. Never second-guess the decisions of your platoon. Compartmentalize everything. Shoot first, don't ask questions later, no matter what.

"I said drop it, Sinclair."

Logan had fully recovered his nerve. He was already halfway down the hall, confident that Sinclair was right behind him. Gunners had a secret compartment, deep in the recesses of their psyches, where they stashed the corpses of all the women and children they killed in the line of duty. For the sake of the mission, if not to avoid going crazy, they learned to ignore that particular aspect of winning the War on Terror. Covering the action from rooftop perches, Sinclair wasn't privy to what happened behind closed doors. He couldn't get the image of that draped arm out of his mind. Sniper duty had made him soft.

Sinclair might have escaped the compound with his honor intact if he hadn't glanced down at the dead rifleman. No wonder he'd been so gullible. He was a teenager at best, possibly the boy whose clothes were strewn across the floor in the next room. Probably the son of the phantom corpse behind the closed door. Sinclair nudged the door open with his automatic. He would never forgive himself for betraying Logan's trust. It shouldn't have mattered whether it was a woman or an insurgent. Judging from the position of her body, it was a mother. Her arms were extended, her limp hand reaching out to the dead rifleman. Was it her son or just some random kid? It may not have mattered, even to her. She had reached out to comfort him, one way or the other.

Sinclair panicked. A traitor had invaded his mind. The warrior in him looked on, incapacitated with doubt, as the traitor violated everything he believed in. He wondered what would have happened if he had cleared that particular room instead of Logan. For days he had fought, killing untold numbers of insurgents without faltering. He had knifed a man whose very breath he could feel on his face without flinching. But the intrusion of kindness into the field of brutality unmanned him. The anomalous presence of civilians seemed to transform war into terrorism. He told himself he wasn't thinking these things. He had been trained not to think these things. He had been trained not to think. Training was everything.

The traitor tried to take refuge in the fact that he hadn't shot her. The refuge itself was a betrayal. The entire compound had been declared hostile, and they had orders to shoot everything that moved. There was no place for equivocation in the military. There was right and wrong. Democracy and the Axis of Evil. The traitor tried to convince Sinclair that the woman lying in a pool of her son's blood defied this moral certitude. Even if following orders was right, she wasn't necessarily wrong, just in the wrong house in the wrong city in a war gone wrong.

If only Sinclair were fighting his Grandpa's war. The enemy had been clearly demarcated. They wore uniforms, for starters. The infantry could readily distinguish between civilians and hostile forces. They measured their honor against the dishonor of Nazis herding families into concentration camps. In Fallujah, women and children refused to be herded out of harm's way. Why were they still there, blurring ethical boundaries? Terrorists had killed civilians by the thousands on 9/11. Marines were in Iraq to punish that transgression, not replicate it.

Sinclair smacked his helmet to clear his head. He was going mad. Battle fatigue sometimes affected his performance, but never his judgment. Orders were orders. Civilians had been evacuated. Collateral damage was inevitable. His training kicked in and he raced after Logan, fleeing the specter of the traitor standing over the corpses of a mother and her son. A warrior descended the stairs with Logan, his weapon at the ready. They had cleared the upstairs of hostile forces.

The living room was still filled with smoke, but they could see well enough to confirm that it remained secured. Logan and Sinclair flanked the kitchen door, trying to assess the action within. They recognized the gunner styles of Wolf, McCarthy, Trapp, and Percy. They were all still alive. An awful lot of firepower was crammed into the nooks and crannies of the kitchen. They were up against four AK-47s, maybe five. The odds were already on their side, given their superior weaponry. But Wolf was playing it safe, biding time until the squad was reunited.

"Ready to engage," Logan shouted into his headset.

"What took you so long?" Wolf said.

"Rush-hour traffic."

"Where's Sinclair?"

"Riding shotgun. What are we up against?"

"Enemy gunners at ten and two o'clock. Two or more in the pantry at four o'clock."

"We're right behind you."

They stormed the kitchen, guns blazing. There were five, not four, insurgents. The three crouching behind appliances bore the brunt of the assault. Nothing much left of them, just hamburger meat. The other two were splayed in a utility closet. Mops and brooms and legs and arms. Detergent leaking from punctured containers spattered their blood with antiseptic blues and greens. The squad whooped it up. They couldn't have executed a better blitz. Just one more compound and they'd be scarfing down MREs with Radetzky's men. By then maybe this bogus cease-fire would be over and they could really kick ass.

A screen door at the far end of the kitchen opened onto a back porch. Wolf was already assessing their next target. Stacked in their usual configuration, the squad regained its composure. They sprinted toward the adjacent compound, peppering the windows and balcony while Wolf opened a breach to the entrance. As far as they could tell over the racket of their own automatics, their charge was unchallenged. They reconfigured on either side of the front door, panting with excitement. Taking fire was nerve-racking, but at least you knew what you were up against. Either the compound was empty or they were in for one hell of a surprise party. McCarthy prepared to break down the door. Percy and Logan primed grenades. They popped the cork and the team rushed into the compound. Wolf and McCarthy sprayed the fatal funnel. Sinclair and Logan hit the corners. Percy scanned the room for traps.

"Clear!"

"Closed door at one o'clock," Percy warned.

"Cover it!" Wolf ordered. "We've got the kitchen."

The door flew open, as if on cue. Trapp and Sinclair let loose, nailing an insurgent. Another one appeared in the kitchen, drawing fire from Wolf. An instant later, two more descended the staircase. The squad was on the wrong end of a double bait and hook. McCarthy and Logan pivoted, zipping rounds up and down the stairs. The lead insurgent's body danced a grisly jig, arms flailing from the impact. But not before somebody got a shot off. McCarthy went down.

Trapp tried to stanch the wound. It was no use. Even American body armor couldn't withstand close-range rounds. The bullet was lodged in what was left of his heart. Trapp keened over the body, rocking McCarthy in his arms. He experienced the loss viscerally, like a severed limb. They were all part of one Corps, a single martial body. The rest of the squad formed a semicircle around them, weapons at the ready with tears streaking their grimy cheeks. Sinclair alone was stony-faced. He couldn't afford to go there. He had to keep it together so the traitor and the coward wouldn't ambush him again.

Before every offensive, Wolf recited the first half of Sun Tzu's military creed. Regard your soldiers as your children, and they will follow you into the deepest valleys. He never recited the second half. Look on them as your own beloved sons, and they will stand by you even unto death. The mere mention of death hit too close to home. He felt personally responsible for the loss of McCarthy. He loved his squad with the same unfathomable intensity that he loved his own family. Technically his job was to keep them alive so they could kill others. Actually he fought to protect them. He kept his eyes and ears open, even as he mourned with his men. The living room was strewn with enemy corpses. A head count revealed that one of the insurgents had escaped up the stairway.

"Percy!" he barked. The whole squad flinched. "Secure the area."

"Yessir."

"Move out. McCarthy's motherfucking murderer is upstairs."

Wolf led the way. There were three closed doors off the upstairs hallway. Russian roulette. He stationed Trapp at the head of the stairs to watch their backs. McCarthy wasn't there to do the honors, so Logan positioned himself outside the first door, flanked by Wolf and Sinclair. He broke the door down and they stampeded in, decimating knick-knacks and throw pillows. Wolf flung open an armoire and they shredded somebody's wardrobe. The veils were gaily colored. The dresses were stylish, a woman with impeccable taste. Sinclair thought he detected the faint scent of her clothes wafting through the smell of explosives. He was almost afraid to look. But no one was hiding in the armoire, which didn't mean she wasn't cowering in the next room or already dead, her limp arm stretched across a bloody floor.

"All clear!"

They repeated the drill in the next room, emptying multiple rounds into a box of toys and a whimsical canopied bed. Logan thought he spotted a muzzle poking between remnants of lace hanging by a thread. They renewed the attack, splintering the wood on all four bedposts until the canopy collapsed. Wolf pulled off the blankets, exposing a stuffed animal. Sinclair did a double take. Its furry little arm wasn't draped across the sheets. Its hand didn't reach out in supplication. Blood wasn't everywhere.

They raced down the hallway to the third and last room. Logan prepared to kick in the door. Sinclair summoned his training. Wolf gave the signal. They stormed the room. Sinclair thought he saw a child in the corner of the bomb-pocked nursery. Delay and you get blown away. He spent his last breath looking over his shoulder at his buddies. They continued to charge without him, pumping round after round into the body of an abandoned doll. Wolf rushed to the window. The enemy, if there was one, had vanished.

In Memoriam

WILLIAM SINCLAIR

November 22, 1983, to April 9, 2004
Lance Corporal
Bronze Star

When they were boys they found a jackrabbit with a broken leg. Pete wanted to splint the leg and nurse it back to health. Sinclair said it would never survive anyway. He offered to wring its neck, but Pete said he shouldn't have to shoulder all the responsibility. They'd better kill it together. Its neck was too scrawny for them both to get a decent grip. Though barely big enough to carry BB guns, their aim was true enough. On the count of three they put the poor thing out of its misery. Sinclair pronounced the death sentence with moral authority remarkable in a boy his age. Its time had come.

They fashioned a bier out of bark and processioned to the aspen grove. Wind had cleared a patch of earth where they sculpted a hole in the shape of the jackrabbit's body. So it would be comfortable. They found a smooth round stone in a dry creek bed and placed it on the grave. To protect it from scavengers. To mark the spot so they could pay their respects. Pete was ready to recite the eulogy, but Sinclair said they needed another stone. There was one rabbit, but there were two of them. They returned to the creek bed. Two round stones mark the grave.